The Bossuet Conspiracy

THE BOSSUET CONSPIRACY

a novel
by Bill Goodson

iUniverse, Inc.
New York Lincoln Shanghai

The Bossuet Conspiracy

All Rights Reserved © 2003 by Bill Goodson

No part of this book may be reproduced or transmitted in any form or by any means, graphic, electronic, or mechanical, including photocopying, recording, taping, or by any information storage retrieval system, without the written permission of the publisher.

iUniverse, Inc.

For information address:
iUniverse, Inc.
2021 Pine Lake Road, Suite 100
Lincoln, NE 68512
www.iuniverse.com

This is a work of fiction. Characters, names, places, and events portrayed in this book are either products of the author's imagination or are used fictitiously. Any resemblance to actual persons, living or dead, is coincidental.

ISBN: 0-595-27971-6

Printed in the United States of America

Acknowledgments

The author wishes to thank the following individuals for their assistance: Pat (Komma Kop) Goodson, Elise Goodson, Dorothy and Miles Snowden, Cindy Holliday, JoAnn Moorman, Bob Stewart, Martha Humphreys, John Dobbins, Mickey Sharp, and John Hay.

Front cover photo courtesy of Harriet Dobbins and graphics assistance by Fulcourt Press.

Chapter 1

Bangkok, Thailand
December 10, 1968

Merton let the spray from the showerhead fall on his scalp and descend over his face and shoulders. His hands slapped out a beat on his thighs keeping time with a Coltrane favorite he was humming. For half an hour he had afforded himself this luxury, alternating hot and cold water as was his wont, awakening the senses and purifying his restless spirit. His brothers back at the Abbey of Gethsemani, marking his penchant for lengthy midday showers, teased him about his "Hour of Shower Power." In his present locale, the conference center near Bangkok, he was far removed from their playful observations.

His inner clock told him time was drawing near for the start of the afternoon session. He turned the knobs to the left and threw back the shower curtain. A towel was waiting on the curtain rod. He grabbed it and rubbed vigorously, letting his mind return to the here-and-now, wondering if the afternoon's offerings would be better received than was his that morning.

His eye caught a puddle of water outside the shower that led the few feet into the tiled bedroom area. *Must have left the curtain outside the stall. Careless of me.* With the towel tucked around his waist he stepped out into the puddle. He could not see that it led directly to the standing fan that was oscillating in the other room. Neither could he see the eyes that were observing him through partly-opened blinds at a back window.

His body was seized with a jolting, searing lightning bolt of pain. He stumbled through the bathroom door, unable to extricate himself from the wet floor and its insistent current. Falling forward, he brought the fan down on top of himself and breathed his last.

The two men in maintenance uniforms finished their business at the rear of his cottage then disappeared around the corner.

* * * *

The New York Times
December 11, 1968

CONTROVERSIAL MONK THOMAS MERTON DIES
Associated Press

BANGKOK—Thomas Merton, famous author and monk from the Abbey of Gethsemani in Kentucky, died yesterday in Bangkok while attending a convocation of Eastern monastic leaders. He was found dead by a friend in his cottage not long after delivering the opening address of the meeting. The cause of death has not been determined, though authorities suspect an accident involving electrocution from faulty wiring of an electrical appliance. Foul play has not been ruled out.

Merton was a celebrated author whose prolific literary career was launched with the publication of his best-selling autobiography, *The Seven Storey Mountain*, in 1948, a few years after he entered the Trappist monastery. His works were acclaimed in both religious and secular circles, but political controversy surrounded his oft-stated opposition to the Vietnam War and to nuclear weapons, leading to unconfirmed rumors that the CIA was watching him closely. Conservative elements of the Roman Catholic Church also decried his embrace of Eastern religions and recently called for censure.

This personal statement from Pope Paul VI was released by the Vatican: "It is with deep sorrow that we learned of the death of Father Louis (Thomas) Merton in Thailand. His contributions to the Church and its contemplative traditions will long be felt. When we say that our deepest sympathies go out to his family and friends, it must be recognized that Merton's circle embraced the entire family of God, including those of all religious faiths, with whom he engaged in fruitful dialogue."

Professor Dan Walsh of Bellarmine College in Louisville, whom Merton often credited with inspiring his call to the monastery, said by telephone interview today, "It's the saddest day of my life. I've lost my best friend, and the Catholic Church as well as religious persons of all faiths have lost their most ardent and talented spokesman."

Funeral arrangements are yet to be announced by his superiors at the abbey in Kentucky pending further investigation of the circumstances of his death.

Chapter 2

▼

September 14, 1993
Nashville, Tennessee

"Before the second Vatican Council, you see, the altar faced away from the congregation..." The priest's monologue was interrupted by the sound of a telephone ringing, barely audible, coming from a side door.

"Excuse me, ladies," he said. "That's the office phone, and I'm alone here. I'm expecting a call." Turning as he walked briskly away, he added, "Phyllis, continue the tour. I'll be right back."

The two girls were dwarfed by the night-darkened, empty nave of Holy Spirit Church. Track lights pointed their way to the altar.

"This is where the action is," Phyllis said, leading her friend past the wooden railing and kneelers worn from use by generations of devout knees and up the two steps to the table.

"I know. I told you our service is practically the same. We do the Eucharist every Sunday. You call it Mass, that's all."

"Well, if they're so much alike, why would you want to change? You love acolyting. I just don't understand." Phyllis, hands on hips, looked squarely at Rachel, who glared back.

"Because...because it's more real, don't you know? All that tradition and history and all."

"It's that stuff you've been reading that Scott gave you, isn't it?" Phyllis asked.

"Maybe," Rachel said. Her brother Scott had been home for a couple of weeks before the fall term started. She had picked his brain about college life, all the important things such as did he ever cut class like a normal guy, did he ever want to cut class just to try it like she did, just for the heck of it? No and no, he had said and told her she'd better decide about her term paper if she wanted to ever get to college so she could be normal like he wasn't and experience delinquency to the max at an institution of higher learning. Their conversation turned serious and eventually led to his suggestion that she pick Thomas Merton as her topic. He had done the same just the last term and was finished with the books which she could borrow for research. These were the books with her father's signature on the inside covers that she tried not to see but occasionally peeked at just to test herself, hoping that by now his name would assume no more importance than if it were a total stranger's.

"Maybe," she repeated distractedly, peering at the far end of the nave. "Hey, show me the confession booth."

Phyllis balked, looking toward the priest's office and the ray of light streaming from the hallway. "I think we should wait for Father Morris."

"Oh, come on. It's getting late. He won't mind."

Phyllis led the way down the aisle to the back of the church. "Okay, this is where the priest sits, and this is where the penitent sits. See the screen there? That's where you talk to each other."

Rachel's eyes widened, white surrounding hazel. "Wow! Just like the movies!" Then a twinkle, and, "You be the priest and I'll be the...whatever you called it." She shoved Phyllis toward the opening of the enclosure.

"I don't think we're supposed to do this," Phyllis protested. She frowned, glancing again toward the priest's office. No activity there. "Okay, but be quick."

Rachel pulled her sweater up over her head and assumed a demeanor and accent not unlike Ingrid Bergman, whom she had seen recently on American Movie Classics, and the impersonation would have been complete if she could have managed one of those picture-perfect Bergman tears but she didn't have time. "Father, I confess that I have sinned grievously. My best friend has brought me to her church for a tour with her priest, and now I've made her do something she didn't want to do, and..." she paused a second and looked at her watch which said 8 p.m., "...and if we don't get home soon, I'm going to make my mother say a bad word." She giggled and Ingrid vanished.

"Oh, Rachel! Let's get out of here."

"Okay, okay." Rachel rose to follow Phyllis' command, paused, and took in the spare insides of the booth. So plain, so simple, she thought, compared to the elaborate trappings of the rest of the church with its multicolored stained glass and gold leaf ornamentation. Hard for her to say which she preferred, but at this moment, simple got the nod.

Her hands passed through strands of hair, then to her neck, and finally defined the contours of her eye-catching hips through the fine, one hundred percent cotton, GAP shorts purchased this summer at the outlets in Pigeon Forge. They had been to Sevierville for a visit with family and braved the crowds for a little shopping while in that part of east Tennessee. She had argued with her mother that the shorts were more expensive than she needed, to no avail. What's in a label? Window dressing. Hormonal correctness. Patch a GAP label over every pimple and smile through perfectly aligned, fenced-in incisors.

"Go ahead and wait for Father Morris," she said.

Phyllis looked puzzled.

Rachel felt for the seat and said she would just stay there a minute.

She stayed longer than that.

Phyllis pulled her out just in time to beat the locking of the church doors.

The scene outside was deserted except for two men leaning against a wrought iron fence near the sidewalk. They raised their heads to eye the two girls, betraying Latino features. Rachel stared at them for a moment and then hurried down the steps to the street.

* * * *

Same time

"I'm Trey. I'm an alcoholic."

"Hi Trey!" the chorus came back.

Around the room went the reciprocating ritual, voices mixing with the thin cloud of smoke that began to fill the limited air space as the hour cranked up. The auxiliary room air conditioner in the window, which the church had generously added to handle the smoke problem, fought valiantly but was going to lose the battle again.

By the time introductions were completed and the speaker had begun, Trey was losing his own battle against boredom. This particular speaker he had heard at least three other times in the past two years, and his script was the same. The story was funny the first couple of times, especially the part about the day the priest visited the speaker's home and his girlfriend pretended to be his wife. He was about to get away with the subterfuge until the bimbo inquired cutely of the preacher's wife and children. Father O'Day apparently was speechless. A ripple of chuckles aroused Trey enough for him to realize that there were newcomers who were hearing this for the first time.

Gratitude. Attitude of gratitude! How many times he found himself repeating that slogan during meetings like this, meetings he could drift through on automatic pilot until something like a chuckle or a cough from the guy next to him brought him out of his reverie. Then he would have to admit that, yes, he was grateful to be in that crowd of grateful drunks, yes, even in that cloud of carcinogens, instead of where he was four years ago.

Four years ago he would have been—let's see, at eight-thirty p.m.— yeah, by this time he would have finished half a quart of Cutty, on his way to a blackout.

Four years and it might as well have been four eons, when earliest recorded history took note of the abyss he sank into, emerging from the other side into a new universe that was nothing short of continuing bewilderment to him. At least he was beginning, at times, to feel like a human being again. Times such as two weeks ago when he was invited to return to his position as clinical instructor at Vanderbilt. The department head met him for lunch first and sat close enough to Trey to give his breath the sniff test. Almost cheek-to-cheek at one point, Trey had doubts for a moment about his chief's intentions. In the end, he was judged safe enough to turn loose on the psychiatric residents again, and he met with them for the first time in four years.

Applause broke up his thoughts, signaling the end of the talk. Madame chairman wound up with the usual invitation to sponsorship and group recitation of The Lord's Prayer. At two minutes before nine the chairs were emptying, and the coffeepot performed its magnet routine.

Trey headed for the exit, avoiding small talk. Someone was at his elbow following him.

"Hey, Trey, what's the hurry?" It was Jack C., his fellow traveler in the ranks of recovering doctors. "We need to talk about Phoenix. The IADAA convention. It's coming up in November. Be here before you know it."

"I'll catch you at the Caduceus meeting Sunday, okay?" Trey threw at him, backing out of the doorway and onto the sidewalk. "I'm sure there'll be discussion about it. Yeah, I'm still planning on going as far as I know. Sorry I have to run." He was lying, not about having to run, but about going. He turned his back on Jack and hurried on to the parking lot, hoping he'd catch the hint.

"Hey fella," Jack hollered, "you look worn out. D'ja ever hear about 'Take it Easy'?" The jibe and familiar slogan were not lost on Trey who was opening the door of his BMW.

Jack was right. Trey knew that if he looked anything like he felt, he could have passed for twenty years older than forty-eight. Forty-eight and holding, except that his graying temples weren't cooperating. He sucked in a lung full of fresh September air, hoping to displace the secondhand poison.

A front from the Midwest was caressing middle Tennessee and found its way to the parking lot of Briarwood Christian Church just as Trey and a couple of others pulled out. Even the car windows whistled an exhilarated tune with the breeze coursing through them, windows that were open for the first time in a week, ready to welcome the beginning of autumn. And just in time to forestall a threatened mutiny by the beleaguered air conditioner.

He turned on to Old Hickory Boulevard for the ten minute drive to Balmoral Estates and his townhouse. Fortunate he was that the church had decided to allow meetings there the last couple of years. Probably the only church around still permitting smoking on the premises, and the room served more than one purpose. There was a handful of fallen men belonging to that church who petitioned for a smoking room where they could hold Sunday school and weekday Bible study classes. The sign on the door said Forbidden Fruit, and children were not allowed so much as a sniff. Some likened it to a brothel, others purgatory. The bluehairs wanted to emblazon a "T" on the chests of the tobacco-tainted men, and if they hadn't accounted for such a healthy percentage of the collective tithe, it might have happened. At any rate, the church was perfectly situated for Trey to catch a meeting on the way home evenings.

The guardhouse was empty again. Same old story of failed promises from Bennett Properties, Inc. Should be called Red Inc., Trey was thinking, according to rumors of impending bankruptcy. Balmoral Owners' Association would undoubtedly be soliciting bids soon for a new management company, hopefully one that could keep a guard at the allegedly protected entrance and stem the rising tide of burglaries and vandalism.

Curving off Dundee onto Ayr Circle he pulled into the neat little parking spot at 105. Another whiff of cool air caught his cheek, and he paused a moment before getting out to enter the empty house.

Empty. That's the word that went with house. The word home wouldn't work. Who ever heard of an empty home? A full house beats an empty home. A pair of treys beats an ace, for sure. He and son Scott played poker a few times this summer. Poker beats Solitaire. He had become intimately acquainted with solitude the last couple of years since Scott had left for college and pre-law at Davidson. He had found that divorce demanded homage to the gods of Solitude.

Scott had been home for two weeks in August after spending most of the summer clerking for Uncle Jonas in the nation's capital. He had jumped at the opportunity to gopher for the chairman of the Senate Armed Services Committee. He got a startling taste of the excitement and contention that often fill committee chambers. On the top of Chairman Crockett's mind this summer was the matter of base closings, and he assigned Scott as liaison with the Base Realignment and Closure Commission's hearings. There he witnessed the parade of indignant, steely-eyed, dig-in-your-heels-for-the-local-economy officials determined to let somebody else suffer.

Scott told Trey of such a group from Anniston, Alabama, who brandished a tale, supposedly true, of the way that the base closing commission's delegation was greeted this spring in their town. It seems the local high school football team skipped spring training that day when they heard of the inspection visit. They formed a human chain at the main entrance to Ft. McClellan, the installation at issue. Then General Perkins, chairman of the delegation, was alledgedly cut down at the knees by a 240-pound linebacker with a Fu Manchu mustache, a young man clearly held back in school a few years to mature into his destiny. The destiny, or dream, of many of these oversized army brats was to play at Tuscaloosa or Auburn, and they weren't going to sit by and let their papas be transferred to some base in Montana if they could by-god help it. Kiss my grits.

Scott, passing messages and ordering lunch boxes, was often allowed into the inner sanctum to witness his uncle juggling complex issues with a firm sensitivity that belied his bullish reputation. Once, in the conference room adjoining the hearing chamber, where wills were often tested and seemingly unyielding knots loosened, he saw Uncle Jonas pause, almost in mid-sentence discussing a pesky budgetary item, to inquire of an aide as to the result of his mother's MRI. He even knew her first name.

Scott delighted in recapping his experiences with his dad at the end of the summer. He found time, too, to visit his grandmother at the assisted living facility, a duty he found easier to handle than did Trey. Scott's affections for the elder Mrs. Crockett were untainted by the scars that marked Trey's history with her.

Trey missed his son's company now, discovering anew that divorce also cultivates one's appreciation of companionship.

Just as he pulled the door release to exit the car, Trey caught a shadow approaching in the side-view mirror. When he stepped out, he could see two men walking toward him. He also noticed for the first time a car, their car presumably, parked on the circle. For some reason this didn't feel good.

"Doctor Crockett?" one of them growled. "Doctor Winton Sevier Crockett the third?" The shorter of the pair's raspy voice, Latin accent, and terse delivery did nothing to quell the anxiety that was beginning to suffuse the atmosphere. They stopped just a few feet from him, their faces barely visible with the backlight from the street. Trey wished he had remembered to turn on the automatic timer for the porch light.

"Yes. What can I do for you?"

"Could you step back inside your car, please? We have something we'd like you to hear. Your tape deck does work, doesn't it?" The south-of-the-border inflection was even more evident.

"Wha…what is this…what is this all about? Who are you?" Trey was preparing to stand his ground until the larger man's meaty right hand grasped his left shoulder and convinced him otherwise.

"Have a seat. No one's going to get hurt. Who we are isn't as important as who we represent. And you'll find out about that soon enough." Raspy was the spokesman for the delegation.

Large Hands stood beside the driver's door, closing it noiselessly. How damn nice that these luxury foreign cars are made so tight, Trey thought. No racket to alert the neighbors.

Raspy opened the passenger-side door, pulling something from his jacket pocket and easing into the seat. The dome light illuminated a mustached, dark-skinned, Juan Valdez-looking Latin.

"Now, Doctor Crockett, would you turn the key so we can listen to this tape? It won't take long, and I assure you it will be interesting. Then we'll be on our way and let you get on with your evening." His English was good, very good.

Trey was thinking fast. Maybe this was a practical joke. If it wasn't, he was not in the best of positions to object. He could hit the horn, but chances are he wouldn't hit it for long. Direct physical opposition looked suicidal. If the greaser next to him was telling the truth, maybe the best course was simply to comply. After all, they could be selling a new Placido Domingo collection. A new direct marketing technique.

He opted for simple compliance. "Okay, fella, let's turn on the tape player and see what you have. I hope it's not jazz. I hate jazz." No one laughed. Raspy found the tape port after fumbling for a few seconds.

The woman's voice was clear, though a little shaky. Trey recognized it right away.

"Doctor Crockett—Trey—I'm taping this at the insistence of these people. I'll be reading what they wrote for me to say, but I do mean what I'm saying. What I mean is that what I'm about to tell you is really going to happen unless you do as they say. Oh, this is Teresa— Teresa Kelly. I guess I just assumed you'd know my voice, but then you might not; it's been so long." Her voice broke up and trailed off.

She cleared her throat. "These people have something on me and my family. I think you know how important family is to me, and if this got out, it would ruin my father. I can't tell you what it is; it's not good.

"They also know about you and me. About my agreement to keep it quiet and out of court and out of your state license records."

She continued after a deep sigh. "What I had to agree to is that unless you cooperate with them fully I will file a complaint with both the state licensing board and the American Psychiatric Association. Their lawyers have drafted the complaint, and the...the gentlemen with you will leave you a copy.

"They didn't tell me what it is they want from you except to assure me it won't get you in any trouble. I really hope you cooperate with them so I won't have to do this. Trey! They won't let me say any..." The voice abruptly ended.

Trey stared numbly at the tape player. After a long pause, Raspy pushed the eject button and removed the tape. Reaching inside his jacket pocket, he pulled out a fat envelope. Without comment he placed it on the seat beside the doctor, opened the door on his side, and walked away. His partner peeled off to join him.

After a few steps Raspy turned back and added an afterthought. "Rachel is a very attractive young lady, Doctor Crockett. You'd better watch her, though. She seems attracted to the Catholics."

There was a long sighing "Ooooooh, shit!" that broke the silence of the darkened BMW, followed by the whispered lament, "I need a drink."

Chapter 3

▼

He didn't take a drink. There were no drinks in the house. He decided long ago that guests could do without.

He needed time to think. Before he opened the envelope he needed time to think. To compose himself. Of all the threats to his sobriety over the last four years, this took the prize. Not divorce, not misadventurous sex, not his father's death. Maybe Rachel.

Yes, Rachel would compare. He felt now like he did the last time he tried to reconcile with her. She was in the finals of the city juniors tennis tournament. He was in the stands, not at her invitation, but at the insistence of his own compulsion that held out hope for the two of them. Call it conscience, call it duty, call it love if you like. Rachel called it a disaster. She was leading her opponent 6-2, 6-4, and 4-2 in the third set when she spotted him in the crowd, and then she proceeded to lose every game and the match. She double-faulted like crazy and whiffed overheads. It was awful. Afterward, at courtside, she walked past him and never gave him the time of day. He could see she was crying, and he hadn't seen her since. That was two years ago.

He slammed the plump envelope on the coffee table knocking the dust off his *Twenty-four Hours a Day* meditation book which was propelled onto the floor in the process.

How ironic, he thought.

He threw his jacket on the easy chair, loosened his tie, kicked off his black loafers, sat on the edge of the couch, and stared at the envelope.

In a few seconds, he was up again and pacing.

His next coherent thought was what sons-of-bitches they were—whoever "they" were—to leave that last emotional ad lib of Teresa's on the tape. Obviously they could have erased it but chose to leave it on for effect. Funny how that part of the tape stood out in his mind. Teresa's voice evoked all kinds of feelings in him, one of which was none other than the old familiar passion.

Whoa, you silly sonofabitch, you've got more important things to think about.

Like what the hell is this all about anyway? What do these people want from me? Raspy said it would all be made clear soon enough. Any soon is too soon. Damn!

He sat down, took a deep breath, and closed his eyes, face twitching with confusion.

Unable to think of a reason to delay any longer, he stretched out his arm and lifted the envelope from the table. Plain, white business-size: no clues there. A piece of clear tape surrendered to his tug, and he removed the contents: a piece of notepaper and three folded legal-size sheets.

Trey read the note first. Typed, it said simply, "Al will be calling you at your office tomorrow to arrange a meeting."

The rest wasn't so simple. Titled "Complaint for the Purpose of Redress of Grievances" with the subtitle, "In the matter of unprofessional conduct by Winton Sevier Crockett, III, M.D." *That's great!* he thought. *Just put it right up front in the title where we can all see it. Why not say, "In the Matter of Screwing His Patient" on the marquee?*

It went on. "Brought by Teresa Lynn Kelly this ___ day of _____, 19__. Drafted by the law firm of Keaton, Brindle, Simmons and James."

So! Keaton, Brindle were in on the deal! That bunch of sleazeballs! How do they manage to keep up a front of respectability?

This wouldn't be Trey's first encounter with them. Sitting on the executive committee of HospiCare Corporation, he had seen their work close up six years ago when they represented a group of smaller hospital owners in an antitrust suit against HCC. What was worse: the assholes won the case.

He scanned the paragraphs, the "factual assertions by the complainant," all numbered neatly for easy reference from 1 to 15, with lots of a,b,c's thrown in. What they said did not make for pleasant reading. All the facts were painfully in order: dates, places, incidents. Appointments later in the day when his receptionist had gone; casual touching leading to caresses; sharing details of his personal life with her; terminating therapy with the presumption that this would free them for more intimacies; finally the inevitable trysts in her apartment.

Trey ran his dry tongue over his lips and looked at the painting on the opposite wall of the room. It was one that came to him in the divorce settlement, an idyllic Caribbean scene with sailboats in the distance. He and Evelyn were there on their honeymoon. Now he wanted a handy-dandy rewind button for his life, anything to avoid reading more of what he held in his hands.

The details were all too familiar, yet at the same time strange. A morbid *deja vu*. A dark presence from a benighted prior incarnation. But it was real, in bold print, in front of him; not only that, it was all true.

The last two paragraphs had to do with "the complainant's damages" at the hands of this satyr, just a hint of what was to come if she decided to file a civil suit in addition to the administrative complaints. Sure enough, the closing statement of the document covered that with: "The complainant retains the right to civil action before proper jurisdiction should the decisions and actions of these bodies be insufficient in her judgment to correct the injustices done her and to prevent damage to other parties at the hands of the perpetrator."

At the very end the usual signature blocks for her and the notary. Trey stared at the blank spaces.

He folded the sheets, slipped them back into their sheath, and tossed the whole thing somewhere in the direction of the table without altering his gaze. He didn't want to read any more. He had seen enough to know that these people had the goods on him. He could deny many of the accusations, but the circumstances were all there, and the testimony of his former receptionist would be damning. To make things worse, Teresa's then-twelve-year-old daughter had been a witness to their trysts; not the sex part, but the fact of his presence in their apartment was less than redeeming.

The truth was that during that time in his life he was a disaster. The Demon claimed him, and judgment was out the window. Alcohol had knocked out the higher brain functions and left intact only the part that worked on his groin area. Now he was paying for that bit of physiological mayhem, in spades.

They had the rap on him. Someone wanted his cooperation bad enough to dig up dirt on both him and Teresa. How much more did they know about him? The gratuitous parting shot from Raspy about Rachel was nothing but intimidation, and what was that comment about the Catholics? What does he know about her? He might as well have said, "Well, now, Doctor Crockett, we just want to be sure you understand that your life is under our microscope, and your children are not off-limits."

Questions raced through his mind:
What do they want me to do?
How am I supposed to hold onto sobriety through this?
Who's this "Al" I'm going to hear from? Capone?

*   *   *   *

Tokyo. Same time.

An innocent-looking helicopter drifting past the skyscraper hovered for a few moments a couple of hundred feet east of the Matsaku Towers. Tinted glass hid the binoculars and powerful telephoto lens with reflection-filtering equipment that were trained on the building's windows. Inside the chopper the click-whirr, click-whirr of the camera competed with engine noise. Then like a hummingbird the craft darted off and out of sight.

That particular nature image was lost on the gentleman who was raising his glass in a toast inside those windows on the 52nd floor. Manuel Matsaku was accustomed to seeing helicopters from the rarefied atmosphere of his company's boardroom. Police, med-evac, television news, corporate, choppers of all types daily graced the airspace around his building, the tallest in Tokyo.

Today he didn't notice the latest of that parade. His sole focus was on the company gathered at his table. The glass of wine, a fine French chardonnay, was raised in turn to each guest, accompanied by the slightest bow.

He spoke their names in flawless English, which was the *interlingua* for the occasion.

"Secretary Eisenberg, General Perkins, Governor Turnbow, Honorable Madame Beason, Secretary Belsasso. May I offer a toast to the success of this venture which upon its realization will be a monument to the ingenuity and cooperative spirit of the people of our countries. May Japanese, Mexicans, and Americans always work together in peace and harmony!"

All stood and raised their glasses with appropriate bows and muted exclamations of approval. With a single gesture he invited the guests to take their seats again while he remained standing at the head of the gleaming table.

Manuel Matsaku. Chairman of the Board of Matsaku Enterprises. A largely self-made multimillionaire who at age fifty stood astride one of the world's largest multinational corporations which included major real estate and timber interests in the United States. And now he was adding Mexico to the atlas of his network, a milestone he anticipated with special fervor.

On her deathbed five years previously, his beloved mother had accepted his promise that one day he would consummate a venture in her honor. A venture that would unite his parental heritages.

Before him, seated in Brazilian mahogany chairs upholstered in the finest silk that worms could spin, were the people who could help make that happen: the U.S. Secretary of Defense who had been personally delegated by President Clinton; the former Chairman of the Joint Chiefs and now member of the Base Realignment and Closure Commission, also sent by Clinton; the Governor of Kentucky; the Speaker of the House of Tennessee and odds-on choice to become the state's first woman governor; and the *Ministro de Comercio* of the *Republica de Mexico* who was President Salinas' designee. Matsaku's generous but oh-so-discreet contributions to selected political campaigns in the USA and other key countries had led to prodigious influence.

"My friends, it is a great pleasure to welcome you to Tokyo and introduce you to what promises to be the most ambitious project ever undertaken by Matsaku Enterprises. It is a personal honor for me that you have accepted my invitation. Let me say, too, that I appreciate very much your understanding of the need for confidentiality in our proceedings. I believe we have made that quite clear, yes?"

This was his first invitation for a response and was answered by five agreeably nodding heads. They were aware indeed of the need for secrecy. That's why they each had found plausible cover stories for their trips. Not even their closest aides knew of their exact whereabouts at that moment. Mr. Matsaku commanded that sort of obeisance around the globe.

The commander continued. "At the risk of boring you, a personal note. This moment carries a deep significance for me." He cleared his throat and cast his gaze at the floor. "It is no secret that my heritage is mixed Japanese and Mexican. My physical features would not allow me to hide that fact even if I wanted to." He was referring to his large frame and bold Aztec/Spanish facial features that mixed curiously with Oriental eyes.

He was starting to move about the room, energizing the monologue with his impressive body.

"Some twenty-five thousand years ago during the last ice age, there began a migration of men and women from the Asian continent across the Bering land bridge." His hands swept the air. "Eventually, the descendants of those courageous people moved throughout the continents of North and South America."

Matsaku was working his way slowly to the far end of the long table, causing the listeners to follow magnetically with their attention. On the wall to his right was a collection of handsomely done artworks: portraits of his mother and father, Delores and Itagaki Matsaku, and paintings of religious figures. Three of these could be recognized as popes: John Paul II, John XXIII, and the most prominently placed one, a likeness of Paul VI. A fourth portrait, that of a monk, was not as well known. It was of Thomas Merton, the American Trappist monk.

Matsaku's migration across the chasm-like room was matching that of his forbears, marking him as a lone adventurer, removed from the huddled crowd. No lacking in his sense of the dramatic.

"Perhaps I insult your intelligence by reminding you of that bit of anthropological history, and if so I apologize. But I risk that to bring into clear perspective my place, the place of Manuel Matsaku, in the scheme of things. My mother Delores was Mexican, of mixed Aztec and Spanish lineage. You see her likeness on the wall there." He made the sign of the cross while continuing to talk.

"My father was Japanese. So you see," and he paused breathlessly, pointing his index finger at his chest, "in my personage resides the reuniting of the ages of man. Twenty-five thousand years of disunion are corrected. The grand crusade is consummated. Quite appropriately, the United States of America will provide the arena wherein Señor Belsasso and I may lead our peoples to the concrete realization of this reunion." A bow in the direction of his Mexican colleague punctuated the monologue.

He pivoted and faced the far end of the room, which had been unlighted. A sharp snap of his fingers brought on ceiling lights trained to illuminate the entire wall. It was covered by a mosaic of brilliant colors and kaleidoscopic images: of cosmic vistas, landscapes, battle scenes, religious figures. The onlookers sat up in their chairs and craned to grasp the vision before them. No one spoke.

Matsaku turned back to them. "I do not expect you to take in this work of art just now. It deserves patient and careful study, and I will be pleased to guide you through its nuances at your leisure when our business is concluded. Suffice it to say that this mosaic portrays, much more beautifully than ever I could with mere words, the substance of my message to you. While I would not presume to emulate my blessed mother's ecumenical religious endeavors, I am privileged to pursue, in my own way, this enterprise which follows in her footsteps."

After a pause he added, more to himself than to his guests, "It is my destiny to do so."

Another snap and the wall was once more in shadows. He walked silently back to the business end of the table.

This interlude provided the others with a chance to reflect on what they were witnessing. General Perkins, red-faced and barrel-chested, shifted in his chair and winced at the pain in his left knee, which was yet to recover from an encounter with a behemoth high school linebacker at Fort McClellan, Alabama last spring. He was wondering if this man was a megalomaniacal, genetically-fractured, mental case and was thinking up a graceful exit. Eisenberg was busy capturing the proceedings in his tape-recorder mind, the facility for which went a long way toward explaining his success in life. He was a legend at Princeton as the only four-point student to never take a notebook to class. The others were hypnotized by the intensity of feeling emanating from their host. General Perkins decided not to run out of the place until the guy was through.

Matsaku paused at his place to sip ice water then moved a few steps toward the north end of the room. "My friends, would you please join me here?" He motioned for them to follow.

"Let me show you the preliminary layout of the project I have in mind for us. We have arranged a model for ease of presentation." With that he reached for a wall switch and illuminated a large table upon which rested a scale model.

"Beautifully done," Pat Beason crooned, her smile beaming, followed by words of agreement—"Yes, yes"—from Perkins and Turnbow. Then she added, "Please explain it," and wished immediately she hadn't sounded so impatient. The Japanese are patient people.

"Of course my dear, that's why we're here," Matsaku replied, confirming her fears. "What you see is a development covering the tract of land that is now Fort Campbell, Kentucky. There are 105,000 acres, the fifth-largest military installation in the United States." He wielded a pointer and used it to make a broad sweep over the model.

"It will be the largest entertainment venue in the world. Allow me to point out the highlights. The centerpiece you see here is the horseracing track, domed for climate control. Equally important are the casinos and hotels, two of each, comparable to the grandest in Las Vegas or Atlantic City, placed at some distance from each other but connected by this monorail system. You can see that the entire complex is furnished with monorails for easy access." His pointer traced the paths of a criss-crossing network that reached all corners of the model.

"At the south end of the tract, separated from the gambling enterprises, is the theme park, Discovery World. It will match anything Disney has done. In fact, we have a lead on acquiring one of Disney's executives to work for us. The discovery theme will be, let us say, universal, in that many of the popular eras among the frontiers of creation and civilization will be featured, from dinosaurs to human migration to Daniel Boone to outer space. We might even include a Garden of Eden, a Biblically-based venue."

He paused allowing his guests to assimilate what he had said before continuing.

"There are housing developments in four areas—here, here, here, and here. Each will provide a special environment, such as golfing in these two locales, or horse stables and equestrian arts, or water sports. The details of course are subject to change. Something for everyone." He smiled broadly and watched their expressions.

"Oh, and here is the airport, large enough to accommodate the new large-body jets which will bring the crowds. So, what do you think? But first, let us return to our seats for more comfort."

He left the spotlight on, inviting them to return later for a more detailed study.

"What I think is..." General Perkins was the first to take up his offer for comment. "What I think is that it's the damnedest thing I ever saw."

"A brilliant idea. It should work," added Governor Turnbow.

Fernando Belsasso, classic Castillian in his tailored suit, slick-back full head of black hair, and elegant manner, cleared his throat. "It is a most ambitious scheme, and I compliment you, Mr. Matsaku, on your vision. But of course you have never been known to be short on vision. I am wondering, well, just how much this will cost, since you have engaged the resources of my country to assist in financing." He delivered his lines with precision as rehearsed with Matsaku during their specially arranged pre-meeting meeting. There were certain items, "sensitive areas," Matsaku had called them, which would be kept from the others.

"Indeed," Matsaku answered, "I anticipated your interest in that aspect. The best estimate now is one hundred billion dollars." The words flowed off his tongue as easily as if he had just priced a new convertible. There was much shifting in chairs and glancing at each other before he added, "A sum within the grasp of this group assembled."

"What about the property acquisition? The military property?" the general asked. "You must know that the decision to close Campbell is one of the hottest potatoes the Base Realignment and Closure Commission has dealt with. The 82nd and the 101st have been battling it out. Hell, they may initiate hostilities against each other any minute! And, of course, Senator Crockett is sitting at the head of the Armed Services Committee. He's not budging on the matter. He says he won't see Campbell closed. In fact, he's just introduced a Joint Resolution to block the Commission's plan."

"I'd have to agree with General Perkins," Secretary Eisenberg interjected. Thin, worried, and obsessive, he saw his role as Clinton would have, namely, to bring a note of moderation to the proceedings. "This is a beautiful plan, but Jonas Crockett is a formidable opponent and could upset the whole thing. I'm sure you're aware that the bulk of this land is in his state, and his people want it to stay there. The president has staked his position, but it's not a done deal by any means."

Pat Beason spoke up again. "Believe me, these gentlemen are absolutely right. Campbell is a red-hot issue for us in Tennessee. I'm sure Governor Turnbow would say the same about Kentucky. One-third of the property is in his state. Even if we plastered a picture of your model there on the front pages of the *Commercial-Appeal*, *Courier-Journal*, and *Tennessean* and promised full employment for everyone within a hundred miles, there'd be tremendous opposition."

Turnbow grunted and nodded agreement, distracted as he tried to drag from his uncooperative memory bank the key operatives of his political machinery in that part of his state. He was often lost in a fog without an aide at his side. His most publicized lapse was the occasion when he introduced Mrs. Clinton as "Hester," thus inspiring a spate of political cartoons with scarlet letters as the theme.

Matsaku lifted a hand, pulled himself up ceremoniously, and smiled. "Yes, I know very well about the formidable and reportedly irascible senior senator from Tennessee. I have been kept informed of the progress of the Base Closure Commission's recommendations. I am aware of the Joint Resolution which may impede our plan."

Putting his wineglass down, he thrust his chin forward and erased the smile. "Please do not underestimate the extent of preparations. Our contacts in the United States have allowed us to anticipate such maneuvering. At this moment we are engaged in two tactics: First, we are examining the membership list of the Armed Services Committee to find allies; second, Señor Belsasso has already been at work on a plan to enlist the services of a close relative of the senator's, a certain Doctor Crockett, a psychiatrist, I believe, who we have reason to think will be able to assist us in this matter. He too is from Tennessee. Perhaps, Madame Speaker, you are acquainted with him?"

"As a matter of fact, I am," she answered and smiled her beautiful, broad, God-given smile that had won many votes…and hearts.

As a matter of fact, she said to herself, I'm more acquainted with him than any of you could possibly imagine, thank you.

Chapter 4

▼

Each time Trey drifted off, a dream awoke him. The dream repeated itself: He was crippled and was in some tropical setting, a vineyard of sorts. He was trying to hobble his way out of the labyrinthine rows. But as soon as he was in view of an exit, a dark figure would appear to block the way, and the labyrinth would magnify in complexity. The vines closed about him, suffocating and menacing. He would awaken in a cold sweat.

He knew just enough about the art of dream analysis to be dangerous. His practice didn't lean in that direction. But this nightmare was from Dream Interpretation 101. The vineyard was his nemesis, the nectar of the gods, alcohol. The exit represented freeing his soul from the daily—hourly—struggle. The dark figure was none other than himself, the self that always got in his way, blocking the exit to freedom, allowing the demons to engulf him.

The specter of his dark side, the cocky and self-indulgent Trey Crockett, was well known to him. It was there in his flamboyant college days of the sixties when he ruled the roost at Davidson College as president of the student government. He was bright enough to carry a high B average even with the torrid social life he led, a social life fueled by lots of money and the liberal use of mind-altering chemicals.

Then for the first time in his silver-spooned life, he came up against a brick wall. Vanderbilt Medical School didn't seem to place much value on his past achievements or his money. Neither did they cater to his lineage: a string of luminaries stretching from his father who was at that time governor of Tennessee all the way back to John Sevier, the first person to serve in that capacity when Tennessee became a state. Not to mention Davy Crockett, the rough-and-ready limb of his family tree.

The medical school faculty gave him no quarter. When he almost flunked out the first year, he found another side to himself: a more humble, dedicated self. Begging—for the first time in his life, begging—to be given another chance, he buckled down to a low-profile student life that would have made Hippocrates smile. He disciplined himself to drink only on Saturdays, gave up smoking weed, and almost gave up sex.

Almost. He was just too damned good-looking. Or so his women-friends said. Too good to waste. With thick sandy hair, square jaw, deep blue eyes, and a well-built six-foot frame, the gods of chastity faced a difficult challenge. Pre-AIDS flings were easy and carefree, such as the one he had with the instructor his third year in medical school.

He had been so virtuous the previous year keeping his pants zipped. Then came the class summer picnic at Montgomery Bell Park when he and Dr. Patrice Bashore, a shapely rising star in the Pediatrics Department, found themselves swimming and cavorting together. There was a lot of incidental, supposedly accidental, touching, and before the last beer keg was drained, telephone numbers were being exchanged. It lasted almost a year.

That was his last affair before he came upon Evelyn Sanders of Louisville, Kentucky, his wife-to-be. She was studying voice at the Cincinnati Conservatory and met Trey on a blind date. He was a psychiatric resident and single and had an interesting family in Tennessee. Her family was well-known in Louisville society, particularly the arts community. No relation to the Colonel, she always explained. The two hit it off and a year later there was a first-class wedding.

Evelyn's music career was short-circuited when Trey's took precedence in their lives. She would often have regrets about that as later events came to bear and as a divorcee she was reduced to giving private voice lessons and a role as church soloist. She would have plenty of opportunity to wonder what life might have been like for her had she never met Trey Crockett.

Indeed, such might have been the case had he continued his liaison with Patrice Bashore. That affair was almost the undoing of his medical career, when Dean Billings got wind of what was happening sometime around mid-year. With a bit of timely advice from fellow students, Trey managed to break loose before calamity struck again. But my! how he missed her lithe body and smooth skin! Pediatrics rounds were not nearly as exciting.

So, yes, indeed, Winton Sevier Crockett the Third was well acquainted with the side of himself that once again was haunting his life. This particular Wednesday morning he was wishing he could do away with that shadow as easily as the one he was removing from his face. Unfortunately, the previous night's encounter with the two emissaries, Raspy and Large Hands, the tape, and the envelope with its ugly truths were not a dream. They were a living nightmare.

Snugging the knot of his tie against the shirt collar, he sighed a sigh as deep as his mother's the day he told her he was going to be a doctor instead of a lawyer. Ruby Crockett had married into tradition and had written the script for her son, who had come along just in time to grace the later stages of her reproductive years. Maybe now he was paying the price for that independent streak. He was never sure that his mother had forgiven him, and now she was reaching an age where she might leave him never knowing.

He stared into the mirror and shook his head. If he were half as devoted to his AA program as he was supposed to be, he'd be planning to make a meeting a day this week. When he first came out of treatment he did that for a year. Lately though, with the Tennessee Impaired Physicians' Program off his back, he had slipped to one or two a week. Sometimes fewer.

Hospital rounds that morning were fast-paced. He was finished by nine. His three patients at Westpark Pavilion may not have gotten their money's worth. Especially the one whose name was Albert. Trey kept thinking: Could this be "Al," a plant by these people, whoever they are?

His usual Wednesday routine involved a short workday. He had two patients at the office from ten to twelve, then a clinical case conference with psychiatry residents over lunch at the medical school, the recent addition to his schedule. That left him free after one-thirty and he usually headed straight to the athletic club for tennis and swimming.

The smell of freshly brewed coffee awaited him when he trudged into the office at 9:30. Melba, his secretary and receptionist, greeted him with a smile which he answered feebly. Theirs had been a comfortable relationship ever since Trey decided to bring her into his confidence. He told her about his near-calamitous history when she came to work for him three years ago. He really didn't have much of a choice, considering the fact that for the first two years she received random calls from the state medical association's office requesting him to submit a urine specimen. He had to either convince her that he was a subject in some research study for kidney disease or tell her the truth. Since truth-telling was his number one ally in those days, he opted for the latter. She reassured him that she could handle it, that this was nothing compared to the last doctor she worked for who was making a comeback following a conviction for Medicaid fraud. She figured she soon would be eligible for a specialty license in rehabilitation medicine.

"You have three messages, doctor."

Trey saw the familiar pink slips in his message box. The first was from the hospital advising that Dr. Wesley was requesting a consultation for one of his patients. The second, from Irene Jenkins, was about her mother who was having some reaction to her medication.

The third was from Al, an attorney with Keaton, Brindle. "A personal call, said you would know about it," Melba's brief message read.

With a few choice muttered words for this less-than-choice law firm, he went straight to dialing for Al Horton, leaving Dr. Wesley holding the bag and Ms. Jenkins' mother in the throes of a skin rash or sluggish bowels.

Mr. Horton came to the phone after a short intermission. "Yes, Doctor Crockett, I believe you were expecting my call. Right?"

"That's right," Trey answered in his best level tone. "What can I do for you?"

"A lot, we think. But I need some time with you to go over the details. When would that be convenient for you…say…in the next twenty-four hours?"

How considerate, Trey thought.

"Actually Wednesday's a pretty good day for me. I have the afternoon off. Are we talking your office or what?" He'd have to cancel his tennis date, which was penciled in on the calendar he scanned on his desk.

"I was told you have a regular tennis date. Maybe you could cancel that so we could get this done as soon as possible. Our client is feeling some urgency. Yes, this afternoon at my office would be good."

"How's two o'clock?" Trey asked, wondering if the sons-of-bitches knew his brand of toilet tissue too.

"Two's fine. We're on the third floor of the Werthan Building."

"That's on Main in East Nashville?" Not a prime-time neighborhood, just enough out of the mainstream to match the firm's reputation.

"Correct. Look forward to seeing you, doctor."

He saw his two patients that morning without flinching. The ability to do that came naturally. Whenever he should be most distracted his focus was keenest. Probably something he had learned growing up in a home with powerful distractions, not the least of which was a father who commanded center stage at all costs. Many a late evening he had spent alone in his bedroom with homework, shutting out the sounds of banjo music or a resounding speech rehearsal going on in the family room below. His mother's applause and laughter supplemented the cacophony.

So yes, indeed, Mrs. McClary and Mr. Guthrie got their one-hundred-dollars' worth from their psychiatrist that morning with never a hint that he had a mess waiting for him in the afternoon.

It was a short walk from his office on Twenty-first Avenue to the conference room in the Department of Psychiatry on the fifth floor of Vanderbilt Hospital. He took in the scene with its bricks and mortar and concrete motif. Once there were lawns and trees in these environs which had burgeoned into a sprawling tertiary care university medical complex in the past two decades.

Bigger is better, he thought. And uglier.

Sack lunches were awaiting him and the eight residents who assembled to pick his brain. The complimentary sandwich, pickle, chips, and brownie supposedly compensated for the meager stipend he earned for this weekly encounter with academe. The Psychiatry Department didn't know it, but Trey would have paid them for the opportunity. He enjoyed the contact with young, inquiring minds.

Initially it was his choice to put a hold on these duties. He wanted time to prove to himself the resilience of a newfound sobriety. There was also the practical matter of making that AA meeting every day for a year, which often consumed the noon hour. A year ago he had requested reinstatement, but with some excuse about changes in the department structure, which Trey took to be a cover story for scrutinizing him closely, it had taken this long to get started again.

Today offered a lively discussion about one of the residents' patients who was having problems reconciling her strict Roman Catholicism with an extramarital affair.

"What do you know about the Roman Church?" Trey asked, throwing the question out to the lowest bidder.

"It's less and less Roman isn't it?" one of the residents, John Robbins, asserted. "I mean if you grabbed Catholics off the streets of Nashville today I bet less than fifty percent would believe in papal infallibility. At least among our age group."

"Are you Catholic, John?" Trey inquired.

Grunts and nods arose from the others, indicating Trey had hit upon an inside subject. John reached into his shirt and retrieved the end of a chain with crucifix and St. Christopher medal.

"Yeah," John smiled, "I'm the only one of this heathen group with a direct line." He glanced upward. "Just you wait though. All these guys'll come flocking to the faith when they get into practice and we compare bad debts. Catholic guilt won't let my patients leave the office without paying."

"Hail Mary and the jingle of the cash register," one of his cohorts chimed.

After a good laugh Trey asked, "Any of you ever heard of Thomas Merton?"

Robbins alone nodded. "Yeah, he was a controversial figure in the church back in the 60's. Anti-war, anti-nuclear, all that stuff."

"Right," Trey confirmed. "He was a Trappist monk at the Abbey of Gethsemani. That's just up the road, near Bardstown, Kentucky. A wonderful retreat." He put in a plug for the residents' finding time for themselves, quiet time, regardless of their religious beliefs.

He then steered the discussion back to the patient. What he didn't discuss was conservative vs. liberal views of extramarital sex. Squirming was not becoming to a teacher just back from probation.

Leaving the conference at 1:25 gave him just enough time to get to his car and drive downtown and across the river. That's the way he wanted it: no slack, no time to think. Except he couldn't help recalling his last encounter with this law firm over the anti-trust matter with HospiCare. His involvement with that health care giant was a legacy of his father who was one of the early investors. Trey lost his position on the executive committee when he went into treatment but was creeping back into their good graces; recently he was assigned to the Finance Committee. He recalled his mother's smile when he told her of that appointment. Nothing pleased Ruby more than her son's fitting neatly into the shadow of his father.

* * * *

He found the offices of Keaton, Brindle, listed on the directory and proceeded to the third floor.

Al Horton was a real porker, the original Mister Five-by-Five. Stout suspenders were the only things standing between him and indecent exposure. He offered a meaty paw to his visitor. "Al Horton. Glad to meet you, Doctor Crockett. Please sit down. Some coffee, water, or cola?"

"No, thanks. Just had lunch."

"It's nice to see you in person, doctor. I've heard of you for quite some time, and of course your father, God rest his soul. He was quite a governor, stumping around the state playing that banjo. Ha! Ha!" He shook his head and slapped his leg, recalling the familiar image of Winton Crockett exciting the crowds in East Tennessee with homespun mountain music.

Trey nodded with barely a smile that said this was old hat and he'd rather get on with the business at hand. One day he hoped he'd meet someone in Tennessee who didn't recognize him as merely the issue of Winton's loins. Or at least not dwell on it.

Al obliged. "I guess you'd rather hear what this is all about though, wouldn't you? Sure." He didn't wait for a reply but bit the end off a cigar, lit it, and then sucked and spit out words at the same time. "You don't (suck) mind, I hope (suck)," indicating the cigar.

Trey shifted in his chair and said nothing. He minded everything about the slug from his cheap toupee—Trey had just realized what it was that made Al remind him of Larry the Stooge—to his overpolished shoes that kept catching their heels on the back of his pants cuffs. The suspenders must have been losing their grip.

"Doctor Crockett, I've got a client, a very wealthy client, who's interested in purchasing some government property. More accurately I should say he and a group of investors want to." He stood, inspected the burning end of his cigar, and walked to the end of his desk where he planted his gluteus maximus, well named in this case.

"He's interested in Fort Campbell, Kentucky, which as you know is mostly in our state. Ever been there?"

"Mr. Horton, I've covered every square mile of this state on the stump with my father and uncle from time to time. Yes, I'm familiar with Fort Campbell."

"Your uncle, Jonas Crockett, I presume, is very much to the point. It's the senior senator from Tennessee, the Chairman of the Senate Armed Services Committee, who appears to hold the…uh…let's say the key to unlocking the doors for my client's enterprise." Al paused with raised eyebrows and Trey remained silent.

"You're aware of his stance opposing the closing of Campbell. Ever since the President made his campaign pledge to reduce defense spending, this thing between him and your uncle has been building. And when the recommendation from the Base Closure Commission came out that Campbell and the 101st be closed down, the senator went ballistic. He's filed a resolution to strike down the President's order, and the fight's on."

"Yeah, I know. You don't have to be a nephew. It's on the front page every day."

"Ah! But you do have to be a relative, a very dear and especially close relative, to influence him to change his position. That, Doctor Crockett, is precisely why you are here today." Al smiled at his guest, lifted his bulk off the desk, and stood staring at Trey who stared back, speechless.

Al shuffled back to his chair, elevated his suspenders with two thumbs, and continued talking. "Actually my firm's been engaged secondarily by a Washington, D.C., firm, which is primarily engaged with the client I mentioned. I get my instructions from them. I understand you've been persuaded—and let me be perfectly clear that I do not know the circumstances—persuaded to assist in this matter. I'll be your contact person for the project."

"You what? You do not know the circumstances?" His voice rose precipitously. "What kind of bullshit is that, Mr. Horton? Which law firm's name was all over that blackmail document I read last night? It didn't look like a D.C. address to me!" Trey was standing up now, walking around the edge of the desk and slamming it with his hand.

Al very calmly swiveled his chair away and took a slow puff on the cigar. "I'm sorry, doctor, to see you upset. Let me repeat that I have no knowledge of any document or the circumstances of your being persuaded to assist; nor am I interested. My job is simply to inform you of your assignment and to coordinate with you as to progress. Now..." as he pivoted back to face Trey "...could I suggest you compose yourself, sit down again, and we can work out the rest of the details."

Trey realized he had blown it with his outburst. These guys may be in the low-rent district, but they didn't just come in on the turnip truck. Whether it was true or not, and more than likely it was not, Al was buffering himself against charges of criminality with these claims of ignorance. The complaint document that was delivered to him the previous night was no proof Al knew anything. Anyone could have typed it and used the firm's name.

Trey took a deep breath and sat down again. "You have no idea how ridiculous this whole thing is, Mr. Horton. Somebody up there in the capital is greatly overestimating the influence I have with my uncle. I thought everyone knew how independent and stubborn he is."

"Yeah," Al answered, "we all know about the senator's style. In fact, I asked the same questions you're asking. They kept telling me you're the closest person to him, that there's a very close bond, and if anybody can help us you can."

Trey was surprised at the thoroughness of these people. They knew about his ties to the senator, that Uncle Jonas treated him like his own. It went back to 1962, when Jonas, who was now in his fifth term, was running for the first time. In the midst of the campaign, Jonas' son, his only child, was killed in an automobile accident. Trey took up the family banner and filled the role his cousin had begun, helping his uncle win the nomination and eventually the election.

Thus began a surrogate father-son relationship that continued to this day. Jonas was Trey's chief ally when he made the critical decision to go into medicine instead of law, a decision his parents had disdained. Jonas saw the wisdom in Trey's rejecting the "political destiny" role inasmuch as he would be perpetually dominated by his father's image. Winton eventually toned down on the subject but largely due to his brother's persuasion. Ruby went silent.

An even more recent event had further cemented the bond between uncle and nephew. Some six years ago Jonas's wife, Jeanne, had suffered a severe mental breakdown. It appeared to most that she had some form of obscure dementia. She was sent to the Johns Hopkins Hospital and a brain biopsy was suggested.

Jonas had been alarmed at this drastic proposal and asked Trey to fly to Baltimore to help with the final decisions. After discussing the case with the neurologist and psychiatrist and talking to Aunt Jeanne, Trey thought they had missed the diagnosis. He saw a catatonic depression masquerading as dementia and suggested a trial of electroconvulsive therapy before resorting to the biopsy. The consulting psychiatrist reluctantly agreed, and after three treatments she miraculously recovered. Jeanne and Jonas would be forever grateful to him for sparing her the hole in her head and for bringing her back to herself.

Al and his cohorts were right. If anyone could do it, Trey could.

"We do have a timetable for this project." Al reached for his glasses and began reading from notes on a legal pad.

"The Joint Resolution...let's see...I didn't have the foggiest about any of this damn political stuff until the D.C. guys briefed me...let's see...here it is. The Joint Resolution must be passed on or before October twenty-first if the President's order is going to be stopped."

"Yeah?" Trey answered, trying to regain his composure. "I didn't know about the deadline."

"If you're interested, I have a faxed copy of the base-closing law here...uh...Public Law..." Al rifled through the mess on his desk and produced a document. "Public Law one-oh-one-dash-five-one-oh. I scanned it. There are very specific deadlines for the Congress to meet in order to override the Base Realignment and Closure Commission and President's recommendations." He tossed the document toward Trey.

"I might want a copy, yeah," Trey murmured.

"Anyhow," Al continued, "what it amounts to is this: before the Armed Services Committee reports the resolution out to the full Senate, the chairman and the necessary votes need to be in our pocket. That has to take place before..." He checked his notes again. "...before October sixth. Yeah, October sixth. That's the actual deadline for your uncle's committee."

Al rested both elbows on his desk and opened his palms in Trey's direction as if to say "It's all yours now."

Trey's mind was a whirl. "I'll need some time to think about this."

"Sure. No problem. Let me know tomorrow what your game plan is. The D.C. firm has funds and connections." He put down the cigar and escorted Trey out of the office with a handshake.

In the elevator an older gray-haired man about the age of Uncle Jonas spoke to him cordially. This is just great, Trey thought. So now I use the love and devotion of my closest relative to save my ass and drag him through the slime with me.

Two things came to mind. The first was that he had to think of a way to approach Jonas. The second was that he wanted some comfort. Not from a bottle. He wanted Pat Beason's body next to his.

Chapter 5

Speaker of the House Pat Beason of Tennessee and Governor Nat Turnbow of Kentucky made the return flight from Tokyo sitting together. The joint business-seeking excursion their respective states had sponsored in Japan had provided them with the cover they needed for the meeting with Matsaku, and it was natural they would have mutual interests to discuss. It was just that none of their colleagues on the flight knew exactly which interest was their prime topic of discussion. That's the way it had to stay, too, so the lid wouldn't come off the deal prematurely.

Matsaku had insisted on no written records of their proceedings, and there would be no correspondence until after November first at the earliest. All communication would be via telephone, and no notes were to be taken. Colleagues, secretaries, etc. were to be told anything to keep them off track. The code name would be "The Delores Project." Of course.

He had also directed that Belsasso was to be the prime channel for all communications. As the others came upon significant developments, they were to communicate with him.

Beason and Turnbow settled into their chartered first-class seats and ordered drinks. The governor stuck to his native and favorite bourbon,

Maker's Mark, while Pat settled for plain tonic water. Engine noise was sufficient to muffle their conversation.

Turnbow began. "Did you see General Perkins turn red when Matsaku went into that monologue about being the…what was it he said?…the key person in whom resided the reunification of the peoples of the world? God! I thought Perk would stroke out on us right then and there!" He shook his head and chuckled.

"I'm not so sure about my own coloring at that moment," Beason replied. "It was a bit shocking to hear someone that powerful become so grandiose in front of people he'd only just met. He leaves no doubt about his personal investment in this thing."

"Right, no doubt. I believe we're in for one helluva ride with him at the controls."

The flight attendant arrived with the drinks along with cheese and crackers.

"A toast," Turnbow proposed, "to 'Delores,' otherwise known as 'Las Vegas East,' and our states' mutual prosperity."

"Mind if I add: to keeping our jobs when this is all over?" Beason said, clinking her glass against his.

"Hey, I don't see how we can lose. You heard him say we don't have to come out in favor of closing the base. He's got a plan to make that happen. All we do is let our congressional delegations fight it out and don't get our hands dirty. Then when that's over we support the purchase by Matsaku and his international brotherhood. The base-closing legislation requires the Secretary of Defense to consult with state and local governments before selling a closed base. You knew that, didn't you?"

"Oh, yeah. That's already come up with Seward Air Force Base when it closed a few years ago. Not the same piece of legislation but same principle. Don't you figure that's why Matsaku had us there today?"

"Sure. Handy having Eisenberg on board, too. Anyway, we'll come out smelling like a rose. The benefits to our economies will be tremendous. It'll make the citizens of Hopkinsville and Clarksville wonder why they didn't think of it themselves. Those towns have been clinging to defense budget whims for years. They'll be kissing our feet on the way to the bank. Hey, that's a nice image: we set up receiving lines or voting booths outside the banks."

Turnbow paused to sip his drink. "Ahhh, nothing like Kentucky mash."

"I hope you're right," Beason sighed. "There are a few major assumptions built into this thing. Like that it won't leak out before the decision to close the base is finalized. There were five of us around that table, you know. And number two, that the religious right won't bring enough pressure to kill the gambling issue in my state or..."

"That's one reason he likes Campbell, don't you see," Turnbow interrupted. "We already have pari-mutuel betting and we're very close on casino gambling. The lottery's been running for over a year. Very popular with the public and the legislature. I know you've had some problems on that, but look at Mississippi. They're turning heads on the Delta. And don't forget that a third of Campbell is in Kentucky, so that issue won't stop the development. The land in Tennessee could be used for non-gambling purposes if worse came to worst."

"You're probably right. Matsaku did emphasize the size of the tract. What did he say? One hundred thousand acres? The fifth-largest military installation? That's impressive when you think about it. Where else could you find a piece of land that size with one owner in the middle of America?"

"Yeah, the location is good too. Interstate 24 runs by it, easy access from the larger cities of the Midwest, beautiful lakes nearby on the rivers, and rolling hills. God's country."

"Speaking of God," Beason said, "did you see Matsaku cross himself when he mentioned his mother's name? And all those religious figures, paintings of popes on the wall of the board room? What's the story there? Do you know?"

"What I know is mainly what I picked up here and there. Eisenberg seemed to be well-informed." He paused to sip bourbon. "You and Perkins had to leave after the briefing, but I hung around with Leon and the Mexican a while. Belsasso was tight-lipped, but Leon was in a mood to talk."

"What do you know? If it's okay to ask."

"No, no problem. What Leon said was that Matsaku's mother Delores was a young nun assigned to a convent in Thailand during World War II. The Japanese occupied that country, and Matsaku's father was stationed there, an officer in the Jap Army. The story is that the nun and the officer fell in love and she got pregnant. Then, according to Leon, her superiors gave her the choice of returning to Mexico or giving up being a nun and marrying the father. She chose to marry him. But…BUT…only on the condition that her child would be raised in the Catholic faith."

"And the child that was born was named Manuel," Beason concluded.

"Right. And his father became one of the leading industrialists in post-war Japan. Steel, I think. Manuel has done well at enlarging their fortune."

"With the grace of God and the hand of the Blessed Virgin Mary guiding him," Beason added with more than a touch of irony.

"Apparently. And he's going to need all that kind of help he can get with this project. Say, what's this about the psychiatrist they're using on Senator Crockett?"

Their conversation was interrupted by Jim Daniels, president of Nashville Gas and Electric Company and chairman of the Tennessee Industrial Expansion Commission. The seat belt lights were off, and passengers were starting to move about.

"Hey, you two are mighty serious-looking. Time to relax, isn't it?" Daniels said.

"Just give us a minute," Beason quipped back, "to finish our plans for a government takeover of all utilities in Kentucky and Tennessee. It won't take us long." She was relieved at the interruption inasmuch as she didn't relish the idea of a detailed conversation about Trey Crockett.

Daniels took her kidding as an invitation to join them, so he perched on the seat arm across the aisle and made it a threesome. "Where were you two at noon? Didn't see either of you at the wrap-up luncheon."

Beason was munching a cracker and used that as an excuse to not answer immediately. Nat picked up the cue as if rehearsed. "I don't know about Pat, but I was in my hotel room resting. My aching back couldn't stand up to the pace. It was mostly ceremonial, anyway; all the important stuff was done yesterday, I hope."

Pat wiped her lips with a napkin. "That was the only time I had left to shop, and I promised my nephew I'd bring him back some artifacts. You know, ancient artifacts like tee shirts and posters of Japanese rock stars. Did we miss much?"

"Just the part where they passed out contracts worth billions of yen. Not to worry." Daniels chuckled.

Pat took the opportunity to tune out of the conversation. She pushed the button to release her seatback, turned her body slightly sideways trying to get comfortable in the unyielding seat, nestled her head into the cushion, and turned her face to the window. Turnbow and Daniels took the hint and continued their conversation.

She closed her eyes and wondered when she would see her handsome, blue-eyed lover and what kind of trouble he was in…this time…

Her thoughts drifted to the last night they were together. It had been one of those hurry-up encounters, wham, bam—not satisfying to either of them. She found herself vaguely disturbed by the longing she felt for one of those slow, warm, and tender evenings that seemed to go on forever.

Chapter 6

"Oh…OOOOH…GOD…OOOH, TREY, BABY, OOOH…" Her breathless exclamations crescendoed, their bodies wet with passion, her fingers clawing at his backside…

When it was over, they lay close for a long time, gently caressing without words.

Whatever the reason Pat Beason had never married, it had nothing to do with sexual hang-ups.

"I wonder if jet lag enhances sexual performance," Trey mused to break the silence. "Maybe I can get a research grant."

"I'd volunteer as a subject."

"I think I can use you in the control group. Of course, you need to be aware that the control group will be required to have kinky forms of sex on a regular basis. I have a release for you to sign indicating you won't hold me responsible for any perversions you suffer as a result."

"I'll sign. I'll sign anything. Just tell me you'll never report it to the Ethics Commission." She rolled over on top of him under the sheet. "If you do, I swear to you I'll nibble you to death, starting here…" she bit at his neck "…and ending…who knows where?"

"Heaven help me," Trey moaned.

Her demeanor changed. She rolled off him and propped up on her elbow, her damp hair falling on her forehead. "You won't believe this, but I had something else in mind when I asked you to come over tonight."

"I guess that's why you started undressing me in the hallway."

"I knew you wouldn't believe me. But honestly I did. Seriously, we've got to talk about a serious matter. Jonas Crockett. Know what I'm talking about?"

Trey bolted to a sitting position. "My God, was it in the headlines? I haven't seen the paper." He looked at her quizzically. "How'd you know?"

"Shhh," Pat purred, placing her fingers on his lips. "I'll be back in a minute and we'll talk about it."

Her trim body, exceptional for forty-five years, sprang from the bed and into the bathroom. A few minutes later she emerged fresh and powdered in a bathrobe to find Trey rummaging through the fridge with just his slacks on.

"Got any diet cola?"

"It's in the door." Her eyes took in his bare torso.

"I see it." He could feel her eyes.

Pat declined his offer to join him.

He popped the top and swilled a long drink. "Who goes first, you or me?"

"I think I'll brew some coffee. We may be here for a while." She pulled out the necessary utensils and proceeded to tell her side of the story.

"I told you I just got back from Japan yesterday and that I was on state business, right?"

"Uh-huh," Trey grunted.

"Well…" she paused and poured water into the canister, then turned and looked directly and sternly at him, "…now what I'm about to tell you is very confidential, do you understand? It has to be just between you and me, got that?" She could be intimidating when she wanted to. She waited for his reply.

"Of course, Pat. I'm your friend, remember?" He stepped over to her and placed a hand on each shoulder. "Your very close friend."

"I'm sorry, I didn't mean to be so harsh. It's just a very sensitive subject. Here, let's go sit while the coffee brews." She led him by the hand to the den where they sat on the couch.

"Okay. There's this rich-as-Croesus Japanese fellow named Manuel Matsaku. Ever heard of him?"

"Sure I have. Hasn't everybody?"

"I didn't know how much you followed international business. No offense."

"None taken."

"About two weeks ago I get this call from him right out of the blue. Never met him before in my life. He tells me I've been recommended to him to assist with the development of a venture in the state of Tennessee, that he's picked a handful of people as a planning nucleus, and that it'll involve the purchase of government property. Then he invites me to a top-secret meeting of this group to coincide with a trip he knows I'll be taking to Japan..."

Trey interrupted. "So that's who the 'client' is that sweet Al was talking about! Manuel Matsaku. Holy shit!"

"Who's 'sweet Al'?"

Trey waved her off. "No, sorry, I'll have my turn. Go ahead."

"So, it was on this three-day whirlwind business tour that Matsaku arranged for a meeting. Didn't tell any of us ahead of time who the other guys were. Turns out it was Nat Turnbow from Kentucky, Leon Eisenberg—yes, the Secretary of Defense, no less—General John Perkins, and then a Mexican I'd never heard of named Belsasso. He's the Secretary of Commerce or its equivalent in Mexico. Holds some big purse strings..."

"Let's see," Trey interrupted, "Perkins was Chairman of the Joint Chiefs, wasn't he? I thought he was retired."

"He is. He's on the Base Closure Commission now and knows all the inside scoop. Big old loud guy. Impressive, though. Didn't mind challenging Matsaku about the political realities, but knew when to suck up. In fact, the whole group was impressive. Except for Turnbow. He's sort of a gullible airhead. Might blunder into trouble in a thing like this."

"A thing like this? What thing?"

"It's a beauty." She went on to describe the scale model she had seen in Matsaku's boardroom and the ambitious plan.

"Christ! Sounds like the workings of a madman. Do you think it could work?"

"You can bet your sweet hairy chest I've been giving that some thought the past forty-eight hours, or however many it's been. My internal clock is all haywire since I got back. The answer is yes. I think it can work. It'll be the Vegas/Atlantic City/Disneyworld of Middle America."

Trey continued to push for details. "Where'd Matsaku come up with this idea, and what's with the Mexican connection?"

"Oh-ho, baby, you just hit the jackpot. Wait 'til I tell you about that!" She patted him on the cheek and rose to get the coffee. The satin gown outlined her rounded rear features nicely.

From the kitchen she continued. "I don't know whether you know about Matsaku's parents. Do you?"

"I'm afraid not. Should I?"

Trey followed her to help with the coffee and to be sure he didn't miss an inflection.

"No. I just don't want to bore you with unnecessary details." She poured herself coffee and Trey fetched the milk and sugar. He was still working on his cola.

Pat explained the unusual circumstances of Matsaku's parentage and his obsession with linking up the present with the past. She divulged the code name, "Delores."

"He's really got a mother complex, big time! Makes a piker out of ol' Oedipus," she added.

She emphasized that her explanation could not do justice to the impression made upon her and the other visitors in Matsaku's boardroom.

"It was…captivating…I guess is the best word. Or maybe mesmerizing."

"I can see that in your eyes," Trey added. "Delores. Huh! Sounds so sweet." He sighed. "Powerful. That's what the son-of-a-bitch is. Powerful enough to pull it off and certainly powerful enough to handle my ass a few times over."

He turned and slumped his way back to the couch. He set the cola can on the coaster, leaned back, and looked at the ceiling with his hands behind his head.

Pat came to rest beside him, her hand on his shoulder.

"Okay," she said, "it's your turn now. Tell mama what kind of trouble little Trey's gotten into."

Trey didn't move. He said, "I thought you said you knew all about it. About me and Uncle Jonas."

She pulled her hand away, seeing that he was not in the mood to play. "All I know is what Matsaku said. That you were being asked to help with your uncle. I assume there's more to it." She put her coffee down.

"Oh, yes, hell, yes! There's more to it, you bet!" Trey got up and paced.

"It seems that blackmail is on the list of acceptable tactics for your honorable Mr. Matsaku." He smiled a fake smile and mocked with an oriental-style bow, hands prayerfully in front.

"I'm cold," he added. He went to the bedroom and found his shirt. He was thinking that Pat seemed pretty excited about Matsaku's scheme. He wasn't so sure he'd have an ally in her, politics being politics. Yet he had no choice but to trust her at this point. He returned to the couch, his white dress shirt hanging out and unbuttoned. The grandfather clock in the hall bonged nine-thirty.

Madame Speaker didn't look up at him when he sat down. She had been thinking, too, about the sudden change of mood in her lover. She wasn't sure what it meant.

"They're blackmailing me with the threat of ruining me. Getting me censured by the American Psychiatric Association. Getting my license. Maybe civil action too. It's serious…serious as a heart attack."

Pat turned to him, taking his hand in a gesture of conciliation. "What in the world? Are you drinking again?"

"No, no. I wish it was that simple. Hell, what am I saying? That's a stupid thing to say. No, it's something you don't know about. In fact, no one does, or did, except my ex. And my former receptionist. She must've been the one they got to for information." He paused.

"What information? What is it, for God's sake?"

"It's bad. I had an affair with a patient. Four, five years ago. It ended when I went into treatment. She ended up a basket case. My lawyers got with hers. They agreed to keep it out of court and the public record as long as I cooperated with my treatment. And I agreed to pay for her to see another psychotherapist who was also in on the deal. That kept my license restrictions based just on the alcohol problem.

"So there are a few others who knew about it—the lawyers, the therapist, and of course Teresa. That's her name, Teresa. I never told you about it. Never a reason until now. Thought it was all behind me. But it seems the statute of limitations hasn't run out yet."

"Oh my God," Pat murmured, stunned. "Why is she cooperating with them?"

"I'm not sure. Except she said they had something on her family, her father, maybe. I'm not sure about that part. I heard it on a taped message Tuesday night in my car when I was confronted by two Latin hoods. My mind was not registering things so elegantly at the time."

"Latin hoods?"

Trey explained the events of the past three days.

"Those guys who brought the tape and the documents, could they have been Mexican?" Pat asked.

"Very likely, I'd say. Especially now that I know about your Mexican business connections." Trey wished he hadn't said "your."

"Hmmm...I wonder..." Pat said, "I wonder if Matsaku knows about this, or if he's left the rough stuff to Señor Belsasso and the Mexican Mafia."

"Is there a Mexican Mafia?" Trey asked.

"I don't know. Well, yes, I think there is. It's called *Ojos Negros*, I think. Means Black Eyes, or maybe I read that in a novel. I don't know. But I can't imagine Matsaku being behind all this nastiness. He's so religious with all that Roman Catholic paraphernalia in his offices. He had pictures of popes on the wall, for Christ sake! I can't see this coming from him."

"Aren't the Sicilians Catholic too?" Trey sneered.

"You'd just have to have been there to understand." Pat shook her head.

"I understand that I've got my ass in a sling, big-time." He leaned forward with his head in his hands. "I've gotta come up with something soon. Big Al granted me a reprieve 'til Monday to get myself together."

"So what's the plan? Can I help?"

"As a matter of fact, I think you can. Why don't you just call up your good ol' buddy Manuel and ask him to call the whole thing off. Tell him if he'll do that for you, you'll give him the best piece o' ass he ever had."

"What an incorrigible reprobate you are!" Pat scolded. "No wonder you stay in hot water!" She poked at him and laughed. "I'm serious. What's your plan?"

Trey began buttoning his shirt and stuffing it in his pants while he talked. "I've got the weekend worked out. Tomorrow I'm driving up to the monastery in Kentucky. Got to get quiet for a few hours. I'll spend the night there at the guesthouse. Then, on Sunday, the real challenge. I'll be having lunch with Uncle Jonas and Aunt Jeanne at their home in

Sevierville. That's where they are this weekend. I told him I had something important to discuss. Ha! Little does he know."

"Oooh, I'm sorry, sweetheart," Pat purred, putting her arms around him.

He took her face in his hands and met her eyes with his. "What can you do for me? Well, I guess the first thing that comes to mind is that you can keep me informed about Matsaku's plans. Most of all I need information."

"You big liar! That was the second thing that came to mind. I know what was first."

They melted together in a long, passionate kiss, the same kind that had started the heated evening in the entrance hallway.

"Such a deal," Trey sighed. He donned his jacket, checked pockets for essentials, and walked arm-in-arm with her to the doorway.

"Stay in touch! Call me Monday!" she called after him.

He drove away on the long gravel driveway that led from Pat Beason's isolated country cottage nestled in the hills of Williamson County. He chided himself for the moment of distrust he had felt for the Madame Speaker. He was looking forward to seeing Brother Jacob at Gethsemani the next day. He knew he could trust his Trappist friend.

Chapter 7

▼

"Yeah, it was a great game. We're three and oh now. Look, I've got to hang up. Mom's got a call on call waiting. Talk to you later." Rachel handed the phone to her mother and punched the button. She picked up the tote bag next to her on the couch.

"Hello, Ruth," Evelyn said. "How'd it go at the lawyer's?"

Rachel heard the fading words and knew what that was all about. Another divorce. She was glad she didn't know their children.

Evelyn walked the phone into the living room, which served also as music room and office. She sold the big house after the divorce was finalized and bought this more affordable bungalow on Woodmont, an older but still respectable neighborhood. The Steinway grand had been sacrificed, too, in favor of the smaller Chickering that she now stood beside, brushing off a speck of lint from the keys.

She was discussing not only her friend's personal crisis but also a community project. Evelyn chaired a group from the Arts Council that was working with the Metro Schools to establish a performing arts magnet school. She was hoping her friend would get involved for purposes of healthy distraction.

Rachel's studies mercifully claimed her attention. This totebag with its contents of three books and a note from Scott had been her constant companion the past two weeks. She pulled that note out first and read it for the umpteenth time.

"These belong to Dad. They are his prize possessions, so take good care of them."

She fretted over the words "prize possessions" as usual.

She put that away and extracted *The Seven Storey Mountain*, opening it to her bookmark. Page 319. Merton's description of his first trip to the Abbey of Gethsemani. He took the train from Louisville to New Haven, which was the closest stop to the abbey. He was met there by a brother who escorted him for the first time to the place that he soon was to call home.

Her reading was interrupted by her mother's voice. "I don't know when I've seen you work so hard on a project. Scott's suggestion was a good one, huh?" Evelyn Crockett perched on the arm of the couch and ran her hand through her seventeen-year-old daughter's red hair.

"Yeah. He's a good ol' brother most of the time. I'd never even heard of Thomas Merton. He's interesting. You were from Louisville. Did you know much about the monastery in Bardstown?"

Evelyn nodded. "I had some Catholic friends who visited there. The Louisville paper carried articles about Merton from time to time. He wasn't exactly a saint, you know. I remember the paper carrying a photo of him in a jazz night club, drinking beer. Rumor had it he was in love with a nurse he met while he was treated once at a local hospital."

"Yeah," Rachel said. "I read about that, too."

"I was in college when he died, but I still heard about it. Big news in literary and Catholic circles."

"Do you remember any mention that it could have been a murder?"

"Vaguely. Only brief speculation, unfounded stuff about the CIA or elements of the Catholic church, as I recall."

"It could have been hushed up, you know."

"OOOOOH," Evelyn sighed, feigning freight.

She took the book from Rachel's hand and flipped to the inside cover where she saw "Trey Crockett" signed in bold black ink.

"So now the whole family's stricken with Merton-mania," she continued, extending her arm so that Rachel could see the signature too. "Your father, then Scott, now you." She handed the book back to Rachel. "Why? You want to visit the place?"

"Gosh, no, I hadn't thought about that," Rachel answered, taken off guard. "Just because I'm interested in the Catholic Church, I'm not ready to be a nun or something." There was a highway map of Kentucky peeking from the tote bag. Rachel poked it back without her mother seeing.

Evelyn smiled. "I'm glad to see you sharing something with your father. How does that feel to you?"

Rachel's crossed leg took up a nervous beat.

"I don't know. It's funny…different. Can't get used to it. I mean, actually studying from a book with his name in it. I wouldn't have touched it before, much less read it."

"Am I hearing the faint sound of forgiveness?" Evelyn cupped her hand to her ear.

Rachel's leg upped the tempo. "What about you?" she asked sharply. "A divorce doesn't exactly sound like forgiveness to me."

Evelyn rose and walked toward the window, pulling the curtain aside. Still a handsome woman at age 46, her face furrowed now with the troubled events of recent years. "No, it doesn't," she finally responded. "I just couldn't believe him any more. Maybe he is really changing. It's hard for me to tell." She turned to Rachel. "You could probably, better than me. If you'd give yourself a chance."

Rachel's leg was still. She stared at the floor, then picked up her pen and note cards. "I've got to work some more. This report is due next week."

* * * *

Weekend tourist crowds in the nation's capital had thinned out noticeably now that it was the third week in September and schools had cranked up across the U.S. of A. But it was business as usual for certain of the employees of the United States Drug Enforcement Administration. In fact, one would never have known it was Saturday with all the activity at the Director's office on Army-Navy Drive.

The blinds were pulled for the slide show at 9 a.m.

Director Harvey Smithers was seated in his leather easy chair which swiveled so that he commanded a prime view of the screen. To his left, on the other side of the projector, were Deputy Director Warden and Special Agent Cox. Cox—fifty, balding, sturdy of build, a little on the homely side with thick glasses and poorly trimmed mustache—was handling the presentation while the other two listened and watched. He was pacing and fretting, impatient to get this over with and make it to his son's soccer game before it was over. His wife's comment that his son asked for a picture of him the other day so he wouldn't forget his dad had hit home.

"We've been tailing Fernando Belsasso for six months since we became suspicious of drug smuggling activity leading to high places in the government. The Secretary of Commerce of our southern neighbor seems to have a few unsavory connections. Here are some close-ups of him," Cox explained as he clicked through a number of slides in succession. "Here's the one we're particularly interested in. See the two guys he's with at this bookstore? This is the middle of Mexico City, and that's Juan Vasquez and Fernando Davila, members of the underworld. That's a briefcase passing hands between them."

"You mean *Ojos Negros*?" Jack Warden asked.

"Exactly, sir. The Mexican Mafia. Vasquez and Davila are coming over to our side, sir. When this picture was taken we were just beginning to work on the conversion, and by now it should be a sure thing."

"Those two are already on our payroll?" Smithers asked. "How'd you do that? It takes the CIA two years average."

"I believe you'd rather not know, sir. You give considerable discretion to our foreign employees. I didn't even ask," Cox answered.

"If I may continue, sir, that shot was taken a month ago. We decided to put a tap on Belsasso's phone at the Mexican Commerce Department."

"Did our man there arrange the tap too?" the Director asked.

"Yes, sir, he did. He's a cracker jack, if I may say so. We've been listening day and night. Nothing to go on, though, as far as any further *Ojos* connections. The Secretary must conduct that business from somewhere other than his office. But two weeks ago we came upon an interesting item. He got a suspicious-sounding invitation from Manuel Matsaku..."

"Who?" Smithers interrupted him.

"Matsaku, sir. Manuel Matsaku, the Japanese industrialist."

"Oh, yeah." The Director nodded recognition, removing his wire-rimmed glasses, frowning, rubbing his eyes. Weary eyes. "He was on the cover of Time a couple years ago. Major mover and shaker."

"Yeah, yeah," Deputy Warden added. "I read that article. What I remember is he's a Jap who's obsessed with the Catholic Church. Something to do with his mother. Weird."

Cox paused to see if his superiors had any other comments before proceeding. Warden looked at him and nodded.

"Mr. Matsaku asked Belsasso to come to Japan for a secret meeting having to do with a new U.S. investment involving Matsaku Enterprises, the Mexicans, and Americans. That meeting took place this past week in Tokyo." The slides began to click again.

"We had to resort to outside shots from a helicopter to get pictures of the gathering. Security in his building is phenomenal. There must be really big secrets kept in that skyscraper."

"Who're we seeing there?" Smithers asked.

"Well, sir, the resolution with this particular camera is good enough, even through the silvered windows, that we've identified all the people in that room. It took some doing with the lady, but the others were a piece of cake. Here's a close-up."

He clicked to a shot from another angle, which revealed all the faces in either full front or profile.

"On the right, standing, is Matsaku. Then counterclockwise we have Leon Eisenberg—needs no introduction—General John Perkins, former Chairman of the Joint Chiefs and now a member of the Base Realignment and Closure Commission, Governor Nathaniel Turnbow of Kentucky, Belsasso, and closest to the camera in profile is the Honorable Patricia Beason, Speaker of the House of the legislature of the state of Tennessee. She's a hot politico, seems to be priming for governor. We'd never have identified her without the help of Agent Morris. He found out Turnbow was in Japan on a joint business trip with Kentucky and Tennessee officials and then got his hands on a list of the delegations. After that it was easy."

Smithers yawned and looked at his watch. "So what's the upshot? I've got a meeting with you-know-who at ten."

"We aren't sure, sir. From all we can tell the meeting was a well-kept secret. No one in defense seemed to know Eisenberg was there. At least no one's admitting it. He was supposedly on a week's vacation in California. You know if he was there though, the President knows it. We have some more investigating to do on the other parties, so this is preliminary. We should know more in a week."

"Just don't be spending time on a wild goose chase, Cox. The President is interested in busting up drug smuggling from Mexico. But he won't be too happy if the Secretary of Commerce of our NAFTA partner is dirty. He's frothing to see the trade agreement with Mexico pass on the Hill, and a scandal like that could set the whole thing back, maybe enough to kill it." The Director paused and shook his head.

"Now the Japanese too. I hope to God they aren't involved. Find out what you can. Yeah, this week."

* * * *

There were two routes to the monastery from I-65. Trey took the scenic route this time, exiting at Sonora. He could do it blindfolded.

He crested the knob just south of the monastery and pulled the car over to the side of the road. A certain peace rolled over and through him, gazing at the collection of buildings nestled in the hills. What was it, he often wondered? The absolute incongruity of the place, this old-world node of serenity here in the midst of Appalachia. The Oz of the Soul.

His first visit was indelible. It was a bone-chilling January night two years ago, and he arrived with newly-acquired recovering friends, Catholic types, who talked him into coming. When he first caught sight of the church's spire and rectangular building profiled against the moonlit sky, and one of his friends whispered, "There it is," he couldn't say a word. Awesome would have come close.

Since then the abbey's architecture had become framed in his innards. He lowered the car window and breathed fresh country air, imagining at the same time a medieval mustiness wafting from the direction of the buildings. It was instead the smell of new-mown hay delivered from nearby acres the monks rented to Nelson County neighbors.

He rolled into the parking lot at 11:30 a.m. It was filled with cars from several states, signaling a full booking for the weekend. This place was no longer a well-kept secret, being the subject of newspaper and magazine articles on a regular basis, as well as being listed in travel books, and not to mention word of mouth.

He walked the path beside the public cemetery that was the preamble to the guesthouse building. The monks were buried in a separate private area on the west side of the church. Trey liked to amble among the monks' graves, reading the simple crosses with their names inscribed. Most guests came looking for Thomas Merton's grave, and he had done that too on his first visit. "Fr. Louis Merton" it had read on the standard small metal cross. "Died Dec. 10, 1968." "Louis" had puzzled him initially, then realizing it was the monastic name given him at his initiation into the order. Strange, Trey had noted, that the celebrated Trappist had been buried just as simply as the others; nothing to suggest fame. Fitting, though, for these humble folk.

Trey entered the heavy wooden doors of the guesthouse with bag in hand to be greeted by the familiar and friendly face of Brother Brendan. He was the receptionist/telephone operator, the cloister's interface with the outside world. A couple of the guests were loitering and talking quietly in the lobby, one of the few areas designated for conversation.

Silence was the general rule and a welcome one for Trey who came to this place seeking respite from television, telephones, and all the other telethings that regularly perturbed his serenity.

Brendan found Trey's name on the guest list in the slot for room 310.

"Is Jacob around?" Trey inquired.

"Let me see if he's upstairs," was the reply, and Brendan punched one of the buttons on his telephone.

"No answer in his office. He's usually back after lunch. Shall I leave a message?" he asked.

"Please. Tell him the problem child is here. I'm supposed to see him at two this afternoon. He'll understand. Thanks."

Trey chatted with the monk for a few minutes, catching up on the latest happenings at the abbey. There were two novices who had signed up this summer, good prospects, and no one had died. "Graduated," they called it. No one had graduated recently. There was a brother in the infirmary though. Dom Philippe Flaget was seriously ill with kidney failure, Brendan explained. He was now eighty-two years old, a Frenchman and a Trappist patriarch who had come to Gethsemani Abbey a few years ago to live out his years on the grounds where his beloved friend Merton was buried. He had endeared himself to the brothers with humorous and wistful remembrances of Father Louis. He also had become a close friend and confidante of Dom Raphael, the abbot.

Trey stowed his bag upstairs in his room. The dormitory-style guesthouse was comfortable, thanks to a major reconstruction job in the late 1980's funded by benefactors such as the Kennedys who had become friends of Merton and the monastery. Rooms were furnished with Shaker-like, blonde maple furniture, and walls were decorated with a handsome series of icon reproductions from paintings by a Gethsemani monk. One of the originals, of the Virgin and Child, held a place of honor in the church's nave near the choir stalls.

Lunch was underway when Trey came back downstairs. Guests were making their way through the cafeteria style serving line and finding seats at tables. Silence was being observed, and except for the taped homily playing quietly over the speakers, the only sounds were those of utensils on plates.

Trey's thoughts were straying from the monk's monotonic, meditative delivery. He was thinking ahead to his meeting with Jacob. The two had grown close since that first winter's visit. Jacob's clear vision and humor could often serve to center Trey's tangled thinking. He was confessor, advisor, and trusted friend, and Trey's sole misgiving was the martial arts thing. It was never clear why a humble, world-renouncing, aggression-eschewing monastic would be attracted to oriental self-defense. Maybe the Lord's buckler and shield were not enough to fend off Satan and his minions. Maybe the ecumenical momentum of Vatican II and Merton's leanings to Eastern practices were leading to cultural exchanges never quite intended by the hierarchy. Or maybe Jacob caught the abbot in a moment of weakness when the latter granted permission for him to attend karate lessons in Bardstown once a month.

At two o'clock Trey found him in his office on the second floor of the guesthouse. He stood outside the glass door a moment watching Jacob sitting at his desk with his back to the door, poring over sheets of music. The forty-year-old musician was assistant organist for the abbey in addition to his duties as guestmaster.

Jacob responded to Trey's knock with a jerk of the head and a quick smile. His youthful features were betrayed only by the salt-and-pepper sprinkling in his short-cropped hair which was thinning in front. He moved gracefully in his sandals and tunic, slight of figure but energetic. They embraced warmly, followed by Jacob's abruptly assuming a karate stance in mock challenge to Trey.

"Still playing around with the martial arts, huh?"

"Have to do something to defend against you heathen Protestants," Jacob responded playfully and with a thrust stopping just short of Trey's midsection. "Now, what's this sudden visit all about?"

"You won't be too happy with me, I fear. It's a long story."

Jacob suggested they walk outside, so they proceeded to the inner courtyard of the cloister, off limits to guests except by special invitation. They sat on a weathered wooden bench surrounded by a flowering hedge which held many a man's secrets in its internecine foliage. Trey took a deep breath, leaned forward with hands clenched, and proceeded to tell his friend of the events of the last few days. From the Mexican envoys to Big Al to Pat Beason.

Hearing of Trey's liaison the previous night with the Tennessee politician was no surprise to Jacob. He was aware of his psychiatrist-friend's undisciplined sex life as well as other assorted defects that had been confessed to him in detail. But he had never heard of the affair with Teresa Kelly.

"Is all of that true?" he asked.

"I'm afraid so," came the answer.

Jacob's smile faded, and he struggled for a response. "And it's Matsaku who's behind it?" he asked.

"So it seems. I'm not supposed to know that, of course. Big Al was silent on the matter, but who am I to turn a deaf ear to information just because I heard it between the sheets?"

"No comment," Brother Jacob demurred, his patience growing thinner by the moment.

"Don't forget I'm a shrink and can read minds. You're put out with me, aren't you?"

Jacob frowned and looked away at the sweeping limbs of the Japanese maple nearby. He didn't frown often. He shook his head. He didn't shake his head often.

"Trey...yes, I'm put out with you. I'm not so sure God isn't, too. You compound one sin with another. You visit here with me, my adopted Episcopal brother. You confess and do penance as sincerely as any Roman Catholic, as any monk, for that matter. Yet I see no change in your behavior. At some point, where the rubber meets the road, or where flesh meets flesh, your life must begin to reflect that God is directing things. That you are experiencing amendment of heart. I don't see that happening."

Both were silent, listening to the breeze in the leaves. Two brothers walked together along the covered walkway around the inside of the cloister. They nodded in the direction of the two seated on the bench.

Jacob continued. "Yet, I know that everything happens in God's time, not mine. I will continue praying for you and ask you to do the same for me and my impatience. Let's also pray that my influence in your life will facilitate redemption."

He turned and smiled at Trey who had been trying to digest what he had just heard. Trey felt not so much shame as he did anger at himself for burdening this gentle man of God with his sordid life. Surely Jacob had come to this place some twenty years ago at least in part to find respite from the complexities of secular life. Trey wasn't making it easy for him.

Jacob made it easier for Trey by redirecting the conversation.

"So...hey...you wouldn't be aware of the coincidence with your Manuel Matsaku and Gethsemani."

"What do you mean?"

"The family has been a most generous benefactor of ours over the years. I'm not surprised you don't know; theirs is a quiet benevolence."

"Come to think of it," Trey interrupted, "Pat, my friend, did say something about his being Catholic with a mother who was…a nun?…is that right?"

"Yup, that's right. Delores Matsaku was a Benedictine sister. She was sent to a convent in Thailand where she met Manuel's father-to-be and fell from grace, obviously. She left the Order but retained a passion for Mother Church."

"And what was her connection with this abbey?"

"She and Tom Merton developed a friendship in the sixties based largely on Merton's growing interest in the commonalties between Christian and Buddhist contemplative practices. It was her idea to convene the conference, the international monastic meeting, that Merton attended."

"You mean when he died?"

"Yup. That's the one."

"And Manuel Matsaku's mother, was she there…I mean, at the conference?" Trey quizzed.

"I don't know. I'm flying blind on this whole subject. 'Twas all before my time here, you know. The family's support has maintained the connection, but I don't know much more than that. Except that when Delores died a few years ago, many of our brothers thought that would spell the end of the support."

"Well did it?"

"I, uh, the last I heard, Manuel was still making contributions. At least, I think so. I don't know. Is this…I mean, could this be important to you in your situation?"

"Gosh, Jacob, I don't know. It just seems so strange that I've come up here today with a 'Delores Project' problem and walked right into Delores Territory. Yeah, it could be important. At this point I'm interested in all the information I can get."

"Hmmmm..." Jacob pondered. "I definitely can find out more about the Matsaku family and their involvement here. Especially Delores. Dom Philippe Flaget must have known her. He was in the thick of things at the time of Merton's death."

"I thought he was real sick. Brother Brendan said he was in the infirmary."

"True. He's getting close to graduation. But he's still coherent. I'll see. It's the least I can do to atone for my ungracious outburst a moment ago."

"You mean today? Could we talk to him today?" Trey asked.

"Nope. Not today. He gets dialysis on Saturdays." He looked at his watch. "He's still up in Bardstown, and he's spent for hours afterwards. I'll talk to him tomorrow and then call you with an update Monday. How's that?"

"Good. That's good. Thanks."

"Now," Jacob said, "how's it going with the kids?"

"Good and bad. Scott had a good summer in D.C. and spent a couple of weeks at home before school started. He's doing great.

"Rachel's a different story. Well, actually the same old story. Won't see me. Hands the phone to her mother when I call. All I hear is 'Hello.' Second hand I hear she's doing famously. Guess a dad is superfluous, huh?"

Jacob smiled. "Give it time. It'll come."

Jacob had to take care of some business before *none*, the next of the daily choir offices, so the two walked back to the guesthouse to their respective tasks. Trey's was to prepare himself for the next day's meeting with his uncle.

*   *   *   *

President Clinton had not been pleased with the news of possible drug connections to the Mexican government that he received from the DEA Director at his Saturday morning briefing. Harvey Smithers' observation to that effect was confirmed by the short conversation he had with the President's Chief of Staff, Marshall Counts, after the briefing.

"Do you think the President wants me to push this investigation in Mexico, or should I hold up a few weeks, you know, until the heat is off with the vote on NAFTA?" Smithers asked.

"It wouldn't look good," Counts answered, "to stall unnecessarily, Harvey. You know how the *Post* is. They've got their bloodhounds' noses to the ground right now sniffing out leaks on drug trafficking. It could backfire. Give Belsasso a code name. Go ahead at a reasonable pace. 'All deliberate speed'. You know the routine. And don't l…"

"…let the sun set on any news that'll surprise you in the morning paper." Smithers finished the Chief's familiar phrase for him, a phrase he was fast growing to despise. He would love to see the sun set on his ass on his way permanently out of town.

Counts smiled and patted him on the back. "That's the ticket."

Chapter 8

▼

The New York Times
December 12, 1968

DEATH OF CONTROVERSIAL MONK NATURAL?

Associated Press

BANGKOK—In the aftermath of the sudden, unexpected death of celebrated Trappist monk Thomas Merton, many rumors have surfaced that could put into question the cause of his death. Sources requesting anonymity within the hierarchy of the Roman Catholic Church have suggested that the CIA might be involved in a plot to have Merton assassinated due to his radical anti-nuclear statements and his well-known friendship with Soviet writers.

CIA spokesman John Powers refused to comment other than to brand such accusations "ridiculous."

Merton was attending a convocation of eastern monastic leaders here and was found dead in his room by a friend. Local law enforcement authorities have assured convocation officials that a thorough investigation is underway, though permission for an autopsy had not been requested at press time.

Other, unofficial sources have suggested that Merton was viewed with suspicion by conservative elements of the Catholic Church, implying that his death might be welcome in some circles. These same sources intimate that a clandestine group known as the Bossuet Society could be implicated. Such statements stand in sharp contrast to the vast outpouring of grief and shock that has emanated from his admirers and friends around the world since his death.

From Dom Philippe Flaget, who discovered Merton dead: "We are all still in a state of shock and disbelief. He was at the prime of his life, ready to embark on new and unexplored adventures of the human spirit."

Funeral arrangements are yet to be announced.

Chapter 9

▼

Aunt Jeanne outdid herself as usual with Sunday dinner. With all her years as wife to the now-most-powerful member of the United States Senate, she had not lost her touch in the kitchen. Chess pie topped off the meal that featured a pot roast, baked squash casserole, and homemade rolls.

"You boys just go on into the den and do your talkin'. I'll clean up. And no backtalk. I don't want you messin' up my kitchen."

Trey pecked her on the cheek. "Yes, ma'am. I know my place. Scrumptious meal, Aunt Jeanne."

"Oh, you'd say that if it was pig slop. Get out of here, you overgrown coondog!"

Trey and his uncle walked into the den.

"Lately, she likes to tell people she needs her nephew Trey likes she needs a hole in the head. Then she explains about the way you saved her from a hole in the head up at Johns Hopkins." Jonas chuckled and patted Trey on the shoulder.

"She gets a big bang out of that. Loves you dearly. She'd never have fixed a meal like that for just the two of us, that's for damn sure. You need to do this more often!"

"The feeling is mutual. I'm sure you know that," Trey offered nervously.

"So," Jonas said, situating his 6-foot-two, 250-pound frame into his favorite easy chair, "what's this we need to talk about, son?" He sunk his silver-domed head into the cushion.

Trey sat in the chair opposite, gulped, and laid it all out to his uncle, omitting only the source of his information about the Matsaku-Mexican venture. He would rather Jonas didn't know about the affair with Pat Beason.

He waited for the explosion.

It didn't come. Jonas Crockett had sat through the entire recitation attentively but calmly. He had shown no emotion. And now, after Trey's last statement, "So I've got to have a plan tomorrow for Al Horton," the senator prepared to speak.

The not-unexpected question: "Who's your source on Matsaku?"

Trey fumbled around. "Uh...it's...well, it's a very reliable source. A personal friend very close to the whole operation."

Then it came. "I asked you, dammit, who it was, not for a character reference!" The mountain of a man projected from the chair like an explosion of the Saturn rocket, jowls a-bouncing. He closed the door so Jeanne didn't have to suffer his profanity.

"You present me with this damn problem of yours, which is now my problem, it seems, and you start playin' cozy with your sources!" Jonas glared at Trey who was withstanding the barrage with difficulty.

The senator turned away, took a deep breath, and walked to the window.

"I'm sorry, Uncle Jonas. When I said it was a personal friend, I meant really personal. Like, it's a woman friend, you know, someone I'm involved with. And she's in politics, and I was just trying to protect her."

"Yes, yes, I see," Jonas answered. "I'm gettin' the picture, son. And it's not a pretty picture like the one I'm seein' out this window, with the hills risin' beyond the creek over yonder. I'm gettin' the picture of my nephew who can't keep his pecker in his pants. My nephew who's been in a lot of scrapes, more'n we like to remember. And I'd sure as hell like to forget this one. Believe me," he emphasized, turning toward Trey again, "I'd like to forget this one. I'd like to walk out of this room and get some coffee, and we could just start this visit all over again, and none of this ever happened."

He took his frame back to the easy chair and sat.

"But...bein' the practical-minded person I am, I know that's not going to happen. So now we'll just crank the reel back a few frames, you can tell me your source, and we'll figure out what to do." He said it evenly, managing a tone-changing half-smile.

"It's Pat Beason, one of the 'Delores' cooperators."

"Hmmmph! Pat Beason. Yeah, one of the insiders, no less. Next governor. A looker. You got good taste. Piss-poor judgment but good taste. Hmmm...Pat Beason. Came from Crossville from a poor background. Went to UT then Harvard Law. Hmmm...Pat Beason." Jonas nodded and drummed his fingers on the cushioned arm.

"At least she's not married. Give me that much credit."

"Folks wonder about her not marryin'. Leaves room for a lot of gossip and speculation. Do you trust her, son?"

"Trust her? Wha...why, sure I do." Trey flashed back to Friday night's misgivings. "Yeah, I don't have any reason not to."

"You don't sound so sure of it. It's damn important we can trust her."

"That'll be okay, I'm sure," Trey replied, pulling himself up. He liked his uncle using the pronoun "we."

Jonas leaned forward with his elbows on his knees, gesturing as he talked. "Now listen, and listen carefully. I'm in a donnybrook with the president over this base closin' thing. It's come down to me and him. Bill Clinton doesn't give a rat's ass about our elite fighting men, the ones who will spell the difference if we ever decide to take out Saddam Hussein and his regime. Besides, I've made my promises to the people who count the most, the people of this state. Las Vegas East won't substitute for my word. I can't back down without sellin' my soul."

He was staring a hole through a speechless Trey.

Jonas continued. "There're just two people in the Christian world I'd sell my soul for, and they're both in this house with me right now. If it comes right down to it, son, I'll do what I have to for you."

Jonas sat back and Trey waited, suspended. There was something else pending in his uncle's pronouncement.

"But we want to stop it short of that. Jam the Jap's plan. Stymie it."

The wizened politician's mind had been spinning plans the whole time he and Trey had been talking.

"We've got three weeks to get this resolution out of committee, and then another two before it's got to be voted on by the full Senate. I'm conductin' hearings on it beginning Wednesday. I've got me an ace in the hole, a former chaplain with the 101st, a World War II hero and one helluva dynamic spokesman. I plan to spring him on the committee next week if I need to. I've got this stage set like a high-falutin' opera at the Kennedy Center, and I'm lickin' my chops."

He paused for a moment then leaned forward again, shaking his head slowly. "I don't want to miss this opportunity. So let's think of how to stymie the Jap." The bushy eyebrows rose into an inviting question mark.

"Okay, okay. I'm all for that, believe me, I'm all for that," Trey said, swallowing hard. "What do you have in mind?"

"I have in mind that there are enough people involved in this thing on the other side—you know, Eisenberg, Perkins, Turnbow, Bel...Belstosso or whoever, and your Pat Beason—that we should be able to put a monkey wrench in their works somewhere. I don't know just how, son, but you don't gather a crop of muckety-mucks like that without at least one Achilles heel in the bunch. Eisenberg is obviously there with Clinton's blessings, so it goes all the way to the top. The Belstosso guy may be one to look at too."

"...sasso. BelSASSO, Uncle Jonas, I believe is the way it's pronounced," Trey corrected.

"All right, all right. It took some doin' for me to pass Spanish at UT. Anyhow, he's bound to be vulnerable, what with NAFTA on the table."

The senior Crockett's mind was astir and he was excited about the prospects of overcoming an obstacle. He'd done this sort of thing before, and it showed.

He continued. "I'll just have to give it some thought. In the meantime, you tell this Al-lawyer-fellow that we've talked and we're comin' up with somethin'. That's all he needs to be told. Just pacify him, son. We're comin' up with somethin'. Pacify him. You know how to do that."

He reached over and patted Trey on the knee in a show of confidence. If he was still put out with his nephew, he was doing a good job of hiding it.

They both arose and shook hands. Trey was relieved, thinking Uncle Jonas would come up with something.

"I'm sorry," he said. "This is a helluva way to treat my favorite person in the whole world. But I appreciate your help. Believe me. I'll do my best to work my way out of this mess. And I promise I won't drink. You can count on that. Things are just beginning to come together for me, getting back on the faculty at the medical school, being appointed to the Finance Committee of HospiCare."

"I know, son, I'm proud of you."

"Say," Trey asked, "who's this chaplain you mentioned? Sounds like a winner."

"Fella's name is Grant Stone. Episcopal priest livin' down in Huntsville, Alabama. Eighty-three years old, but fulla piss 'n' vinegar. Jumped into combat four times in the Big War. Damnedest preacher you ever heard. Could fill up Thompson-Boling arena up at UT with his voice without a microphone. I swear it. I'm not exaggerating.

"Heck," he continued, "you want to know somethin'? Let me tell you what I heard. Back a couple of years ago when Bush was tryin' to get ol' Mitterand to come around on the Middle East, this fella Stone turned it around for us. I'm not kiddin'. He was over in France for one of those D-Day celebrations and had an audience with ol' President Mitterand. Right after that, the French were like putty in Bush's hands. The scuttlebutt had it that Father Grant Stone laid it on the man so convincingly about US-French relations that Mitterand had tears in his eyes."

"Sounds like you've got your spokesman, all right," Trey said.

"Damn right. If he could soften up Mitterand, God knows, by the time he gets through testifyin' about those young paratroopers dyin' in his arms at Normandy, he'll have the Armed Services Committee on their knees prayin' that the 101st and Fort Campbell be blest with long life by the Lord God Almighty His by-God self. Ha!"

Jonas enjoyed the images he conjured. They both laughed.

Trey pulled out of the driveway for the three-hour trip from Sevierville to Nashville. He tried to avoid looking at the tape player. For the past four days, every time he got into his car he could hear voices, those of Raspy and Teresa Kelly. The echoes hung in the air.

He started singing to himself to drown out the unwanted reverberations.

"Had a dog an' his name was Blue;
Had a dog an' his name was Blue.
Had a dog an' his name was Blue;
Betcha fi' dollar he's a good dog, too."
And then the refrain,
"Oooooh, Bluuuue; you good dog, you."
Long and sad-like.

He used to sing that old mountain folk tune with his Dad picking the banjo. The hills of East Tennessee rolling by outside the car window joined in with the harmony just as they had in his youth.

He took the four-lane to the interstate. Four-lane. This part of his life's landscape was different than it was in his youth, what with interstates, Dollywood, Pigeon Forge, Gatlinburg. He passed the family farm at Catlettsville. Rented out now since his father died and his mother moved to a retirement home outside Nashville. Uncle Jonas and Aunt Jeanne were his remaining family contacts in Sevier County. His sister Abby had long since left these parts when she married a Virginian.

His reflections took him back to school days and classmates. He had always regretted in a way going off to private secondary school. Ties were broken with his neighbors in Sevierville, seemingly forever. Battleground Academy, or BGA as it was known, had taken him to Franklin which was like going to a foreign country. He'd had his thirtieth class reunion this summer, and there were precious few classmates from these parts. Middle Tennessee was different from East Tennessee was different from West Tennessee. Geography was different. Speech was different. Politics were different.

Oh, yeah, politics were very different. There was an attempt early on in statehood history to pull East Tennessee into North Carolina. Those folks always seemed to believe they weren't really a part of ordinary Tennessee.

Trey crossed the French Broad River where he had fished and canoed with those lost companions in a time long passed.

Other thoughts crowded in: whether Jacob had been able to learn anything about Delores Matsaku from Dom Philippe Flaget; what clever machinations were emanating from the mind of Uncle Jonas; the image of the Reverend Grant Stone reducing steel-hearted senators to tears; how he would stall Big Al the next day; whether he could really trust Pat Beason.

Oh, Blue, you good dog, you. Good ol' hound dog.
Life was so simple for ol' Blue.

Chapter 10

▼

A powerful female politician must a) be at least five-foot-seven, attractive, and more intelligent than her male counterparts. Or b) have a strong and sonorous voice. Or c) look back on the line of a wealthy, political family.

If a and b but not c are correct, mark the box beside the name "Pat Beason."

Five-foot-eight, Elizabeth Taylor eyes, Connie Chung voice, Law Review at Harvard. Not wealthy or political in her lineage, however. And a loner in many ways. For instance, she carried on a solo law practice at a time when such was all but unheard-of in a city the size of Nashville.

"Single-minded." "Goal-oriented." "Power-hungry." Such were the descriptors often applied to her by the press.

That's what Special Agent Cox was discovering about his subject.

Phil Cox had seven days to ferret what he could about the lady politician, the profiled figure in the window of Matsaku Towers about whom Washington knew very little. He had built up a file on Kentucky's governor which was complete enough for their purposes, and Smithers had told him to lay low on Belsasso, or "Dineros," as his name had been encrypted, for the time being. Eisenberg and Perkins were already open books what with confirmation hearings and years of national public exposure.

So Patricia Fleming Beason was Cox's sole focus this week. Born February 3, 1948, in Crossville, Tennessee. Never married. Valedictorian, Crossville High 1965. Undergraduate at the University of Tennessee, graduated summa cum laude, class of '70. Harvard Law School '73, Doctor of Jurisprudence '75. Joined group law practice in '75, then solo since 1981 when she won her first term as state legislator. Spearheaded Governor Lamar Alexander's educational reform package which propelled her to statewide prominence and led the way to her becoming Speaker in 1991. Articulate debater, tough inside fighter, loves to wheel and deal.

Cox picked up some of those tidbits Saturday afternoon from the computerized newspaper files in the DEA's Data Room which was networked with the Congressional Library. Others he acquired by calling Claude Bishop, an occasional contact with the Drug Enforcement Division of the Tennessee Bureau of Investigation, on Monday morning.

"Whadda ya wanna know 'bout her?" Bishop asked.

"Just tell me whatever comes to mind," Cox replied in good open-ended interrogator style.

"Well, she's a damn good looker, for starters. But we're not supposed to notice anymore, are we?" The fifty-five-year-old weathered Viet Nam veteran betrayed just a hint of sarcasm in his bow to political correctness *a la* 1993. "Don't answer that! I don't want to have to testify at your trial one day that we even discussed it."

"Okay, cut the crap and get to my question." Cox sighed.

"She's probably our next governor. Won't say she is or isn't running, but everybody knows she'll announce the next month or so. Primaries are next spring."

"Why'd it take her five years to get through college?" Cox asked.

"Huh?"

"Her resume' shows a five-year gap between high school and college graduation."

"I think you must be the first person ever noticed that. How the hell do I know? Probably work-study. She's the type. What difference does it make, Sherlock?"

"Okay, okay. Next question: What's her claim to fame besides, of course, she's beautiful and smart and has a Harvard law degree?"

"Like, how has she made her mark so far? Is that what you mean?"

"Yeah. What's she done?"

"Let's see, the main things would be, I guess, educational reform, for sure, and, oh yeah, she negotiated a compromise between the Tennessee Hospital Association and the Insurors' Federation. Came up with legislation that spelled out how reimbursement rates were to be set. She got HospiCare Corporation and Blue Cross together across the table from each other without bloodshed for the first time in recorded history."

"What's HospiCare?" Cox asked.

"What's HospiCare? Are you kiddin'? Just the biggest hospital chain in America! Where you been the last twenty years, Cox?"

"Not in Nashville, Claude. I can't stand country music. I don't think the President likes it either, even if he is from Arkansas. You don't play "Honky-Tonk Angel" on the saxophone. Tell me more about Pat Beason. Why's she single?"

"Hey, man, I don't know about that. I keep my nose clean."

"I'm not asking for a personal testimonial. What's the street talk?"

There was a pause.

"She's not...she's straight, as far as I know, if that's what you mean. And..." his voice lowered "...there's all kinds of gossip, as you can imagine, her bein' a looker and all. I mean, about her and other guys. Prominent guys and so forth."

"Okay," Cox interrupted. "I get the picture. You've told me what I was wondering."

"Well, Cox, you better get your bureaucratic butt down here sometime to see how the other half lives out in the boonies."

"Thanks, Claude, I'll do that. 'Fact, I'll probably be there this week to check out the lady at close range. I'll let you take me to lunch and show me around."

"Hey, I'd like that. Things're gettin' just a little too routine for me around here."

"Thanks for the info." Cox signed off.

Cox pushed the intercom button for Spike Field, his African-American partner in the Mexican drug-smuggling investigation.

"Spike. Good Monday morning to you."

"Yeah? What's good about it? Is your butt all wreathed in smiles after the Saturday briefing with Smithers?"

"Why is my butt all of a sudden the topic of everyone's conversation?" Cox replied.

"Because, my good friend, you keep it shined up so pretty sitting at your desk while I do all the real work."

"Well, all that's about to change, Spike ol' buddy. Get your bags packed for Music City, USA. That's Nashville, Tennessee, in case you didn't know. We're leaving this afternoon. I'll tell you all about the briefing on the plane."

"Huh?"

"I don't have time right now. It's Lois' birthday and I've got to order some flowers. This damn job is about to ruin a good marriage. If there is such a thing."

*   *   *   *

Trey slept well Sunday night. No nightmare. Maybe it was because he had gone to the Caduceus support group meeting Sunday when he got back to Nashville from east Tennessee. Maybe God was rewarding him for being a good boy and for putting up with Jack C., who was still bugging him about going to the national convention in October.

Trey had been to the last three of those and was ready to pass on this year's, but he didn't want to appear less than enthusiastic. Jack had a big mouth, and it was important for Trey to give no appearance of backsliding. Rumors spread fast in the medical community, especially about the "impaired physicians," as they were officially tagged. "Repaired" would have been a kinder word.

Monday morning he returned Scott's phone call he had found waiting for him on the machine.

"Hey, Dad, where were you this weekend? I tried several times."

"I was out of town. At the monastery Saturday visiting with Brother Jacob. Then I dropped down to be with Uncle Jonas and Aunt Jeanne yesterday. Why? Anything up?"

"No, not particularly. Well, yes, there is. I mean, besides just wanting to keep up with you. I'll be coming home this weekend. Remember? Monday is Founders' Day, and school's out. I was wondering if I could bring some of the guys and use the lake house. You know, last water-skiing of the season and all that."

"I don't see why not. I haven't planned anything. Maybe you should check with your mother to see if she and your sister have any plans. I don't think so, or I would have heard from her about it by now."

Evelyn, his ex-wife, was always good about clearing the use of the cabin on Old Hickory Lake well in advance, and she often did so in Rachel's behalf. There had been no request from that side of the fractured family regarding the weekend, so Trey felt confident in allocating the premises, ski-boat, jet ski, etc., to his son.

There were few pains in his life like the one he felt when thinking of Rachel. He longed for the day when she again would rush into his arms and he would twirl her about and her red hair would fall all over his face. He imagined himself saying, "I love you, I love you, my little puddin'," while she clasped her arms around his neck and answered, "I love you, my little pie."

"Puddin'" and "pie" had been their respective nicknames, love code-names that were reserved for only their use when Rachel was a little girl. When she was HIS girl. A million years ago.

"Okay," Scott replied, "I'll do that. I won't mind, though, if Rachel wants to come over. I like showing off my baby sister now that she's half-civilized. In fact, I think sometimes that she's overdone the business of being lady-like. I guess Briarwood tends to do that to the girls, doesn't it?"

"Either that, or they rebel and become little hellions. Be grateful she's opted for lady-like."

"Will I see you next weekend?" Scott asked.

"Sure…at least I don't see why not." Trey was thinking of the past weekend and knew that the near future was an unknown quantity to him. He wasn't ready to tell Scott.

Trey continued. "Call me again Thursday or Friday so we can give each other a better reading. And I'll call the marina to be sure the ski-boat's fixed. They said it was just a dirty carburetor, so it should be ready. But you know how they are."

"I appreciate that. I know it's a pain a lot of the time."

"A royal one. But I'll get you back one day. I'll fix you good by giving you all the boats and other gas-powered equipment. Then I'll retire and never look at a carburetor again. I'll forget what a carburetor is. Yeah, when I get Alzheimer's, that's the first thing I'll forget."

"Hey, speaking of forgetting," Scott said, "I keep meaning to tell you that Rachel has your Merton books now. The ones you loaned me last year for Religion class."

"What's she doing with them?"

"She needed a biography subject for a report, and I thought of him. It's okay, isn't it?"

"Oh, yeah. I'd forgotten about them, to tell the truth. But I could use them now for a…a project I'm doing. I'll tell you about it this weekend if we have time."

"That's a deal. I'll call you later. Love ya, Dad."

Thank God for Scott. Thank God he's not like me.

Trey finished getting ready for his workday, hoping to hear from Brother Jacob and his uncle. He picked up the morning paper off his driveway.

There it was in headline:

"PAT BEASON RUNNING FOR GOVERNOR"

With the smaller sub: "Democrats hail expected announcement." She was calling a news conference Monday afternoon for the formal hat-tossing.

Thanks a lot, Pat, for letting me in on the news. Maybe I trust you more than vice versa.

Her explanation came later that morning.

"I'm sorry, Trey, for not telling you about it Friday night. I really wanted to, but John Grider—my campaign manager, I guess you know—had me take an oath of silence until he called the newspapers and stations last night."

Trey had called her at his first break to offer congratulations. Her phones were ringing off the hook but his secretary had managed to get through with persistence.

"Let's get together to talk about campaign financing." She was counting on major donations from the hospital lobby, and she wasn't referring to the place where people enter the building. She meant the PAC. Trey was her contact with HospiCare, the kingpin of that confederation.

"And, oh yes, I'd like to hear about your progress with, you know, your problem," she added.

They agreed to meet at her place for dinner Tuesday night. She had a campaign staff meeting scheduled tonight and every Monday night for the foreseeable future, hopefully all the way through the primaries and into November 1994. Trey understood completely. Campaigning had been etched into the marrow of his youth. He had attended many such meetings with his father and uncle on the hustings.

The psychiatrist was running late for his appointments all day, trying to work in the extra telephone conversations between patients. Eventually he decided he couldn't do this all week. He asked Melba to cancel some appointments and free up an hour each morning and afternoon until further notice. She cheerfully obliged, asking no questions.

That afternoon he received a fax from the Abbey of Gethsemani, Trappist, Kentucky. Brother Jacob was definitely on task and as clever as ever.

Dear Trey,

Methought it best to commit this to writing since we are often hard to connect. Righteo? After all, fax is fax. And fast.

Our beloved Dom Philippe Flaget recouped enough Sunday that we could talk without tiring him excessively. He was concerned about your predicament and would like to meet you. He seems to have known Delores Matsaku intimately and also knows Manuel, though less well. He corresponded with Delores until her death.

He was reticent in relating more details to yours-truly. But he would be willing to talk to you personally. I think he wants to lay eyes on you to be sure this isn't some figment of my imagination. If you strike him the right way, I have the notion he may be willing to tell you a great deal more. I could be wrong, mind you. I'm not as gifted with intuition as perhaps you are.

I just reread the previous paragraph and had the oddest thought that you might come up here and strike the poor sick fellow. Please resist. In the name of all that is holy, resist.

Let me no (sic) that you can't come. Get it?

In His Peace,

(Jacob)

Trey chuckled and shook his head at the linguistically twisted wit of his friend.

Yes, Trey would let him know that he could come.

He faxed a reply:

Dear Jake,

No, I cannot refuse to decline your unoffer.

Will there be a place for me up there this Saturday night just in case I show up in spite of whatever the first sentence above means? Would Dom Philippe likely be able to talk to me on Sunday?

I trust this strikes you as appropriate.

Peace,

(Trey)

The answer came back later in the day that Trey was welcome Saturday and that Jacob would prepare Dom Philippe for the visit.

In the meantime Trey put in a call to Big Al who took Trey's evasive report with a grunt and a reminder that there was a two-week deadline staring them in the face.

"You do recall, don't you, Doctor Crockett, that by October sixth the committee vote will be in and that today is September twentieth?"

"Yes, Mr. Horton, those dates are now embedded into my very biorhythms," Trey replied between his teeth. "You know, Mr. Horton, I've just got one nerve left, and you've managed to get on it every time I've talked to you."

"I've noticed that, doctor. I'm trying not to take it personally. I know you're under a lot of stress with all this."

Mister Sanctimonious, Trey thought. Add that to Mr. Gluteus-Very-Maximus on his list of surnames.

They terminated the conversation agreeing to touch base by phone daily.

In addition to the Beason headline, the morning *Tennessean* had a front-page article on the Senate Armed Services Committee hearings. Trey got around to reading it at five o'clock when he finally had a cancellation. The mayors of Clarksville, Tennessee, and Hopkinsville, Kentucky, were scheduled to appear before the committee today pleading the economy and tradition of their locales.

Senator Jonas Crockett was quoted as saying: "We've got a little over two weeks to listen and deliberate. I can't speak for the rest of the committee, but I don't think even the UT-Alabama game could get my attention for the next sixteen days. I'm glad they're not playing until later in October."

Jonas Crockett had played football at the University of Tennessee, and nothing interfered with his attending the Alabama and the Vanderbilt games each year. Particularly this year when Alabama was the defending national champion and his alma mater had a new coach.

Trey read the article and pictured his uncle's jowls bouncing as he matched wits with the reporters interviewing him for that story. And wondering what plan was hatching in his fertile mind. The next quotation gave evidence of his determination:

"It's clear that the President has been hell-bent on closing our base. However, his reasons are anything but clear. Maybe there's more to it than meets the eye. Maybe we're going to find out."

Trey was reading between the lines, wondering if the interview had taken place after his visit with his uncle. He glanced back to the beginning of the article. There it was:

"In a telephone interview Sunday evening from his Georgetown home, Senator Crockett..."

So, Trey thought, is he going to use the Delores thing against Clinton? My God, if he does, my goose is cooked! Surely not...not with his ace-in-the-hole, Father Grant Stone, waiting in the wings, he wouldn't have to resort to that...surely.

Chapter 11

▼

Special Agents Cox and Field had just about had it up to here with the prima donna politician. Tennessee's would-be next governor had been too preoccupied with press and television interviews Monday and Tuesday to grant them an audience.

After their arrival from D.C. Monday afternoon their first stop had been the office of the candidate. It was a mob scene. They never even got close to her and barely saw her as she rushed out with a host of associates at 5:30 p.m.

"I'm sorry, gentlemen," her receptionist had said to them. "I'm sure she'll find some time tomorrow. I left your business card with her. If you'll call back, oh, I'd say around ten in the morning, I should be able to tell you something."

Well, at ten Tuesday morning the Honorable Madame Beason was still unavailable, and at twelve, and at two, and at four.

"Let's go to her house tonight," Phil Cox said.

"Are you crazy, white boy?" Spike Field responded.

They were having late-afternoon coffee in the cafeteria of the TBI building in downtown Nashville, hosted by their guide, Claude Bishop.

"Hell, no, I just wanna get this done and get back home before the weekend, that's all. I've got plans with my family, y'know, and I don't want to waste any more time on this dame. I want to meet with her, explain that we know about her trip to Japan, ask her a few questions, that's all. And college...I want to find out what took her five years to get through. I don't know, just curiosity got the better of me. And I want to get it over with, d'ya understand? Bishop, will you explain it to him?"

"Me? Don't look at me. I'm just your tour guide. You want to go to Ms. Beason's house tonight, I'll take you there. But I'm not goin' in with you. I'll stand lookout in the car. I don't think my boss at the Bureau would want me questionin' the next governor. Especially about her college career. That's ludicrous. Besides, it's your show. Which I don't exactly understand, by the way. I mean, why you're pickin' on this lady. Why not one of the other guys in on the deal?"

"That's simple. They don't want us checking around on the President's men, Eisenberg and the general. It wouldn't endear the agency to the administration. And the consensus is that Kentucky's governor is some kind of loudmouth fool we'd best steer clear of. That left the Mexican and your Ms. Beason, a no-brainer."

"Yeah, well," Bishop warned, "I'm glad it wasn't 'cause you thought she'd be an easy touch for information. You'd be in for a surprise."

"That's getting to be more obvious by the hour," Field said. "Okay, okay, I'll agree to this caper. Under protest, for the record. You know where she lives?" he asked, nodding at Bishop.

"Roughly. I can get directions." And then he added, "You know, this little project is gettin' more and more interesting. I thought it was just a nuisance to start with, but you guys are growing on me." Bishop chuckled and hitched his thumbs in his plaid suspenders.

At 7:30 that evening Bishop, Cox, and Field pulled off U.S. Highway 31 South, otherwise known as Franklin Pike, at the driveway marked by a mailbox with "Beason" on it. Just ahead of them another car, a BMW, had pulled into the same driveway. Bishop stalled a minute to give the first car time to gain a lead then eased forward. The driveway was a long curvy one with tall boxwood hedges.

By the time they could see the house, the driver of the BMW was entering the front door with a German shepherd wagging approval. The visitor was of the male gender and definitely not a stranger from the dog's friendly reaction. Cox took down the Tennessee tag number of the BMW with the help of field glasses, and Bishop slowly backed the Chevrolet out of sight of the house. They would wait to see how long he stayed. The shepherd barked in their direction a couple of times then rested on the porch.

Trey made it all the way to the den this time before she got to his belt. Both were too preoccupied to have seen the other car backing out of the drive or to have wondered why Jake was barking. Both were possessed at that moment of particular sensory arousal that precluded ordinary observations such as noticing federal agents in their driveway. Other brain hormones were at work, an endocrine fireworks display that would have intrigued a PET scanner.

The conversation in the Chevy ran from pennant races to women to politics. After a lull, Bishop asked, "Anybody ever tell you you looked like Bill Cosby?"

"Not exactly. Just that we all look alike. Does that count?" Field said.

"Nah. You got his impish grin. Anybody ever said that?"

"No. I didn't go to Temple University, but I've been to Philadelphia. And I do like Jell-O puddings. That's the closest I've been to Bill Cosby."

"Where did you go to college?"

"University of Maryland. How 'bout you?"

"Tennessee Tech. I'm sure you know where that is."

"Tech? Of course. Everybody in D.C. knows about Tennessee Tech. Great…uh…great Reading Department, right? They did teach you to read there, didn't they, Bishop?"

"Naw, I got that in graduate school."

"Hey, you guys keep that up and I'll have to put one of you out of the car," Cox said.

"Speaking of reading," Bishop said, "have you seen the new Grisham book?"

"I just now finished *The Firm*," Field answered. "I'm usually about a year behind with books and necktie fashions. Hey, you notice how the FBI always gets the spotlight in these novels? Why is it the DEA can't be heroes sometime? There must be a civil rights issue in that somewhere."

"According to my wife," Cox said, "we're the biggest suckers within fifty miles of the Potomac, the hours we keep. Maybe she's right. I don't know how long I want to keep this up."

"Aw, cut it out," Field said. "You've been in some kind of funk lately, probably going through the change. Go get some hormones. I saw a pharmacy back in that last shopping center we passed."

The three visitors finally gave up at nine-thirty. They had no way of knowing what was going on inside the legislator's house, that the tastes and smells of another political race had whetted her appetite for sex into something of a frenzy. Trey had his hands full that evening with barely enough stamina left for the serious discussion afterward. Discussions about campaign financing and about Delores.

That dialogue was underway as the agents grumbled their way back out on Franklin Road and headed north.

"Hell," Cox complained, "whoever the guy is, he's good enough to outlast us. This is ridiculous."

"Yeah. I won't say I told you so," Field chided.

* * * *

Grant Benton Stone. Soldier-priest. Or was it priest-soldier? No, it was soldier-priest. Anybody who knew him well would agree.

Why else would he wear clerical robes made of green/brown camouflage parachute material? Why else would he take his sermon texts ninety percent of the time from the Old Testament lesson and stumble each time he had to read the words "swords into plowshares?" His was a God of War and Vengeance and Burning Bushes in the Trenches of Normandy. Why else would he travel every five years to the beaches of France to commemorate the Invasion Crusade?

Father Grant Stone. Decorated with the Silver Star, Purple Heart, and French Legion of Honor, for starters. Chaplain to the courageous men of the 101st Airborne Division with four combat jumps in World War II to his credit, more than any other chaplain in history.

Now eighty-three years of age and living in semi-retirement as Priest Associate with the Episcopal Church of the Advent in Huntsville, Alabama, he had lost none of the fire that was his trademark.

"Hello, Father Stone speaking," his deep bass boomed into the telephone. An elephantine voice was another trademark.

"Father Stone, this is Robert Hughes calling from Washington, D.C., the nation's capital." It was 5 p.m. Thursday, September 23.

"Yes, Robert, thanks for reminding me of that. What can I do for you?" the terse reply came.

"Ah...yes, sir...ah, well, I'm a staff member for the Senate Armed Services Committee. You know, Senator Crockett's committee?"

"Yes, yes, I've been expecting your call. I saw your name on the last correspondence from the senator. What's happening up there in Gomorra, son? Are they still trying to dismantle the greatest fighting machine on the face of God's earth?"

"Ah...well, sir, ah...I guess you could say that, sir. I mean, sir, that I'm sure you would say that. The thing is that Senator Crockett asked me to call you to let you know that he will need your testimony after all. He asked me to schedule you for next Tuesday if that's convenient with you."

"Certainly, young man," the priest replied, confident that the odds were with him on the inferred age differential. "I'm sitting on ready. I've had my parachute and duffel bag packed for the last two weeks." He laughed heartily.

"Ah...yes, well, good, sir." The aide returned the laugh weakly. "Well, sir, if you could arrange to be here on Monday. Then you could spend the night before the hearing begins at 9 a.m. Tuesday. It would probably be less...ah...more comfortable for you that way. And I'll be glad to help with those arrangements, sir, if you like."

"That won't be necessary, son. I've testified before at Senate hearings. I've been to Washington, D.C. That's your nation's capital, you know. The letter from Senator Crockett explained things well enough. About being reimbursed for expenses, et cetera. I'll be at the hearing at 9 a.m."

"Good...ah...that's good, sir. And oh, yes, I believe you understand the need for some discretion in the matter. I mean, the senator would like to place your name on the agenda at the last possible minute which will probably be Monday for...ah...for strategic purposes. I think you understand."

"Yes, soldier, I understand." They said their good-byes.

A great grin spread across the priest's face as he cradled the telephone. He sat in his chair for a moment before the grin changed to a resolute countenance. He arose and walked to the bedroom closet. Reverently he removed his dress blues with the rows of ribbons and other decorations lacing the breast of the jacket.

Holding the outfit up to his front, he straightened himself and turned to address the mirror on the closet door.

"Mister Chairman, distinguished members of the committee, ladies and gentlemen." His demeanor was firm, his voice commanding.

"It is an honor and a privilege to appear before you today. I can think of no other duty save that to my God and my church that could move me so deeply than to speak for the preservation of the 101st Airborne Division and Fort Campbell, Kentucky. In fact, I believe firmly that the hand of the Almighty has particularly blessed this fighting unit. I hope to make that evident to you, also, in the next few precious minutes..."

Then he paused, frowned, and amended, "...in the next few providential minutes..."

He placed the blues on his bed, went to his desk in the study, and began writing the text.

*   *   *   *

Friday evening Trey placed a call to his uncle in Georgetown. It had been four days since he had talked to him. Monday night the Senator had told him to keep stalling and that he was working on the problem.

"Listen, son, what with NAFTA and these Campbell hearings, my plate's full. You'll have to forgive me for not gettin' back to you sooner. The good news is that I think we can use this Bel-stos-so thing to our advantage."

"Good. Tell me about it." Trey decided he would desist in correcting his uncle's pronunciation.

"Mind you it might not work, but I hear—I hear, you understand—it's been leaked to the White House that the Mexican is involved in this secret plan to buy the army property in order to realize personal gain from it. Understand, I have no idea where this rumor came from, and I don't really want to." If you can put a wink in your voice over the telephone, he did it.

"I understand," Trey injected with a half-smile.

The Senator continued. "Like I say, it might not work, what with the sorry state of affairs in international business ethics. Clinton and his boys might just laugh up their sleazy sleeves, shrug their puny shoulders, and forge ahead pell-mell, if you know what I mean."

"Yes, sir, I know what you mean."

"But I'm pullin' out the stops. We've got Father Stone from Alabama on tap for Tuesday morning. I told you I was going to put him on the stand?"

"Yes, sir."

"Yeah, well that's confidential so let's keep it under our hats. I'm not announcin' him 'til the last minute on Monday. You haven't told anybody about my ace-in-the-hole, have you, son?"

"No...no...uh...no," Trey lied. He did tell someone—Pat Beason—Tuesday night. Did he swear me to secrecy? I should have known better. Damn!

"Good, that's good. Not even your girlfriends. No, especially your girlfriends."

Damn!

"In the meantime, you go ahead and work it from your end, from the Mats-ee-oo-koo end, and find out what we might be able to use. You know, from that monastery place." He very carefully mispronounced the foreign name.

Thank God he's not chairman of Foreign Relations, Trey thought.

So! Uncle Jonas was working the problem with a strategy that sure beat the heck out of anything Trey could come up with. At least so far.

* * * *

A few minutes later

Scott's chin rested on his arm which rested on the car door which was open ostensibly to allow egress of the young lady in the passenger seat.

"I'll put a sack over your head so you won't have to look at him and vice versa. How's that?" he asked.

"I wish you wouldn't be so silly," she answered with a pout, leg bouncing.

"Who's being silly? I didn't ask you to do this, you know. It was your idea to come along. What's the worst thing could happen?"

"He'll look at me and say, 'Rachel who?'"

"Okay," Scott said, springing into action. "Hand me the books. I'll take them in. You stay here." He stood upright and held out his hand.

The leg stopped. She bent over, face in hands, shook her head, and groaned. "Uh, uh, uh."

Then she wheeled toward Scott, who was watching his sister's struggle. She looked him straight in the eye and pleaded, "Be patient. I just need to get myself ready."

He held out his hand to her. She sighed deeply and accepted the invitation. She and Scott and the tote bag walked to Trey's front door.

"We won't be long," Scott reassured.

He rang the doorbell a couple of times.

"You sure this is where he lives?" Rachel asked.

Before Scott could answer, Trey opened the door and stood stock-still.

"Hi, Dad," Scott said.

"Uh…hi, Scott," Trey answered anemically, "…and Rachel," the latter barely audible.

"Hello, Dad," Rachel said, managing a quick smile and tucking herself safely into Scott's side.

"Come in, come in," Trey finally said, backing away.

Another uncomfortable silence, then Scott said, "Rachel wanted to…to…"

"I wanted to return the books myself," she interrupted, extending her arm with the bag towards Trey. "Thank you for letting me borrow them."

"Sure. Thanks for returning them. In person, I mean. Glad you could use them. Sit down. Here. Let me make room." He bundled an afghan and pillow together and held them in front of him. He looked like an activated air bag.

Scott and Rachel sat down.

"We don't have long," Scott said. "I've got to get to the lake and get it ready for the group. Some are coming in tonight, some tomorrow. Is the boat ready?"

"Yeah. Supposedly. But don't hurry. Stay a while. This is a…well, a special occasion." He looked at Rachel; she took in the room around her. Trey, realizing he had the wad in his arms, laughed nervously and put it down.

"So, what are you doing on Merton?" he asked Rachel.

"It's a biography term paper for social studies. Due next week. For some reason, I volunteered to give mine first, the oral presentation."

"If you need the books longer, that's okay. No hurry."

"No, I've got all my note cards done. Thanks. It was a big help."

"Don't I get a little credit? It was my suggestion, you know," Scott said.

"I'll give you a line in the credits, don't worry," Rachel said and poked at him.

"Which book did you like best?" Trey asked her.

"Hmmm. I guess *Seven Storey Mountain*. I like it better coming directly from him rather than someone else writing about him." Rachel became animated. "He really had an interesting early life in France and England and the United States. Well, sad, too, losing both his parents early. He was so much into life, though, music, college, social life. And then to just shut all that down when he became a Catholic, to be so willing to give it all up for his religious life…"

"I had the same reaction when I first read it," Trey said, sitting back in his chair and relaxing for the first time. "His college life, meeting the people and places that began to change him, and then, bam! It was like a runaway train, his desire to be a monk."

"Yeah, I ought to use that in my talk…runaway train." Rachel said, nodding dreamily, also visibly relaxing. "Gives me shivers," she added, and shook herself.

"Does it make you want to become a Catholic?" Trey asked, recalling the parting shot of his Mexican visitors.

"I don't know. Not really, I guess." She squirmed.

"Look, I'll leave you two here if you like, but I've gotta get going," Scott interrupted.

"No," Rachel said, getting up. "I'm going with you."

They walked to the door. Rachel managed to stay on the opposite side of Scott from Trey. Scott the buffer. No threat of touching or handshakes or hugs. That would be pushing it. All sensed it and honored it.

"Scott, you will drop by Monday afternoon on the way back. We need to talk."

"How about five, five-thirty?"

"I'll be here."

They waved goodbye. Rachel walked away without looking back.

Trey closed the door slowly, pensively. He went to the window and looked out at Scott's car to be sure he wasn't dreaming. He sat on the couch where Rachel had just vacated. Yes, it was warm.

He closed his eyes a moment and breathed deeply. Then he looked around again. He felt like shouting, but he contained himself. The voice inside said Uh-uhn. Careful. Take it easy. One swallow doesn't make a summer. Don't get your hopes up too much. It'll hurt even more.

He calmed down, reached into the tote bag, and pulled out the first book he felt. It was Monica Furlong's *Merton: A Biography*. It brought him back to the real world. He checked the index for references to Dom Philippe Flaget, of which there were many. The aging French Trappist who was now dying of kidney failure in the Gethsemani infirmary was a long-time friend and correspondent of Merton's. Flaget had counseled his American friend frequently during the last decade of his life. "Consoled" may be a more accurate way to describe the relationship as Merton suffered mightily under the pressures of censorship from his superiors.

Trey scanned the latter pages of the book having to do with Merton's Asian journey and sudden death. On December 10, 1968, after delivering a speech to the assembled international group of Benedictine monks, Merton was found dead in his dormitory room, the apparent victim of either a heart attack or an electric shock from a defectively wired electric fan.

Trey wondered why Furlong's account was absent any speculations as to possible foul play. He had read of such in other biographical renditions.

He also wondered what Merton's friend Flaget would have to say about his death. And about Delores Matsaku.

Chapter 12

▼

"Praise the Father, the Son, and Holy Spirit, both now and forever...The God who is, who was, and is to come...at the end of the ages."

The echoes of that Benedictine postscript reverberated off the white brick walls of the cavernous church. In near-perfect unison the fifty-odd monks in choir intoned the final solemn, deliberate words of the daily office of *sext* on Saturday noon.

The choir stalls were arranged in two rows on each side of the chamber so that the monks on either flank faced each other. At the far north end of the church was the sanctuary with altar and chairs arranged for mass. The high-ceilinged rectangular nave gave way to that circular, vaulted holy space where the Eucharist was celebrated daily for not only the monks but for guests as well. The eternal candle burned behind the altar and another lighted the iconic image of the Virgin and Child, which was placed near the stalls.

Trey always said the place was enveloped by Grace. There was a distinctive odor in the church difficult to define, a curious admixture of the brick and wood interior and incense. Trey thought it probably the smell of God. He was kneeling at the rail in the balcony, lingering to watch as Jacob took his leave of the choir stalls with the others. They caught a glimpse of each other for an instant, and Trey detected a slight nod from his friend signaling acknowledgment of their appointment just after this service.

There were a dozen or so guests in the balcony, some of them electing to stay on for a while in meditation. Or maybe they just liked to soak up the ambiance of smells and sights and unaccountable mystery that prevailed in this chamber. Trey would have done the same if he weren't preoccupied with his other mission.

"Dom Philippe's not having dialysis on Saturdays now. The doctor in Bardstown decided the schedule was too demanding on him. He's in pretty good spirits today actually," Brother Jacob said. "Even we monks can get grumpy sometimes, especially when we're taxed with ailments that sap the vitals."

The pair was making the short trek under the covered walkway that led from the quadrangle to the infirmary.

"Has he said any more to you about Delores Matsaku?" Trey asked.

"Nope. Not the first syllable about our *femme du jour*." Jacob opened the door to the annexed building, which had seen heavy duty in recent years, what with the aging population of the abbey. The average age of the monks had crept upward from about forty some twenty years ago to fifty-something now. The average population was a mirror image of that trend. Monastic vocations were apparently not a late-twentieth-century-sort-of-thing.

"But…" Jacob added, putting a hand on Trey's chest to hold him up a moment, "…he's said a gracious plenty about you. Or more correctly, he's asked a-plenty and I've told him, well, a medium-plenty, all of it the truth, mind you, but not necessarily the whole truth, you'll be relieved to know. I do consider your aberrant sex life to be a confidence, so if he's to be told it'll have to come from you. Don't be surprised, though, if he asks you some right cogent questions about yourself. Feel free to ask yours truly to leave the premises at any time during the meeting."

"Thanks for the warning. No, I think I'd like you around to rescue me in case the going gets tough. We probably need a signal system for you to let me know if I'm saying the wrong thing. Maybe a wink. Something short of a kick in the groin if you don't mind."

"Methinks you've chanced upon a dandy remedy for your rampant concupiscence, my friend. But no, I'll not kick, just stick to a wink, I think." His eyes twinkled.

Jacob pointed out the capacities of the infirmary to Trey as they walked down the hall. Fourteen private rooms, sitting area, library, and pleasant views out picture windows. There was a minor surgery room with examination table and surgical lighting equipment, a pharmacy, and a small lab. One of the monks was a former lab technician in the military and could perform routine urine and blood examinations. The facility was considered by many to be an exemplary infirmary for a monastery to have on campus.

They came to Dom Philippe's room. Jacob knocked softly without an answer. They opened the door and slipped inside. On the bed lay the small frame of a man. His eyes were closed, his countenance in repose. A sallow complexion covered angular facial features of the Frenchman. A lightweight blanket covered him to the chest, leaving his pajama-clad arms free at his side.

A bible lay open under the watchful touch of his right hand. He breathed easily and deeply with a soft snore that was audible to the two guests when they reached his bedside. He had fallen asleep while reading.

Brother Jacob nudged him. "Dom Philippe," he whispered with the French pronunciation. "Dom Philippe," he said a little louder with a heftier nudge.

"Hmmmn...mnyumn," came the awakening sounds. Flaget opened his eyes and blinked them twice before things began to register well. Then he smiled and spoke in a hoarse whisper.

"Brother Jacob and his friend Doctor Crockett. You came. Please," he indicated the chairs, "have a seat." Between the French accent and the hoarseness, Trey had difficulty understanding.

"Thank you, we will. May I prop you up or raise the head of the bed for you?" Jacob offered.

"Please, yes." He made a circular motion with his hand which meant he wanted the bed cranked up. The abbey had recently ordered new electrical hospital beds, but they had not arrived from Louisville yet. "And I could use a sip of water."

Trey poured a cup of water for Dom Philippe.

He held out his hand in greeting. "Yes, I'm Trey Crockett, Jacob's friend, and I'm so pleased to meet you, sir." They shook hands gently.

"I understand you have some questions for me. Pardon my bluntness, but I tire easily and you might prefer I not dissipate my strength on small talk."

"No, sir, I mean yes, sir, I understand quite well. No, sir, I mean about your bluntness, that's quite all right." Trey winced in the direction of Jacob who shrugged his shoulders.

"How may I help you?" came the reassuring response.

"Well sir, I'm, uh, I'm interested in the connections between Delores Matsaku and Thomas Merton and this monastery." Trey's mouth was dry.

"And just how do you plan to use this information?" Flaget asked pointedly.

Trey glanced at Jacob and found a steady clear-eyed visage that simply said to tell the truth. He pulled himself up into a bolder position.

"It's a long shot, you see, but I'm looking for leads that may help me out of a jam, a predicament."

"I see. Jacob has told me something of this jam. If you don't mind, please refresh the memory of this dying old man." His voice faltered.

Trey obliged the gentleman. He told all, even the parts about Teresa Kelly and Pat Beason.

After the narrative was finished, Dom Philippe asked for more water. Then he said, his voice crescendoing ever so slightly, "You're a brave man, Doctor Crockett, to give me such detail. I believe Brother Jacob omitted some from his rendition. I could wave you off easily at this point with the proposition that the precious memory of my friend Thomas Merton should not be despoiled by colluding with such a nefarious undertaking as you have brought to my bedside."

There was quiet.

"Perhaps I will."

"Sir?" Trey gasped.

"Perhaps I will ask you to leave now."

Quiet again.

"But first, I should give you the opportunity to change my mind on the matter. Tell me, doctor, what greater good than the preservation of Mother Church and the blessed reputation of a saint would be served by my cooperating with you?" He paused, and turned his head to face Trey directly.

"Let me put it to you this way," he continued. "If there were something about Delores Matsaku which I and only I knew, something which connects her with Thomas Merton in a way that would jar the soul of her son and all the Church and at the same time could bring scandal and disgrace to many, including myself…please, doctor, inform me now as to just why I should divulge that to you."

Both Jacob and Trey were dumb. They had not foreseen what would eventuate from the interview, but this sort of disclosure they were definitely not expecting.

Trey looked at Jacob again. No help. Just a you're-on-your-own look.

"Well, sir, I, uh, don't know just what to say to that. I guess my first impulse is to apologize to you for this intrusion into your life. At this time, especially…"

No wink from Jacob.

"…and to excuse myself," Trey continued.

"And leave me go to my grave with my unholy secret, eh?"

Jacob spoke up. "We are sure, dear brother Philippe, that your conscience will be clear with God and your brothers, that you have no obligations to us in any way. Perhaps it would be best if we did as my friend suggested and leave you to rest. I know your energy is limited."

Jacob arose and Trey followed his lead.

"I am sorry to disappoint you, my friends. But if you should decide you have more to say to me, if there were some way for me to further God's kingdom by intervening in your predicament, I welcome your return to my bedside. Provided, of course, that all this takes place in a timely manner." He raised his bushy eyebrows. "Otherwise, you will need a divining rod to summon my secrets." He didn't smile.

Trey and Jacob took their leave.

"I feel like the world's number one jerk," Trey said as they exited the infirmary.

"So what does that make me? Number one jerk-accessory? I don't think I accept that. No, I submit you acquitted yourself admirably in there. You recognized a...shall we say a near-jerk situation...and avoided it with class. I was proud of you, Trey."

"Thanks. And thanks, too, for bailing me out. You spoke up just in the nick of time. Of course I was hoping for a miracle. That he would change his mind. I don't know what I'll do now." Trey kicked at a clod of turf on the walkway.

They walked together back to the quadrangle, the midday sun spraying the buildings and gardens.

"When will I see you again?" Jacob asked.

"I don't know. Things are moving along at a pace right now, but I'm stalled. My goose is about cooked. Just hope Uncle Jonas comes through. I'll let you know."

* * * *

Another Saturday morning. Another briefing with the President.

What DEA Director Smithers had to report was less than adequate by most standards, but exactly adequate by Clinton's. That is to say, agents Cox and Field had discovered nothing illegal in the business between Manual Matsaku and the persons he assembled with him in Tokyo. This meant there were no stains on Mexico's Secretary of Commerce that could surface, at least from that direction, while NAFTA negotiations were at their peak.

Which made Bill Clinton smile. Not the come-hither smile of the lustful philanderer but the self-satisfied smile of a fast-graying man whom many judged to be more like a boy, playing at being the President of the United States. He was pleased that Eisenberg was keeping his nose clean, too.

After the meeting, Chief of Staff Marshall Counts summoned Smithers aside to debrief the debriefing. Sort of like petting after the climax; hard for Smithers to summon the interest, especially with someone who turned his stomach.

"You should know what we've learned about Belsasso from Eisenberg. We didn't bring it up in the briefing because we don't want it leaked. Very sensitive, you know."

Counts looked around again to be sure they were alone. "Aides of Jonas Crockett came to us with the same information and more. It goes like this: the Matsaku thing is linked to closing Fort Campbell, Kentucky. Apparently he wants to form an investment conglomerate with Mexicans and Americans to buy the property and build Las Vegas East, but with horses and a lot of other amenities, too. Belsasso—'Dineros' we're calling him—is supposedly arranging the Mexican financing, which with the underworld associations you guys have uncovered could be very embarrassing to the President. And there's a good chance he's planning to profit personally. Not only that, but Matsaku's group is trying to get to Jonas Crockett by blackmailing his favorite nephew, a psychiatrist from Nashville. That's how the senator knows about this. It's a friggin' mess."

"Yeah," Smithers said, "it fits with what Cox and Field reported when they tried, unsuccessfully I might add, to interview the lady politician from Tennessee. You know, Pat Beason, the one in the pictures we saw last week. This Doctor Crockett was seen going to her home when they tried to talk to her. Stayed with her a couple hours. At least it was his plates on the car the man was in. It fits with what you're telling me. Don't know exactly how the shrink figures with Beason yet."

Smithers scratched his head. "You say he's being blackmailed. Hmmm...wonder if it has anything to do with Pat Beason."

"That's your department, Harv. Maybe your guys would have more luck with him than with her. Didn't I hear she's running for governor?"

"You heard right. That's why Cox and Field never got to her. Too busy with the campaign kicking off, or too busy with the good doctor. It's not clear."

"And the Secretary of Defense and General Perkins are in on the deal?" Smithers asked.

"They're there as consultants. Not much involvement. The President wanted to help the Japanese if he could for a lot of reasons as you can imagine, what with trade sanctions up in the air. I'm not at liberty to discuss it." Smithers could tell when Counts was weaseling and he wondered if there were some foreign campaign donations in the mix.

"So, what do I do with this information besides follow the lead on Crockett's nephew?"

"Not a thing. The President's deliberating his position on Fort Campbell. Crockett's threatening to leak the Matsaku-Belsasso scheme unless the President backs off. We don't know how to do that and save face. It's tricky with the Senate hearings going on and the NAFTA agreement before the House. You see, the other option is to close Fort Bragg and the 82nd. You know how strong Bill came on during the campaign about trimming defense, so something has to go. He's to the wall on it. So is Jonas Crockett. It's getting dirty."

"I gather you don't want any more dirt surfacing on Belsasso...er...Dineros?"

"You gather correctly."

"We might be gathering some anyway. Cox put a tap on the Honorable Madame Beason's office phone. I'll keep you posted."

* * * *

"Praise the Lord and pass the ammunition…"

Grant Benton Stone, D.D., former Capt. U. S. Army, hummed that tune and looked through his suitcase for the third time, checking off items on his travel list: underwear, socks, clerical dress shirts folded and starched from the cleaners, clerical collar, travel kit with bathroom materials, spit-shined extra pair of black dress shoes, pajamas, bathrobe, bedroom shoes, and of course the picture of Dorothy.

He always took this picture of his wife on trips. She had accompanied him on various and sundry missions to France and Washington and Texas and California and wherever else he was called to speak. The retired officers' conventions, and in particular those having to do with World War II, often favored him with invitations to provide keynote speeches, and Dorothy was at his side.

That is, until she died six years ago. Now she accompanied him in a five by seven framed photo that was his favorite and which he kept on his dresser when it wasn't in his suitcase or on a hotel bedside stand. He tucked it tenderly between two shirts on this Sunday evening.

He gave his dress blues one more inspection in the hanging bag. He usually wore them along with his clerical collar at Washington events to enhance the mystique. They would get perhaps their final outing the next summer, he thought, when he planned to attend ceremonies in France surrounding the fiftieth anniversary of D-Day. He wouldn't miss that for the world. He would miss Dorothy. He planned to stay with a French family in Ste. Mere Eglise, the Normandy town where his outfit had jumped in.

He set the alarm clock for six a.m., though he would probably be up before that time. Then he made his rounds of the front and back doors, checking locks and turning on the outside lights. Even in the pleasant southern town of Huntsville, Alabama, older citizens were well advised to use routine security measures.

A shadow from the corner of his eye caused him to do a double take at the back door. Turning off the kitchen light to get a better look, he saw a neighbor's dog and heard barking in the vicinity of the flower garden.

Probably a raccoon. Raccoons had been troublesome pests at times in the semi-wooded neighborhood. He and Dorothy had picked this 1800-square-foot bungalow sitting on one-half acre largely because of the abundance of hedges and trees and the creek that formed the back border of their property. These features that afforded a measure of isolation also afforded habitat for native varmints.

Father Stone opened the back door to get a better look. It was Princess, the Mayes' black lab from next door.

"Princess!! Stop that now! Get away!" His commanding voice got the dog's attention, but instead of a threat the canine took the message as an invitation from her neighbor with whom she had developed a congenial relationship over the years. She wagged her way up the porch steps, bringing paw prints of garden mud and attempting to leave her mark on Father Stone's bathrobe.

"Down! Down!" He petted her head, took one more look around, and went back into the house. Princess resumed her noisy vigilance.

He went through the papers on his dresser before dousing the lights. There they were: plane ticket for Delta flight 1107 departing Huntsville/Decatur 8:10 a.m. CDT Monday September 23, arriving Washington National 11:15 a.m. EDT; hotel reservation for the Comfort Inn Downtown; letter from Senate aide Robert Hughes with instructions and telephone numbers; and finally his typed speech. All present and accounted for.

Lights out, soldier! God's playing taps.

Chapter 13

▼

Jacob made rounds Monday morning in the infirmary. He always tried to get in a quick visit with the brothers there before settling into his duties in the guesthouse.

Arriving at the door of Dom Philippe, he hesitated but ventured in. He found him sitting on the side of his bed with Brother Thaddeus serving breakfast.

After greetings, Dom Philippe opened the subject. "How is your friend Doctor Crockett? Have you heard from him since our visit?" His voice was stronger than in several days.

"No, but I plan to stay in touch. He left a bit disheartened, as you might guess."

"I pray I wasn't too harsh with the man. Sometimes I shock myself with my own reactions. God knows what it does to Him. I suppose He can still muster forgiveness for an old monk, don't you think?"

Thaddeus cleaned up the tray and excused himself.

"You were only protecting the integrity of Mother Church, hardly an unforgivable sin," Jacob consoled.

"You probably wonder, dear Brother Jacob, what it is that is so in need of my protection."

"I would be less than honest if I denied that."

"So that you don't put this all down to terminal senility, I'll tell you this much: There are letters in Dom Raphael's safe, correspondence between Delores Matsaku and Cardinal Swenens, which harbor the secrets to which I alluded."

"Cardinal Swenens of Rome? Pope Paul the sixth's Cardinal Swenens?" Jacob asked. "I thought he died years ago."

"Yes, your memory is good on all counts. Madame Matsaku came to know him well during the contentious and historic days of Vatican II. These letters were written in 1968..."

"Nineteen-sixty-eight?" Jacob interrupted. "That's when Merton died."

Flaget's eyes pierced Jacob's. He almost spoke, thought better of it, paused, then continued. "The letters contain information which could bring disgrace upon the Church. They are under seal, a trust that must remain sacred." He turned to lie down. "I think I need to rest now. Please excuse me."

"Of course, of course." Jacob turned and left.

* * * *

Scott arrived at his father's apartment on Monday afternoon as planned. Stone cold sober. Yes, he was a temperate version of his father. He was endowed with the looks and brains but not the appetites. He was, in fact, the only member of Sigma Chi fraternity at Davidson who had never been drunk in his life. This attribute had gained him the nickname "Arrow" from his fraternity brothers. An arrow from the quiver of an errant archer. But a "straight arrow" nevertheless.

There was a seven-hour drive awaiting Scott for his return to Davidson that night, but he wanted to spend time with his dad.

There was no doubting he was at the right house when he heard the music that penetrated the front door. Anne Murray's sultry voice was unmistakable, warbling one of her hits, "A Love Song." His father had been a fan of hers for years and had a habit of turning up the volume to drown out insignificant interruptions such as his only and devoted son at the front door. After fifteen seconds of parking on the doorbell, Scott resorted to his key.

Anne serenaded the figure of his dad lying on the couch with eyes closed, clearly caught up in a blissful reverie and oblivious to the visitor. Scott stood for a moment gazing at the scene, reluctant to intrude on such serenity. Let-sleeping-dogs-lie had a corollary: Let transfixed fathers be. Then he saw, barely noticeably, that Trey's right foot was keeping time with the rhythm, and he concluded that the person in the figure was at least partially attached to the real world.

"Stick 'em up!" Scott yelled and threw himself onto the supine figure. He was met with a startled "Yeow!" and beloved Anne's melodies met with serious competition as the two wrestled noisily off the couch and onto the floor.

"You...you young punk you!" Trey grunted. "Think your ol' man's a pushover, huh?" He pinned Scott's shoulders to the carpet. "So there!"

"Okay, okay! I give!" Scott pulled himself from his under-position. "But I'd have taken you if I weren't worn out from all the water-skiing." He stood up and straightened his clothes. "Mind if I turn down the volume?"

"No, you never did like Anne Murray. I'm sure you'd rather hear...who?...Madonna? You got no taste in music, son." The elder Crockett assumed an erect posture along with the younger.

"There, that's better. We can talk in a normal voice. You're lucky I wasn't a burglar."

"I don't hand out pass keys to burglars. Or perhaps I should withhold that statement until I've had a chance to inspect the lake house after the weekend. I trust the stereo and TVs are still there." Trey walked to the kitchen for a cup of coffee.

"I'm hurt. I'm really hurt you should insinuate that about me and my friends. I'm just glad you didn't ask about the boats."

"What about the boats!?" Trey's startled face appeared around the kitchen door.

"Kidding, Dad, just kidding. They're in fine shape. The boats ran swell. Thanks for looking after everything. My friends appreciated it too. Said you must be a real cool guy. I told 'em we had special feelings." Scott sat on the couch and picked an apple from the bowl on the coffee table. "These real?"

"What? Our feelings?" Trey asked, puzzled. Then he reentered the room and saw what his son was holding. "Oh, that. Yeah, you can eat it." There was a pause for the first crunching bite. Trey sipped coffee.

"You were right about us having something special. I'd say we get along exceptionally well considering what's gone down the last few years." Trey sat in the easy chair.

Scott nodded agreement, his mouth unavailable for comment.

"And I can't begin to tell you what Friday night meant to me. Thanks for bringing Rachel. Was it really her idea?"

"Yep. And she wouldn't let me call you ahead of time. Wanted it to be a total surprise. I think she wasn't sure she could go through with it. Almost backed out at the last minute."

"It was the best surprise I've had in a long time. Believe me, I've had the other kind lately, too."

Scott's chewing went on Pause mode.

"Which is what I wanted to talk to you about."

"What is it, Dad?" Scott whispered.

"It's...a bummer...a real bummer."

For the fifth time in the past ten days, Trey rehashed the developments, this time to the person who counted the most. It was the most difficult telling, more than to Uncle Jonas, more than to Brother Jacob and Dom Philippe, and certainly more than to Pat Beason.

By the time he finished, the apple was turning brown in Scott's hand and Trey's coffee was cool.

"Wheeww..." Scott whistled through his teeth.

"Yeah. My sentiments exactly."

"Don't you think Uncle Jonas can pull it off, Dad? I mean, I saw him at work this summer, and I wouldn't put anything past him. Honestly. He's slick."

"I'd think so, yes. But I don't know. He keeps telling me to work it from the Matsaku angle to get him to back off the deal. The one lead I have, and it's a thin one, is the ailing monk. He knows something about Delores.

"Jacob called this morning to give me the latest. Dom Philippe softened a little and opened up to him. Told Jacob there were letters in the abbot's safe, some sort of correspondence between Delores Matsaku and officials in the Catholic Church and possibly connected with Merton."

"You mean his death? Connected with Merton's death?" Scott asked.

"That's the idea."

"Well, heck, let's just get Jacob to find out what's in those letters."

"It's not that easy. They've never been out of that safe, and it would take next to a papal decree to unseal them. So says Dom Philippe."

"Hmmm...well...how about Pat Beason? Thought of asking her to help with Matsaku?"

"Yeah. Might have to before it's over. She's not likely to make any waves, though, with her nomination at stake. I haven't pushed her." Trey paused a moment. "And I guess I'm not really sure how much to trust her."

Scott's shaking head registered chagrin.

"I know, I know. You don't have to say it. What am I doing in a relationship with a woman I can't trust?"

"You said it, not me."

"But you thought it."

"Okay, mind-reader."

There was an uncomfortable silence broken by Scott.

"Tell me what I can do to help. You know I will. Anyway I can."

"You've already helped by listening. Beyond that I don't know. Be on stand-by. Who knows what the next ten days will bring. Could I use you for a character witness? Or to rub out two Mexican goons and one sleazy lawyer on Main Street?"

"Seriously, Dad."

"I'm sorry. For one thing, and I know it's unfair to ask, but please don't breathe this to your mother or sister yet. I might need to tell them. If it's about to hit the press or something. God knows I'm afraid what it'll do to Rachel and me. Probably set us back another four years. It might work better coming from you instead of me. Could you do that?"

"Don't worry about it. I'll do whatever."

"And Mother," Trey sighed, "What to do about her? She's been through enough with me already. Never has forgiven me, I'm afraid. Not for my drinking. Not even for my choosing medicine over law. Now this."

"When have you seen her?" Scott asked.

"It's been a while. I see accusation all over her face. My imagination, huh?"

They hugged.

Scott looked at his watch and scurried about to get on the road.

* * * *

"Tell me again about your arrangements with Father Stone," Jonas Crockett asked above the noise of the room.

The scene in the Senate hearings chamber at 10 a.m. on Tuesday was just short of chaotic. Aides were scrambling in and out of the room, delivering written and verbal messages to Senator Crockett and other members of the Armed Services Committee. The press and major networks were waiting impatiently. C-Span was definitely stymied for its live coverage and was showing three-day-old footage of last week's hearings instead. NAFTA debates on the floor of the House would have provided a good substitute, but those didn't commence until after noon.

The problem was that Father Grant Benton Stone was a no-show. Staffer Hughes had talked with him Sunday at his home to confirm arrangements including flight number, time of arrival, motel, and travel to the Senate building. Hughes was upset but not nearly as upset as Jonas Crockett.

"Tell me about your arrangements with Father Stone?" the senator repeated, cornering Hughes at the end of the committee's table. Both leaned in to hear.

"Yes, sir. I, ah, talked to him Thursday night to ask him to be here today. He agreed readily, said he'd received our correspondence, that he was eager to testify."

"No hesitation at all?" Crockett asked.

"None, ah, no, sir. Declined assistance on reservations, etc. Said he'd been to hearings before. Sounded confident. Cocky, I'd say."

"Okay, okay. Then what?"

"Well, sir, just to be on the safe side I FedExed him detailed instructions about the hearings, transportation, and all, and gave him my home and beeper numbers to call me as soon as he arrived Monday. Then to be doubly safe I called him again Sunday. He'd gotten the information and was packing his bags."

"And you didn't hear any more from him?"

"Yes, sir, ah, that's right. Last night I called his hotel and he never arrived. Checked the airline and he wasn't on the flight. I called his home. No answer. I don't know what else to do."

"Call up our next witness, that's what you do. Let's get on with it, dammit. Maybe he'll surprise us and parachute in through the window here." His jowls were alive as he growled the hearings back into session.

Major General Robert Bjork, U.S. Army, retired, commander of the 101st during Viet Nam, was prepared to testify.

At 11:55, just before he was ready to call a lunch recess, the senator was handed a message by Hughes. It said, "Urgent phone call for you in the office re Father Stone." He gaveled the break and hurried to the committee's anteroom, Hughes trailing.

"This is Jonas Crockett."

"Just a moment, senator. We have your party waiting."

"Hello? Senator Crockett?"

"Yes, this is Jonas Crockett."

"Senator, this is Father Jon Monroe of the Church of the Advent in Huntsville, Alabama. I'm calling from Father Grant Stone's home here in Huntsville. I believe you were expecting him in Washington today, weren't you?"

"Yes, I most certainly was. We've been worried about him. Is somethin' wrong?" He motioned for Hughes to listen in on the other extension.

"That's what I'm calling about, sir. A most dreadful thing has happened to Father Stone. He was found dead in his bed this morning by his maid."

"What? Oh, no, I'm so sorry to hear that. My God, father, how did it happen?"

"That's the dreadful part, Senator. The maid smelled gas in the air as soon as she entered the house this morning. She had a key that she uses when he's out of town. It seems the gas stove in the kitchen was left on, unlit. Dreadful, just dreadful."

"Oh, my God, I'm so sorry. Any idea why?"

"Well it certainly wouldn't have been intentional. His bags were packed for the trip. The way we found out about his appointment with you was by some papers laid out on his dresser. We knew you must be wondering what happened to him."

"Thank you very much for calling. Of course we were wondering. He seemed very eager to testify on the Fort Campbell matter. This is just awful."

"Yes, it is. I'm sure he would've made a fine impression on your committee. He told us he would be out of pocket a few days this week. Didn't say where. No one I've talked to had any inkling he was going to Washington. Sorry to be the bearer of such news, Senator. And he was looking forward to next year's fiftieth celebration of D-Day. It's just dreadful."

"Yes, I'm sure it's much harder on those of you who knew him well. Thank you very much for calling, and God bless you, Father."

"And you too, Senator. Oh! I should tell you that the maid found the back door unlocked and, well, she said there were muddy tracks in the kitchen. Dreadful. The police got here after the ambulance."

"I see. Well, I'd appreciate it very much if you'd pass along to me anything else you learn about that. Good-bye now."

"Of course. Good bye."

Jonas sat staring at the phone a moment, then coolly looked at Hughes and said, "I bet my best coon dog he was murdered, and I'd hate to hazard a guess as to who did it. I'd hate to speculate that Belstosso or Matseeookoo or Billy Boy could've ordered it. I wouldn't even begin to speculate that, now would I, Hughes?"

"Ah...no, sir, ah...I'm sure you wouldn't, and I'm sure you haven't, either. No, sir." Hughes suppressed a grin with a frown.

"Get me Jim Stennis on the phone, Hughes."

"You mean the Director of the FBI, sir?"

"That's exactly who I mean!" The senator slapped the heel of his hand on the desktop and leaned back in the chair. "I'll stay right here 'til you get him. Bring me my file from the other room there, and how about a ham sandwich when you've got a minute?"

* * * *

Word traveled fast. By mid-afternoon Marshall Counts and other White House staffers had received news of both Father Stone's death and the official request by Senator Crockett for the FBI to join the investigation. By four-thirty President Clinton had made a private decision to offer a compromise to the senior senator from Tennessee. He sent a message asking for a meeting with him over dinner.

* * * *

It was ten o'clock that night when Jonas finally was able to take off his shoes and rest in his own home. Jeanne rubbed his neck.

"I'm gittin' too old for this."

"You've been saying that for at least fifteen years."

"Yeah, but now my whole body's sayin' it. It's a regular Greek chorus. Can't you hear it?" He bent his knee and the cracking sound confirmed his assertion.

"Tell me what happened with the president."

"First off, he said if my resolution did pass, he would probably back off closing the base altogether. He doesn't want it to go to the Hill for an all-out fight. I think he was softening me up.

"Then he came up with an offer to back off Campbell and the 101st if I'd agree to push for closing Bragg and decommissioning the 82nd. Said it's not worth it to him, with the taint accumulating on Belstosso and now the possible murder of the priest."

"Why, that's just wonderful, honey. That's what you were hoping for, wasn't it? You ought to be celebrating."

"Not exactly, no. I told him I couldn't agree to go after Bragg. I couldn't do that to my Carolina friends. Jesse and all of 'em."

"So, what kind of deal did you strike? You worked out something with him, didn't you?"

"Then he got down to penny-ante stuff, like preserving a battalion or two of the 101st and transferring them to another base. That man just doesn't realize how important the airborne divisions are to our defense. If we are ever going to finally put down Saddam Hussein and his like it'll have to be with the Screamin' Eagles."

He took her hands in his around his neck and kissed her fingers. "Honey, no, I didn't work out anything with him. I wrestled with my conscience this way and that. The good people of my state, my nephew who's like a son to me and you, that poor Father Stone. It was all a-jumblin' in my mind and heart."

Jonas then stood up and faced his wife, becoming more animated. "But the more I sat there and listened to that silly, draft-dodgin' womanizer, that poor excuse for an ordinary man much less a president, the more I realized I didn't want to work out something with him. I just wanted to take him to the wall on this and expose him for what he is. I swear, Jeanne, it just got all over me! Maybe I wasn't very statesman-like, but I just told him basically to take his offer and shove it!"

"Oh dear, Jonas honey, oh dear." Jeanne reached out to him again. "I'm sure you did the right thing. But what will you tell Trey?"

"The truth."

Chapter 14

Trey stayed up until midnight Tuesday watching his uncle at work on C-Span replays, wondering along with the newscasters exactly what had happened to the committee's star witness. News of Father Stone's death was not released until later in the day, and details were lacking.

The item got a mention Wednesday on GMA, with newsanchor Morton Dean citing "…a disappointing day for Senator Jonas Crockett, Chairman of the Senate Armed Services Committee, whose hand-picked witness, an Episcopal priest from Huntsville, Alabama, was found dead in his home yesterday. Father Grant Stone, a former army chaplain with the 101st Airborne, was to testify in favor of the Senate resolution that would overturn President Clinton's plan to close Ft. Campbell, Kentucky, and decommission the 101st. This unforeseen development could be a setback for the senator in what is being characterized as a major showdown with the president. Details of the priest's death have not been disclosed."

The *Tennessean* carried little more than that except for an uncharacteristically brief quotation from the senator. He was reported as saying that "the fate of the 101st Airborne Division does not hang on the testimony of one witness, regardless of reputation."

Trey was hoping to hear from his uncle today, thinking surely there would be more to the story. Surely Jonas would have the answers. Surely Father Stone wasn't murdered.

"Melba," Trey addressed his receptionist, "interrupt me if Uncle Jonas calls."

"Same rules as last week, doctor? How about Mrs. Beason? Interrupt for her, too?"

"Yeah, I guess so. Yeah. Mrs. Beason, too. Thanks."

"How about Mr. Horton?"

"No, not him. Take a message." Trey had not confided in Melba about his problem, but she knew something was up with her boss. He had not been his usual affable self these last few days. He had left messages hanging over to the next day. Two of his patients had asked if anything was wrong.

Rounds at the hospital had been brief that morning with just two patients to see, leaving him with twenty minutes before his first office patient at ten. He sat at his fifth-story window looking west over the Vanderbilt campus, over the tops of aging oaks and magnolias and maples, over the barely visible tops of redbrick and sandstone buildings in the distance, aging with the trees.

In the foreground he saw trees that were younger, smaller, and less numerous, any greater density being proscribed by the high-profile and massive invasion of a megacomplex known as Vanderbilt Medical Center. Twenty years and a few quadjillion dollars after his graduation from the medical school, this was hardly the same place where once all the professors knew his name and vice-versa.

But he wasn't exactly the same either. Following his near-disaster with the passionate and shapely pediatrics professor, he had become a model student and graduated in the top ten percent of his class. He even settled down to one woman long enough to marry Evelyn Sanders.

He was an exemplary psychiatric resident at Cincinnati, capturing the title of Chief Resident in his fourth year. Then there were two years of Air Force duty after he married Evelyn.

Ah, yes. "Off we go, into the wild blue yonder…"

That's when the hinges began to come loose, when the pressure of competitive medical training was off and the talented mind of Trey Crockett went into semi-idle. It was during that time that the devil's workshop cranked up its machinery and Trey had the opportunity to revive the vestiges of his old self.

"Cunning and baffling" is the way the Big Book of AA describes the process of progressive alcoholism. In subtle ways Trey slipped back into the cunning and baffling life of booze and women.

When it finally had come tumbling down around him, there was nothing subtle about it at all. There had been one glaring calamity after another. The sole bright spot had been his lawyer's keeping the Teresa Kelly affair out of the courts. And now the wheels were coming off.

The most damaging consequence of all, though, had been the loss of his daughter. It was like she was dead, at least until last Friday.

Often when Trey had time for moments of reflection, like now, his mind turned to Rachel. He pulled her photo out of his wallet and held it in front of him, between him and the window that had opened up this train of remembrances.

The picture was a snapshot of Rachel and him taken at her thirteenth birthday party, a spend-the-night happening that took place just months before his world caved in. He and Evelyn separated not long after that, and soon thereafter he was the target of an intervention by Dr. Greg Dodge, director of the Tennessee Recovery Network, otherwise known as the "impaired physicians' program."

The photo captured Rachel and him in an ecstatic embrace, their faces wreathed in smiles. It was their last photo together. In fact, it was the last one of her of any kind that he possessed. She declined to send him even her school yearbook pictures.

When he was in treatment at the Alcohol and Drug Treatment Unit at Oak Valley Retreat in Memphis, he had made the tough decision, after much argumentation with his counselor, to come clean with his wife and children. Well, almost clean. On the advice of counsel, he told no one of the affair with his patient.

In the intervening three years since his treatment, Trey had nourished a deep resentment toward that counselor. The confessing of his nefarious ways and asking for forgiveness had made no great difference with Evelyn; she had already made her decision to divorce. With Scott, their relationship was strengthened; the process of making amends worked in the case of his son.

It was different with Rachel. Trey tried to talk his counselor into leaving her out of the sessions. She was just fourteen years old. But he insisted. It was a bad mistake. She didn't speak to him for three years.

Counselors make mistakes. Patients get angry with counselors who make mistakes. Trey nurtured the anger, one of the top-ranking, confusing emotions of that era, right up there along with suicide-contemplating depression. The prospects of losing his daughter and his career weighed heavily. The medical career had been barely tolerated by his father, and the shadow of that family icon still hovered over his predicament, leaving him often in despair.

The intercom buzzed and Melba's voice interrupted his morbid reverie. "Ms. Bottoms is here, Doctor Crockett."

Bottoms is up. No wonder she comes to see me.

* * * *

On Wednesday morning the Tennessee state legislative hearing room was filled with political science and social studies students. Mrs. Roberts had just quieted her charges.

"It's a great pleasure to welcome you students from Briarwood Academy here today. I'm Weldon Simmons, aide to Governor McWherter. The governor asked me to deliver his welcome, too, and to wish you a rich learning experience as you delve into the workings of the government of your wonderful state of Tennessee. Your school has a strong tradition in the classroom and on the athletic field, and I know you are proud to wear its colors.

"Your first speaker today is indeed the First Speaker. That is, she is the Speaker of the House of the Legislature. She is the first woman to hold that position and is doing a remarkable job of leadership. You can imagine, I guess, what it's like to try and ride herd over a hundred and twenty politicians. Ha! Ha!" Simmons blushed, realizing he was the only one laughing.

"Anyway, I know you'll enjoy hearing what the Honorable Pat Beason has to say." He started the round of applause and walked to the side as Pat Beason strode to the podium.

"Thank you, Mr. Simmons. And thanks to the governor and to Mrs. Roberts for arranging this field trip. I'm happy to participate. It was a few years ago—quite a few—that I was sitting out there in your seats when my high school, Crossville High, made the same excursion to the state capitol."

In the middle of the room sat Rachel Crockett next to her friend Phyllis, her eyes glued to the speaker.

"So let me tell you some of what I know about how this state government works…"

A half-hour later, she wound up her prepared remarks. "I'd be glad to answer any questions." She looked at the clock on the wall. "We have a few minutes left before your next speaker."

Rachel's hand shot up with a spate of others.

"Yes," Beason said, pointing to a boy near her.

He stood. "I'm Ben Fuller, a reporter for the Clarion. That's the school newspaper in case you didn't know." He held up his pen and notebook for all to see. There were hoots and catcalls. He bowed to the crowd. "I've seen on the news where you're running for governor. Why do you want to do that? To be the first woman governor in Tennessee?"

"You'll make a good reporter, Ben. You go straight to the jugular." General laughter mixed with boos ensued. "There's nothing I'd like better than to launch into a campaign speech, and I do appreciate your noticing, but I think, Ben, that it would be inappropriate to do so in this particular meeting. I'll just say that there's much more than gender at stake in the race." She smiled. Ben sat down, scribbling ostentatiously.

Beason pointed to Rachel next.

"I'm Rachel Crockett, and I'm not a reporter, so I won't embarrass you, I hope." She glared at Ben. Scattered applause from the crowd. Pat Beason tried not to register recognition of the girl's name.

Rachel read from notes. "With all of the interests you try to serve in politics, how do you preserve an ethical, moral, public and personal life?" No catcalls.

"Now that is a very good question, and one that no honest politician should shy from." Pat Beason's voice was steady, her bearing sturdy.

"It is necessary, I find, to maintain a constant vigilance, a deep awareness of the values that drive the decisions I make, the causes I embrace. And we can't count on Ethics Committees for this purpose. Unless the individual, the person in office, unless I—I," she paused and pointed to her heart for effect, "am possessed of those character traits that you are talking about, then there's little hope for honest government. Or meaningful life, for that matter.

"I'm not sure I've answered your question. There's a deep and unfortunate distrust of politicians in America today. I only hope that I can be one to help reverse that trend. And you, too, Rachel. Maybe you can be up here in my place one day."

Rachel remained standing and began clapping. Soon the entire audience was on its feet and joining her. Pat Beason smiled demurely from the podium.

* * * *

Phil Cox and Spike Field spotted Claude Bishop's stocky frame and plaid suspenders at the baggage pickup. With suspenders like that, Phil had noted, he didn't need a rose in his lapel. A few minutes later they were departing Nashville's airport and on the way to Bishop's office downtown via Briley Parkway and I-40. Ten a.m. Wednesday traffic in this city seemed like nothing compared to D.C.'s.

The Drug Investigation Division of the TBI was on the eighth floor of the Clement Building, named for the late former governor, Frank Clement. He was the darling of the Democrats who had delivered the keynote speech for the Democratic National Convention in 1952 in a losing cause.

Bishop's office was another losing cause. It was hopelessly disorganized and cluttered. Bishop amazed his guests, however, by reaching into an obscure desk drawer and delivering exactly what he wanted: a cassette tape with recorded messages collected over the past week from Pat Beason's office telephone.

"You listened to the whole tape?" Cox repeated the question he had asked in the car.

"Yes, damn it, how many times do I have to tell you?"

"Until I hear nothing but sincerity in your voice. Which might mean eternity, considering you're an uncivil servant."

"And just what do you call yourself, mister Special Agent?" Bishop retorted while inserting the tape into the player.

"Civilized. I'm a civilized servant. From a civilized part of the world. Where the politicians cooperate with government agents and grant them interviews, not shun them like…what do you say here?…poor white trash?" He winked at Spike Field.

"Don't hook me into this fight," Spike interjected with a grin. "Ise jes' 'long fo' da ride, boss."

I've marked the tape so it'll stop at the interesting parts. The first one is from last Friday, and it's a conversation with Señor Belsasso, your drug-smuggling suspect from Mexico City." He leaned back in his chair and hitched thumbs in the suspenders.

The voices of the two parties were very clear.

"Madame Beason? So glad to hear from you again." The man's accent was definitely Latin.

"Thank you, Señor Belsasso. Good to talk to you too. I thought I would bring you up to date if that's okay. Do you have a moment?"

"Why of course. I always have time for such a beautiful lady with such a beautiful voice, and, of course, with such useful information."

"I've learned from my source that Senator Crockett plans to bring in his star witness to the hearings next Tuesday. He's Father Grant Stone, an Episcopal priest and former war hero, a chaplain with the 101st Airborne. That's the army division that uses Fort Campbell. I guess you remember that though."

"Yes, yes, I recall. Tell me, is the priest still active in the military?"

"No, no. He's in his eighties and retired. Lives in Huntsville, Alabama, now. From what my source says, he's an exceedingly persuasive spokesman for the military, and the senator is depending on him heavily."

"Did you say Tuesday?"

"At nine on Tuesday morning. I thought you would want to know for strategic purposes."

"Of course. You never know when such information will be useful. It's helpful to be able to anticipate events and to assure Mr. Matsaku that we are on task. Thank you very much. Let's see, that's Father Grant Stone, you say, in Huntsville, Alabama? Okay, I have that. Good. It seems our little Delores communication network is working quite nicely. I heard from Secretary Eisenberg just yesterday."

"Very good. I'll stay in touch. You do the same."

"*Adios*, Madame Beason."

"*Adios*, Señor Belsasso."

Bishop hit the Pause button.

"Well, I guess we know who the source is. El Doctoro," Field offered.

"Yeah. He's gettin' double-screwed," Bishop agreed.

"Unless he knows she's feeding the Mexican this information," Cox said to Bishop. "After all, Doctor Crockett has a stake in Fort Campbell being closed. He could be working behind the scenes against his uncle."

"Hmmm…maybe. I doubt it. That's one of the oldest established political families in the state. Goes all the way back to old John Sevier, first governor. They don't turn on each other."

"You're probably right," Cox replied. "Say, did you guys get that reference to…was it Delores? What was that?"

"I heard that. Must be a code name," Field said. "File it and let's hear the next passage. So far, so good."

Bishop obliged. The tape whirred then stopped again.

"This one was Monday about 2 p.m. She's calling El Doctoro Crocketto."

"Hello, this is Trey Crockett."

"Trey Crockett, this is Pat Beason. Remember me?"

"Sort of. Your voice is familiar. Come to think of it, there's a lot of you that's familiar."

"Uh-huh, I thought you'd remember. But I'm all business today. What gives?"

"Actually, I'm expecting a visit from my son Scott to give him the low-down on my predicament."

"That's what I'm calling about. Any news?" Pat asked.

"Nothing good. I struck out at the monastery. It seems that the monk I told you about—Dom Philippe Flaget—is sitting on some valuable information about Delores Matsaku and has access to written correspondence to back him up. Stuff that could loosen some hinges in the Roman Catholic hierarchy. Whether that would cut any ice with Manuel Matsaku, I don't know. But it's my only lead so far."

"That doesn't sound like striking out to me."

"That's because you haven't heard the end of the story. He wouldn't give any details of what he knew because of the possible consequences to the church. I have to convince him that my ends justify his means. Somehow I just didn't believe saving my ass was good enough." Trey sighed.

"Did he offer any hope? I mean, is he going to live long enough for you to convince him?"

"Oh, I think he's tough enough to last through the next couple of weeks, if that's what you mean. And he's lucid. I guess I still have a prayer."

"Well, for what it's worth, I'll offer mine up too. What did you say his name was?"

"Dom Philippe Flaget. He's French. How's your *parlez vous*?"

"Probably about as *bon mot* as yours. Anyway, good luck."

"Thanks. I'll need it. So what else is happening? How's the candidate?"

"Off and running. How's my ace fund raiser?"

"I'll know more about that after the HospiCare board meeting this week." Trey answered. "Will I see you sometime soon?"

"I hope. Not this week, though. Every night's taken. I've got to go now. Keep me informed. Love ya."

"Sure, babe."

Pause button.

"The poor sucker doesn't know, does he?" Cox asked of the other two. They shook their heads in unison.

"Do you feel like Boy Scouts? Let's go do him a good deed and, well, make a patriot out of him at the same time."

* * * *

Big Al was getting pissed. It began to show in subtle ways.

"Just what the hell do you mean, Doctor Crockett, that your uncle hasn't come up with anything yet? Do you realize it's Wednesday the twenty-ninth of September and you have less than a week to turn that cornball Cleghorn around?"

Trey loved it now that the tables were turned. His tone grew softer as Al's cranked up. "Well, Al, yes, I know that. I'm sorry I don't have anything more to tell you than this. Am I correct to assume, counselor, that your fee in this matter is contingent?"

"You can assume whatever you damn well please, doctor, but it just makes an ass out of you, not me. I think I've heard enough out of this conversation. Good fucking day!" The phone clicked dead.

Just as he was getting ready to leave his office at noon, Trey took a call from a Phillip Cox with the Federal Drug Enforcement Agency who was in Nashville with his partner. Mr. Cox wanted to meet with the doctor that evening if possible. He and his colleagues had some very important things to tell the doctor about the Delores project. Yes, they knew the code name. Trey agreed to meet with them at his home.

In the meantime he had his usual Wednesday lunch and conference with psychiatry residents at Vanderbilt. They were subdued that day in their white coats that were as long as their faces, and soon the reason was obvious. There had been a suicide on the inpatient unit the previous night.

Trey had to remind them that such tragic incidents go with the territory if you work with disturbed patients, and that it happens to almost all psychiatrists sooner or later. It was just happening sooner to this group of cohorts-in-training. John Robbins was the main focus of their concern, for it was his patient who had hung herself from the shower curtain rod in her bathroom. They had moved her to a less-secure room because all thought it would be safe.

"The head nurse had been after maintenance for two months," John explained, clearly distressed, "to have the shower rods replaced with collapsible ones. The crew arrived this morning. About six hours too late."

Trey dismissed the planned case presentation and allowed the young doctors to debrief and decompress. Trey's mind wandered at one point to the news of Father Stone's death. Surely that wasn't a suicide, but what was it?

Trey did his own decompressing at the athletic club that afternoon pounding overheads at the net.

* * * *

The printer in the communications room of the FBI in Washington chattered. The clerk on duty noted the time and waited for the first page to fall into the basket. She picked it up and read:

enter code:
blue roses
verify:
menagerie
accepted. begin message.

Wednesday, Sept. 29, 1993
1330 hours
Huntsville, AL
Agent R. Wrenn 053127

Arrived Huntsville 1030 hours, met by Field Agent D. Johnson. Escorted to Huntsville Police Department where I was briefed by homicide detective Ormond. Went to the home of Father Grant Stone at 2208 Fagan Springs Drive. The scene was properly cordoned. Precautions looked good and investigation thorough. Prints found on the back door handle and stove switches match the victim's. No signs of struggle. Mud tracked into kitchen still present and being cast while we were there. Shoe and dog tracks on back porch as well as in flower garden in back yard. Photos all good quality.

Statements from two persons so far:

1) Mary O'Neil, the maid. She comes every Tuesday to clean and iron, had her own key to front door. Smelled gas in house when she entered Tuesday and found gas on at the stove, turned it

off, found back door unlocked, opened doors and windows, then found priest dead in his bed. Suitcase packed and papers on his dresser with airline tickets, etc. Called 911 for help. Called church. Police and ambulance came. Muddy tracks in kitchen noted by police. Rev. Monroe came.

2) Reverend Jon Monroe, rector of the Church of the Advent where Father Stone was employed part-time. He was called by maid who found body. He knew nothing of Stone's appointment at hearings, and no one at his church seems to have. Only knew that Stone was going to be away this week. Says Stone was in good health as far as he knew, 'robust.' Stone assisted at services on Sunday. Monroe last saw him leaving church accompanied by two military visitors who had identified themselves as newcomers to the city in training at the missile school at Redstone Arsenal in Huntsville. They were Latin in appearance and accent.

So far no one else has come forward with more information. Getting good cooperation from locals. Plan to stay on this week, help with investigation. The two Latin soldiers are being traced at the missile school, no luck so far.

End of report.

Trey listened intently to his uncle long-distance.

"Sure. Go ahead and meet with them. Let them be the ones to uncover the dirt. Billy Boy's more likely to listen to his own people, so let them tell him what kind of mischief Señor Bel—whatever the Mexican's name is—is in."

Jonas Crockett through this phone call was registering his permission for his nephew to talk with the federal agents. He also was passing along the latest news from the FBI on the Grant Stone case.

"It sure looks like foul play. Poor ol' feller. Not much to go on yet except some muddy tracks in his kitchen and an open back door. And, oh yeah, he was last seen with a couple of Latin-lookin' military types who were visiting at his church Sunday."

"Did you say 'Latin'?" Trey asked.

"Yeah. That's what the FBI reported. Supposedly in training at the Army Missile Command. We have these programs all the time where we train our allies in the use of missiles. They haven't been able to verify these guys yet. My aide checked with the Pentagon, and they don't know about any current program with Spain or Italy or Mexico. The uniforms these guys wore apparently fit the description more of the Mexican army than anything else."

"That's getting kind of scary-sounding, don't you think?" Trey offered.

"Well, yeah, anything Mexican has a stink on it at this point as far as I'm concerned."

"You're not the only one. Don't forget I had an encounter with two Mexicans just a couple of weeks ago."

"I seem to remember that, yeah. Well, son, you go ahead and talk to those folks. See if they can help. You know my position." He had told Trey all about his encounter with a conciliatory Clinton and his decision not to cooperate, to take the president to the wall.

The conversation ended with small talk about family just in time for Trey to respond to the doorbell. Not even time for him to digest the full impact of what his uncle had told him, that this thing was going down to the wire.

* * * *

Cox and Field and Bishop introduced themselves, showed their I.D.'s, and accepted Trey's invitation to sit in the living room of his home.

Cox kicked it off. "To get straight to the point, doctor, we'd like your help in a matter that has to do with drug-smuggling from Mexico. In our investigations of certain high-ranking Mexican officials, we've stumbled on this plan involving the Japanese and Mexicans to purchase Fort Campbell, Kentucky, and convert it into an entertainment and gambling enterprise. The code name is Delores. You familiar with that?"

"What makes you think I would be?"

"Well, now, Doctor Crockett, let's just say that sources close to your uncle have been in contact with the administration, and we are aware of the blackmail threat against you. And, in addition, we have another source of information close to home," he raised his eyebrows at this point, "who shall have to remain nameless, who tells us other things. Things that you are probably not aware of and which would be of utmost interest to you, let's say would be in your best interest to know about."

"You just lost me," Trey said, shaking his head.

"I'm being vague on purpose, doctor. I'd like to get your agreement to a cooperative venture before being any more specific. I think I have information that could save you from even more trouble than you're in if you'll help us."

"What is it you want me to do?"

"What we, the Drug Enforcement Administration of the United States, want you to do is to help us provide information to Mexico's Secretary of Commerce. His name is Belsasso, and he might be involved in some things he shouldn't be. I believe you've heard of him from Ms. Beason?"

"You seem to know a great deal. Yes, I've heard of him from knowledgeable sources. But I don't know what I could possibly do to help you with him. I don't know the man."

"The Honorable Ms. Beason does know him, according to our source. And she's using you as a source of information, Doctor Crockett, in her dealings with him. We've got proof of that."

"Wha...what did you say? Did I hear you right?" asked a stunned Trey.

"You heard me right. I'll be happy to share the evidence with you as soon as I know you're on board. Like I said, we could save you from more trouble if you'll work with us. But we've gotta work fast. The

Post has wind of Belsasso. There's a leak somewhere, and everybody and their brother are getting calls from reporters to verify this and that. We can't sit on it. It's like about to be on page one pretty soon. By then our options will be very limited."

Trey was pacing. "Okay, okay. You just hit me with a broadside and I'm trying to get my breath." He reflected on Uncle Jonas' permissive response, sighed, and continued, "I'll do what I can for you. Sounds like a worthy cause for my country, patriotic and all that."

Claude Bishop's hand rubbed across the cassette tape in his jacket pocket, and he spied the tape player in the stereo console across the room. Trey didn't realize what was in store for him: he was about to hear yet another recording by one of his sweethearts, and it wasn't going to be Anne Murray.

After the assembled group listened to the taped segments, Cox and Field proceeded to outline for Trey a plan to arrest Fernando Belsasso—*Dineros*—with the help of converted Mexican agents Vasquez and Davila. For illegal drug smuggling as well as conspiracy to commit murder and blackmail.

Trey was going to help them get it done on Monday of the next week.

Chapter 15

▼

Manuel Matsaku kept a shrine in his office as well as in his home devoted to his mother's memory. Five years had passed since her death, and there had not been a day go by that he had not paused to meditate on her memory. When traveling he took along a framed photo of her, one that was taken in Rome with Pope Paul VI and Cardinal Swenens during the latter days of the Second Vatican Council in 1965. He also took the rosary beads she had given him when he was confirmed in the church at age ten.

He kept the photo and the beads resting on the altar of the shrine at his home. On this Thursday morning in September the rising sun's rays streaming through the picture window caught the glass covering the picture and reflected a dazzling beam into his eyes. He was kneeling on the cushioned riser.

He often meditated on this particular image of his mother. It reminded him of her passion for not only the church but for this particular pope. She became quite close to Paul VI during Vatican II, especially in 1965 during the fourth session when the final vote was taken on the document *Nostra aetate* ("In our times"). Its English subtitle was *Declaration on the Church's Relations with Non-Christian Religions,* and Delores Matsaku was a mover and shaker behind the scenes promoting the most liberal language for the final version.

Her immersion into the Buddhist culture of Japan while maintaining a strong Christian faith fashioned her into a champion of ecumenical causes. The Pope's chief lieutenant, Cardinal Swenens, enlisted her enthusiasm to advantage.

When Pope John XXIII convened the Second Vatican Council in 1961, it was generally understood that one of his agenda items was to heal wounds incurred during World War II between Catholics and Jews. The perceived indifference of the Church to fascism and its atrocities had left a legacy of bitterness. The pope wanted the Roman Church to take a distinct and unmistakable step in the direction of reconciliation, not only with Jews but with all religions.

The path was not unimpeded however. Conservative elements of the church opposed any ecumenical movement and sought to water down the language. Delores Matsaku, though not a voting delegate, was able to exert personal influence upon the ranks of conservatives, all except for a particular reactionary enclave known as the Bossuet Society. This was an unofficial, unsanctioned, underground group of priests and monastics in France who were disciples of the archconservative chaplain to the *Chapel Royale* of Louis XIV, Jacques Benigne Bossuet.

It was widely believed that most of the 250 adverse votes on the *Nostra aetate* came from members of that anonymous group. The other 1,763 affirmative votes were cast for this dramatic document which read in part:

> The Church, therefore, urges her sons to enter with prudence and charity into discussion and collaboration with members of other religions. Let Christians, while witnessing to their own faith and way of life, acknowledge, preserve and encourage the spiritual and moral truths found among non-Christians, also their social life and culture...The Catholic Church rejects nothing of what is true and holy in these religions...the precepts and doctrines...often reflect a ray of truth which enlightens all men.

Many of the dissenters stalked out of the Council chambers when the vote was finished. It was rumored that the Bossuet Society burrowed further underground vowing retribution upon those who fashioned this liberal movement which they saw as heretical to the Church's ageless mission.

It was in the hall outside the Council chamber after that vote that the picture of Delores, Swenens, and the pope was taken. Joyful weariness was written on their faces.

Manuel had heard his mother tell of the drama of those days, had sensed the humble pleasure she took in being a part of that historic event, that turning point in the annals of church doctrine, that molding of a document which bespoke the yearnings of her heart.

Now he had the opportunity to pursue her dreams in his own life, in his own way, with this international—call it ecumenical—business venture which united his mother's heritage with his father's.

The final twenty years of her life Delores Matsaku was much more reticent in public life. Manuel dated it from the last project in which she participated prominently. It was the international monastic convocation that took place in Bangkok in 1968. He recalled that she had returned from that meeting morose at the death of her friend and correspondent, Thomas Merton.

Delores Matsaku had never regained her enthusiasm for ecumenical projects after that. The later death of Paul VI and then the early and sudden demise of his successor, John Paul I, only hardened her stance against public exposure. Rumors of foul play in the death of the latter had been particularly odious to her. She simply hadn't the stomach for fighting the battles any more. Now it was her son's turn.

He could recall her curiously ominous, hoarsely uttered words in those last days, when he pledged to her his determination to commemorate her life with a gigantic venture. "My son," she had said, "our wills may be firm, our intentions lofty, but God's plan is mysterious and humbling." She spoke from experience.

Manuel crossed himself and arose from his meditations backing away from the shrine in a Buddhist posture of bowed reverence. He opened the door to find his butler awaiting him bearing a portable telephone.

"A call from the United States, sir. From Secretary Eisenberg. Would you like to take it here, or shall I take a message?"

"I'll speak to him. Thank you, that will be all."

He removed himself to the room he had just vacated.

"Hello, this is Manuel Matsaku speaking."

Leon Eisenberg exchanged greetings with him.

Matsaku got down to business. "What can I do for you? Do you have news for me?"

"Well, yes, I do. It's not all good, but could be worse. First, the good news: It seems the vote on the Armed Services Committee is moving in our direction. Latest tally is eleven for the resolution and eight against, leaving out the chairman. That's a net change of one since two weeks ago when the hearings began. Two more and it'll be out of Crockett's hands."

Eisenberg continued. "We're working on those two as hard as we can. I believe your influence on Senators Wilford and Jansen could be quite helpful at this juncture. The timber interests in Washington and Alaska have been attentive to your wishes in the past. They just might be the two swing votes we're looking for. We do have the chairman's nephew working with us, the psychiatrist from Tennessee, but we don't want to put all our eggs in that basket."

"Very good. Yes, I hope that my connections with those gentlemen may be of some use. Now, what about the bad news?"

"Well, sir, there seems to be an ill wind blowing from south of the border. Our colleague, Señor Belsasso, has been attracting attention from the administration. I'm not at liberty to divulge all, but caution is advised. It seems that a couple of Mexicans have been implicated in the murder of a priest, an American, who was supposed to testify for Senator Crockett this week. The investigation is still fresh and no one has been arrested, but suspicions are running high around here that Belsasso might be involved. The FBI found that two Mexican citizens flew into Huntsville, Alabama, where the priest lived, on Saturday by commercial airline with visas stamped by the *Departmente de Comercio* of Mexico."

"That's very disturbing news, Mister Secretary. Very disturbing. I am grateful for your taking me into confidence. And I assure you that you may trust me with this information. Tell me, now, just when do the hearings terminate? It is sometime soon."

"A week from now; by next Wednesday the vote must be taken. It could be sooner, perhaps Monday, if all the witnesses have been called and the committee agrees to go ahead with it. Then the NAFTA vote in the House is Tuesday. It's going to be crunch time around here, sir, and the Belsasso thing could explode. Hope it doesn't. The President is quite concerned."

"Yes, yes, of course." Matsaku paused a moment. "Well, it might be time for me to pay a visit to my friends in the United States. Perhaps I can look out for my, and our, interests better on a personal basis."

"I'm sure you would be welcome," Eisenberg said. "I'll be glad to help in any way."

"Thank you. I'll look at my calendar and start making arrangements when I get to the office. Good day."

This wasn't the first clouded news Matsaku had heard lately on Señor Belsasso. He dearly hoped that his partner wasn't finding it impossible to resist the notorious siren call of corruption indigenous to his country's government.

Returning to the altar he knelt again and spoke aloud, softly, deliberately. "Beloved mother, I am guided by your spirit in this matter. I honor you with this project which bears your name. Your son has no wish greater than to bring together your heritage with his father's in a grand and beautiful manner. I pray the Holy Mother of God will protect us in all this to allow no harm or dishonor to mar your memory."

* * * *

Rachel turned the last page of the flip chart, straightening the creases so all the class could read the prepared text. Then she paused to be sure she had their full attention as she approached the conclusion.

"I call it 'Merton's Last Stand'," she said, using the pointer to indicate those words in headline. "And these are the reasons I think his death was intentional, not an accident." She had them listed.

"First, he was under surveillance by the CIA because of his affiliation with Soviet writers. Second, conservative elements of the Catholic Church considered him dangerous. Third, there was no autopsy performed. Fourth, there was no investigation into his death, not by the Thai officials or any others.

"And last," she added, "I didn't list this one because it just occurred to me this morning. It could have been suicide. He was torn between his Christian roots and his newly-adopted Buddhist beliefs. Maybe that was just too much for him to bear."

Rachel turned to Mrs. Roberts standing by a window. "That's the end of my report," she said.

"Let's all thank Rachel for volunteering to give the first biographical report, and such an interesting one," the teacher said. The class followed her lead with applause. "Would you like to take questions?" she asked.

Rachel nodded. "Sure."

Two hands went up. Rachel pointed to Alice.

"You described Merton as kind of a playboy in his early life, got a girl pregnant and all that. Wasn't becoming a monk for him like trying to run away and hide because of guilt?"

"That's a common way of seeing a monk's life. It's what I always thought, anyway. Until I learned about Merton. His becoming a monk was, well, more like going toward something rather than away. Know what I mean?"

Alice nodded. Rachel pointed at John.

"What does Merton's life do for you? Like, here you are living in a big city and there he was off in a monastery. What's the connection?"

Rachel fidgeted a little. "Hmmmm. Well, let's see. I'm not really sure, to tell the truth. Except I'm thinking of becoming a Catholic." She blushed, and some laughs followed. "And," she continued, "I'd sort of like to visit the monastery to see what it's all about." She smiled and held her hands out. "Anybody want to go with me?"

To a mixed chorus of yeses and noes, she took her seat.

*　　*　　*　　*

Trey's mission on behalf of the DEA on Thursday was threefold:

- Convince Uncle Jonas, as a member of the Senate Commerce Committee, to arrange for Fernando Belsasso to be invited to come to Washington this weekend on urgent NAFTA business. It's called "conniving" in some circles.

- Slip news of the ostensible reason for the invitation to one Pat Beason so that she could, in turn, pass on the tidbit to a possibly wary Belsasso. It's called "disinformation" in some circles.

- Plan to be in Washington himself on Monday and Tuesday in case his affidavit was needed to make a case on Belsasso. A drug payoff was being arranged for the Secretary of Commerce. It's called "entrapment" in some circles.

As regards the first item: It might have seemed a simple enough matter, Phillip Cox had explained to Trey, for the President to ask for Belsasso's presence just prior to the NAFTA vote on Tuesday. However, given the international tensions such a deception was bound to precipitate, Clinton preferred to share the responsibility for such an invitation. And who better than his current nemesis, Jonas Crockett? His presence on the Commerce Committee offered a perfect opportunity. Clinton's hand was being forced on this matter, what with the *Post* sniffing around.

As to the second matter, Trey relished the thought of planting something in Pat Beason. Something different.

And for the third task: Trey had agreed reluctantly to cancel his appointments on Monday and Tuesday in order to be available in the nation's capital. His was to be a backup role in the eventuality that the drug case on Belsasso wasn't strong enough. The two Mexicans who were involved in blackmailing Trey and possibly in the murder of Father Stone could now be traced indirectly to Belsasso. Trey's descriptions of Large Hands and Raspy were matching up with those from witnesses in Huntsville, and Cox should soon have the visa pictures of the two Mexicans who flew into Huntsville's airport two days before Stone's murder. If those faces matched Trey's remembrance of his two visitors, his statement could be just enough to tip the balance in favor of a warrant from the District's prosecutor.

He called Pat to arrange the rendezvous. "How about tonight?"

"Sorry. I'm meeting with you-know-who."

"Campaign managers be damned! I want you more than he does!"

"Prove it," Pat taunted.

"What if I told you I'd have some interesting news after the Hospi-Care board meeting this afternoon. News of such things as campaign contributions."

"Oooh...now why'd you go and say that? Okay, you win. I'll make an excuse."

Trey also spent a couple of hours Thursday playing phone-tag with his uncle. He had finally reached him about noon and explained the previous evening's meeting with Cox and Field and Bishop.

Yes, the senator had said, he would be glad to cooperate with the president in getting Belsasso to D.C. this weekend, assuming Clinton would pave the way with President Salinas. Yes, he could make a convincing case that the Secretary's presence would enhance NAFTA's chances in the House. After all, Jonas Crockett himself was an outspoken proponent of the controversial trade bill, perhaps the only damn thing Clinton had done right in his estimation. Yes, he would try to call the Mexican that afternoon if Billy Boy would pay him the courtesy of a personal request for his help. He'd like to hear that hoarse pseudo-Yalie Razorback voice pleading once again.

* * * *

Trey was able to reach Scott later that afternoon.

"I said I'd keep you up to date. Things are happening pretty fast." He briefed Scott on Stone's death, the DEA's involvement, and his agreeing to help them with Belsasso.

"We may be real close to a showdown. If there's any way you could let your mother and sister know, I guess this is the time to do it."

"Sure, Dad. I said I'd do anything you asked."

"Just leave off the Pat Beason part if you can."

"Sure. No problem."

* * * *

Pat Beason was in a testy mood Thursday night when Trey arrived. No hallway clutches. She was regretting her decision to see him and it showed.

She ushered him into the den that doubled as a study. Campaign materials were everywhere.

"Running for governor sort of takes over your space, doesn't it," he said, nodding at the clutter. He sensed her wariness but tried not to show it. Did she suspect something? He tried to act normal. How would he act if he were acting normal? He wasn't too sure, but he had to take the plunge.

"Something wrong with my sweetheart tonight? You don't seem yourself," he said, taking her arm before she sat down on the partially cleared sofa. "I'm noticing that I've been here two minutes and my pants are still on."

"Sorry to disappoint you, dear. I suppose I am sort of all-business these days." She turned to him, tossed her head, parted her lips, wet them with her tongue, and kissed him fully and passionately, pressing her body against his.

When he pressed her close to make better contact, she pulled away from him and seated herself.

"I…God! that's powerful!…I think I'd better keep my clothes on tonight. When we make love I'm no good for anything, and I've work to do. John "manager from hell" Grider agreed to cancel our meeting tonight on the condition I would work on the speech for next week."

"That's okay. Don't worry about me. Sex is way down the list for me after…uh…now just what are those other things that Maslow said are supposed to be important in life?"

"Well, one of them is to raise money for your favorite charity which I hope is also HospiCare's. How'd the meeting come out today?"

"You got some coffee? My brain is screaming for caffeine."

"As a matter of fact, I do. I've learned a few things about you the past two years. One of which…" she paused while pouring a cup in the kitchen, "…is that you stall when you have bad news. Am I right?"

"I can't pull a thing on you, can I?" Trey answered, hoping he was wrong about that conclusion, what with the agenda he had in mind for the evening. "Actually, it's not bad news. It just isn't good yet. The finance committee decided they might serve your cause better by assuring the Tennessee Hospital Association's position on your candidacy. If we can get that group's PAC into your trough first, then you won't be seen as just our candidate. We can always ante up more after that's done." He leaned back on the sofa with hands behind his head, a confident if not smug pose.

"No, that doesn't sound bad at all. So maybe I can't read you so well after all, unless, of course, there's something else you're hiding from me."

Trey tried to keep his composure. "Me? What would I be hiding from you?"

"Oh, I don't know. Just a hunch." She cooled her coffee and kept her eyes on him over the cup. "Anything going on with your uncle and the Fort Campbell thing?"

"Not much that I know of," he dissimulated smoothly. "I was going to ask you the same thing. Any news from your Japanese guru?"

"Not a word. I'm laying low on that one 'til the dust settles." She flashed back to yesterday's talk to the students and the ethics question raised by Trey's daughter.

"Can't say I blame you. Could get nasty. Washington's hot as a firecracker these days with NAFTA up for grabs. In fact, I heard from Uncle Jonas just today that he was asked by Clinton to invite the Mexican. What's his name…the Secretary of Commerce?"

"You mean Belsasso, Fernando Belsasso?" Pat perked up.

"Yeah, that's his name. He's being invited to Washington for the NAFTA vote. Clinton apparently thinks his presence will help, and Uncle Jonas is on the Commerce Committee. I guess it's Clinton's way of extending the olive branch to Uncle Jonas. You know, asking for his help. He's with Clinton on NAFTA anyway, so he said he was glad to." Trey shook his head. "Politics! I don't know how you do it."

"It's all very logical, like a chess game. Just takes a little intelligence and guts."

Trey looked for any signs of disbelief from his paramour. He saw none. Maybe he had pulled off Step Two of his assignment. He sipped coffee in mute celebration. Cheers, he thought. Cheers for the good guys.

"So," Pat said, studying the floor, "Jonas climbs in bed with Bill to get Señor Belsasso to Washington so Bill can salvage his floundering administration with a last-minute save on NAFTA." Then she continued wryly with a nod of the head. "Yeah, logical." She stared right at Trey. "But I don't believe it."

Trey squelched a gulp and prayed that Pat didn't notice it. "Wha…what do you mean, baby?"

There was an uncomfortable pause.

She put her cup on the side table and rose to explain while pacing in front of the couch and continuing to stare at him. "I've been around enough now to smell a rat in the barn. Clinton's up to something." Her finger was waving in the air now, her fertile imagination stirring along with it. "I don't see Bill Clinton putting that much stock in the Mexican's presence. It must be for another reason."

Then she stopped and whirled toward Trey. "Do you know the reason?" Trey could sense accusation in her tone. Or maybe it was only insistence with a touch of arrogance.

Trey stood at this point in order to match her eye to eye. If there was a showdown coming, he wanted at least equal positioning. "No, I don't. I don't have the foggiest idea what you're getting at," he said with his dead-level best sincerity.

They matched stares for a long moment; she blinked. "I'm not sure either, but if I were your Uncle Jonas I'd watch my backside. Clinton might be setting a trap for him. I was thinking you'd have a sixth sense about it. But maybe you're naive. Or maybe I'm paranoid." She sat down again.

"I saw your daughter yesterday," she said matter-of-factly.

"Where?", Trey asked, sighing with relief at the change of subject.

"Her class attended a government forum at the Capitol. She's smart, and cute, too. Asked me a tough question about ethics."

"How'd she know you were selling your body for votes? I swear I didn't tell her."

Pat stood and straightened her blouse. "You really should get to know her better. Has a lot more class than you. Just like Jenny." She picked up the picture of her niece off the end table and wiped the glass with her finger.

"Who is that, anyway?" Trey asked. "I don't remember seeing it." He reached for the framed photo of the young woman.

"That's my niece, Jenny. Helen's daughter. It's her college graduation picture. Yeah, I just put it out there."

"Favors you. Must be special?"

"Sure. Well, actually, it's a long story. Maybe I'll tell you someday." Her voice broke and she turned away. Rachel's and Jenny's faces flashed in her mind.

Trey set the picture down and put his arms on her shoulders. "Hey, is something wrong? Didn't mean to be too nosey."

She pulled herself upright and shook her head. "No. It's okay. Nothing, really nothing." She smiled and walked away.

"Okay. Tell you what, honey. I'm going to be real generous and leave you to your speech writing. I count myself lucky to have wrenched you away from Grider tonight, so I won't push it."

Pat didn't object, and they said their good-byes, each more than a little perplexed with the way this relationship was going. And Trey wondering what's with niece Jenny.

Chapter 16

Crossville, Tennessee
Friday afternoon, October 1

Pat stretched and took a seat on her mother's living room couch, feeling the familiar texture of heavy ribbed cotton under her hands. The furniture was the same as it had been for at least forty years. Same pictures on the walls, too. High school graduation photos of Pat and her sister Helen and assorted prints of Old Masters.

On the console television set stood frames with other family portraits that included Helen's wedding picture and the two grandchildren, Jenny and Paul, at various stages of maturation. Gordon Beason's likeness was kept in the master bedroom where his widow could treasure it in private.

"What's this you're doing here? Did I catch you in the middle of something?" Pat leaned over and surveyed the assortment of papers and snapshots spread on the coffee table. She had surprised her mother with a visit today.

"Just a minute and I'll tell you about it," her mother called, putting the finishing touches on the tea service.

Pat's curiosity kept her fingers moving through the items. She recognized her own handwriting on one of the envelopes with the address:

Mr. and Mrs. Gordon Beason
2208 N. Grove St.
Crossville, Tenn.

The postmark read May 15, 1967, Knoxville, Tenn. *May, 1967!* Pat thought. *That must be...* She picked it up to remove the contents just as Mother appeared, arms fully loaded.

"Don't get into that just yet, dear. I said I'll tell you about it." She poured two cups full and both helped themselves to sugar and lemon.

"It's providence you showed up here today. Helen called this morning and we had a long talk. It seems that Jenny's getting serious about this young man she's been seeing."

"The one she works with at TVA?" Pat asked.

"That's the one."

"How serious?" Pat's brow furrowed.

"Enough that she's wanting to know more about her real parents. I guess that's natural when you start thinking about having children of your own. To want to know more, I mean."

"So what does Helen say about it?" Pat sat back and gritted her teeth.

"She wants to tell her, I think. Well, you know, she's still studying it and talking with George. She'll be calling you, of course." Mother blew and sipped her tea.

Pat looked around the room at the photos. She hadn't touched her tea. "So that's what this is about," she said, nodding at the coffee table.

"Yes. Haven't had this batch of stuff out in Lord knows how long. Smells it, too. Can't get the musty out of that basement no matter what."

Pat got up and walked across the room, picking up the photo of Jenny in a cheerleader outfit, blue-and-white pom-poms perched niftily on her hips. Big smile. Familiar smile.

Mother watched from the corner of her eye.

"Providence. I think so," Pat said. She walked back toward Mother, who now looked her straight in the eye.

"The reason I came today was to talk to you about Jenny. It's bound to come out sometime, with my political life. Somebody's going to get curious about my five-year college career. You can't hide things like this anymore. I intend to be the first woman president, you know."

Mother smiled and nodded.

Pat continued. "Yes, that's right. I haven't changed my mind, Mother. Governor, then President. Maybe Vice-President somewhere in between if I absolutely have to."

"I know, I know. I believe in you, dear."

Pat sat down on the couch again near her mother and held both her hands. "Things get nasty when there are big stakes. Jenny could get hurt. For that matter, you and Helen could get hurt."

Mother squeezed her daughter's hands. "Maybe you don't know it, but I've been expecting this for some time. Hoping, like any mother would, that the time wouldn't come but down deep knowing it would. I'm thinking about you more than anything. I know what you've been through. From the very beginning, and all these years. I know."

"We don't talk about it, do we?" Pat said. "It's time we did. I don't know how to start." She picked up her teacup and sat back, relaxed for the first time since she arrived.

Mother picked up the envelope Pat had spotted earlier and removed the letter from it. She read aloud the first sentence: *I went to the doctor today, and I'm afraid I have some disturbing news for you.* Then she was quiet, scanning the rest of the first page.

Pat picked up another envelope, this one with a logo and return address for "St. Mary's School, Mobile, Alabama." Postmark December 18, 1968.

"You and Dad came to see me that Christmas. I'll never forget it."

Pat broke the next silence. "You know, what I'm thinking is I want Jenny to be proud of me. Ha! So much for maternal instincts! I ought to be proud of her for what she's done, overcoming the adopted-child stigma, graduating college, good job, good sense. Instead, I'm wondering what she'll think of me."

"Don't be too hard on yourself. It's been a long time."

Pat rubbed her brow and frowned. "No, Mom, don't be soft on me. Politics is rough. You can't stay squeaky-clean and get where I'm going. When the mud starts flying, I'll have to grab a handful myself. You'll be reading about things in the papers, maybe real soon. Some of it will be true."

"I'll always believe the best of you."

"You've got to; you're my Mom. It's in your contract. But Jenny, that's another story. I don't want her to find out about her and me at the same time the Ethics Commission features a headline story with my mug shot."

"That's not going to happen, is it?" Mother's composure began to crack.

"No, I don't think so, but you never know. There's a deal going now that's risky for me. Confidential."

"I understand."

"So," Pat continued, "there you have it. Jenny's curious. I'm feeling the urge to open up the subject. Helen and George and I need to talk, and they're in Memphis. Jenny's in Chattanooga."

"And politics won't wait," Mother added.

"Right. Got any ideas?"

"I've got the idea that God's going to take care of this. He won't let you do anything to hurt that precious Jenny. She'll be proud of her mother."

Pat's eyes shifted from her mother to the floor and back again.

"So, Governor Beason, are you staying the night? I didn't see a bag."

"No, I'm not. Supper, if that's all right. But I've got to be at the office in the morning."

"Come help me get it started. Just so happens I've got a pecan pie in the freezer. I know that's what you really came for."

The two walked arm-in-arm to the kitchen.

* * * *

The doorbell rang at 423 Woodmont Drive. Evelyn Crockett turned on the porch light and looked cautiously through the glass.

"My God! Scott!" She opened the door and he walked in with bag in hand.

"Hi, Mom. Surprise."

"I'll say. What in the world?"

"Well, give me a hug," he said, holding out his arms to her.

"Of course. A surprise hug, too," she said, still puzzled.

"Where's Rachel? Did she have a ball game tonight?"

"No. She's here. They had an off-week. She just got out of the shower, I think. Are you going to tell me what this is all about? Everything okay?"

"No. Afraid not. It's not me." They walked into the den. "It's Dad. Dad's in trouble. I didn't want to tell you on the phone. So I decided to come home this weekend. Spur of the moment type thing. I think we need to be together.

"I know, I know," he pushed on, "I was just here last weekend and what kind of a college bum am I who's on the road all the time when he should be studying." He sighed. "I know all that. I missed one class. Just trust me, Mom."

"Why, of course," Evelyn said, trying to pull herself together for whatever was to come. "Here, get your jacket off. Would you like some coffee or coke?"

"No, thanks. I had coffee on the road. Had to keep my heart rate up with the speedometer. It's a wonder I wasn't…"

"Who's that, Mom?" came the familiar voice down the stairway.

"It's Scott, honey. A surprise visit. Come on down if you're decent."

"Scott? Scott who? Not my brother Scott!"

"Yes, the one and only!" he called to her.

Rachel came bounding down the stairs in her bathrobe and wrapping a towel around her hair. "It IS you!" They hugged. "You caught me at my best," she said, pulling her robe tighter around her. She looked at both of them standing stiffly and asked, "What's wrong?"

"I need to talk to you about Dad. He doesn't know I'm here. But he asked me to tell you about it. I'm the designated messenger."

There was an uncomfortable pause. Scott shrugged his shoulders and sighed before continuing. "This will take a while. Do you need to…" he waved his hand at Rachel, "…to do something before we start?"

She touched the towel and shook her head. "No, I'm okay. What's wrong with Dad?"

"Last weekend, Dad and I had a long talk, and it wasn't easy to hear…"

They sat in the den, Rachel and Evelyn on the couch and Scott in the easy chair.

He told them the story, minus Pat Beason. There was hardly a blink from the listeners.

"…so now you can kill the messenger," he said, and sat back in the chair for the first time in ten minutes.

No one looked at the others. Rachel chewed her lip in time with her agitated leg. Evelyn stared at the lamp. Scott drummed the chair arm.

Rachel spoke up first. "Well, is there any hope? I mean, what's going to happen?"

"Who knows?" Scott answered. "The vote will be next week. Dad wanted you to know before anything about him came out in the news."

"So let me get this straight," Rachel continued, holding her hands in front of her. "If Uncle Jonas' committee votes to override the president, Dad will get disgraced?"

"And lose his license in all likelihood."

"And it looks like this…Matsaku is murdering people?"

"Looks like."

"And the monk, the one who's dying, Flaget—I just read about him in those books—he knows something about Thomas Merton's death, something that could stop all this?

"Could."

Rachel got up and paced.

"This looks like an all-nighter," Evelyn said. "Should I brew coffee?"

They didn't hear her.

"Let's go up there," Rachel said to Scott abruptly, still pacing.

"Up where?" Scott asked.

"To the monastery."

"Kentucky?"

"Yes. Gethsemani."

"Who?"

"Us. You and me."

"Why?"

"To talk to Flaget."

"You're crazy. When?"

"Tomorrow."

Evelyn had forgotten about the coffee.

Scott started to speak, paused, frowned, looked into the air. Rachel had stopped pacing and was looking expectantly at him.

"Let me ask Dad," he said, getting up for the phone.

"No, no. I don't want Dad to know." She blocked his path.

"Why not? It's pretty important to him, you know."

"It's just…something I want to do…" Her voice trailed off and broke up, tears forming. "I'll tell you about it later."

Scott reached to her and took her in his arms. Their mother joined them.

Chapter 17

▼

"Want me to drive?" Scott asked. "I looked at the map and can probably get us there quicker. My foot's a little heavier than yours, too." Rachel acquiesced. She preferred he drive anyway. Interstates made her nervous, especially in metropolitan areas.

Scott maneuvered the Accord to I-65 North, following the signs to "Louisville." Once they were comfortably out of the Nashville area, he set the cruise control, relaxed, and reached over to tousle the hair of his little sister.

"Okay, sis, time to let me in on some of your secrets. What were those tears all about last night?"

"You really want to know? It's funky."

"Yeah."

"I had a dream the night before Really, a nightmare. It woke me up. It was awful." She shuddered.

"I'm warning you. It sounds crazy. Okay, I was cheering at a sports event. It was a strange mixture: like a football game being played on a tennis court. I was a cheerleader at one moment and a player the next. Then Dad appeared and walked onto the court. I picked up a tennis racket and started beating him with it until his face was a bloody pulp. He was begging me to stop. A crowd gathered. I was...killing him." Rachel's voice broke.

"Then I woke up in a sweat. My heart was going like mad and my whole body was shaking. I was so relieved it was a dream."

"I guess so," Scott said.

"See, I've had lots of dreams about Dad. But there's never been any violence. It took me an hour to go back to sleep. I just lay there and kept wondering if I was…was killing Dad.

"The next morning at breakfast I decided I had to do something. I don't want to have another dream like that. Maybe visiting him with you last Friday was a start in the right direction."

"You're putting an awful lot of stock in dreams, aren't you?" Scott asked.

"Well, they are supposed to tell you something aren't they? Something about yourself? We talked about that in Sunday school one time. A psychologist—he was religious and all that—spoke to our class about it. Said God spoke to people in the Bible through dreams, so probably he speaks to us now. That dreams aren't just jumbled-up junk. Said we should pay attention to them but don't try to figure out every little detail; it'll drive you crazy. Just get the overall feeling from it."

"So," Scott surmised, "you got the overall feeling you should do something for Dad. Is that it?"

"I don't know. Guess so," she mumbled.

She turned her head and looked out the car window at the passing scene. "Goodlettsville" the exit sign read.

"You sure you know the way up here? It's about a three-hour drive, I figure," she said, pulling out her Kentucky map and holding it in front of Scott.

"Here, look at this map. I marked the route in Hi-Lite. There are two ways to go according to the fellow I talked to. We'll go by Bardstown. It's a little more direct." She pointed to the highlighted area exposed by her unfolding the map.

"On second thought, just keep your eyes on the road. I'll navigate."

She studied the markings in silence for a minute; then Scott spoke.

"I still don't know exactly what the heck we're doing on this trip. You expect these monks to just hand over secret papers to a couple of kids? All of Merton's letters have been donated to different library collections."

"What's your point?" Rachel asked.

"My point is that these papers in the abbot's safe haven't been released. That tells you something right there, now doesn't it?" Scott was excited but skeptical.

"I'm counting on Jacob to help us," Rachel said. "When I talked to him this morning, he sounded pleased we were coming, you know, said he'd be sure we had a place to stay."

"Well, I think I'm just along for the ride," Scott said.

"Think again, big brother. We're the Mission Impossible team."

Before long they were crossing over into the Eastern Time Zone and then turning off I-65 and onto the Bluegrass Parkway toward Bardstown.

* * * *

Trey was striking out with his phone calls on Saturday morning. He couldn't reach Scott at Davidson. His son's roommate knew only that he had gone out of town for the weekend. There was no answer at his ex's, so he left a message for Evelyn to call him. He was anxious to know if Scott had talked with Rachel.

The doorbell rang as he hung up from his last call. Trey imagined it was Scott making a surprise visit, but not so. It was Federal Express. He signed for the envelope and saw that it was the expected missive from Phillip Cox. He opened it while walking back to the den. There were two photos and a note. It took him just a moment to recognize the two men. A recent night in August came flashing back to him, dark figures in the backlit driveway of his front yard. Raspy and Large Hands.

He read the note:

> Dr. Crockett:
>
> These are the passport photos of 'Capitain Jorge Mendez' and 'Capitain Felix Gonzalez', aliases I imagine. Give me a call at 302-551-4438 after this arrives. And get a fax for your home, please. FedEx is dinosaurish.
>
> Yours truly,
>
> (Phil Cox)

He dialed the number and reported to Cox the positive identification.

"Good. That's very good," Cox replied. "You might have to pick 'em out of a lineup soon. I've got your hotel reservations here in D.C. for tomorrow night through Tuesday night at the Capitol Hilton. I'm sure we can wrap this up for you by then, and you might be all through after Monday. Call me when you get here. Okay?"

"Sure. Sounds good."

* * * *

Jonas had been convincing in his call to Belsasso and even managed to pronounce his name correctly. His aide had rehearsed him for a full three minutes before he had made the call. "-Sasso...Bel-SASSO. Okay, okay, I got it. Place that damn call quick before I lose it again." Then he had muttered, "Shit! Never heard anybody fumblin' over 'Crockett'."

The senator had argued that the president and NAFTA supporters might need the Secretary for last-minute compromises and that his presence would lend credibility to such deals.

Belsasso had told Crockett that he would check with President Salinas and then his schedule to see if some appointments could be shifted to accommodate the wishes of his American colleagues. He had pronounced the senator's name "Crow-quette'" and Jonas winced as they hung up.

It was now Saturday morning. Fernando Belsasso sat at his desk conversing with *Ojos* operatives Juan Vasquez and Fernando Davila. They were interrupted by the phone ringing.

"Yes, put her through." A pause. "Hello, Madame Beason, and how fine it is to hear your voice again." He smiled broadly and nodded, rotating his chair away from the desk as he listened.

"Yes, as a matter of fact, I did hear from Senator Crockett. What do you know of the matter?"

"Aha. Well, now, it does seem that my presence is needed. I suppose it has nothing at all to do with Delores, as far as you can tell? I wouldn't want that to become the subject of my visit. Timing would be bad, don't you think?" He rotated back to face the guests.

"Yes. Well, I am considering very strongly the invitation. Your input is welcome." He smiled again.

"And let me thank you again for the information regarding the monk in Kentucky. It is helpful to be able to anticipate their strategy. Please let me know if there is something else I can do to facilitate our interests while I am in your country. Good day to you, madam."

"Gentlemen," he said in measured tones after lighting a cigarette, addressing his underworld confederates who were awaiting the end of his telephone conversation, "we're flying to Washington tomorrow. I will go by Department jet. Make all your arrangements to pick up the payoff coming to us. You will fly commercial. Before you leave, call and tell me of your arrangements. I want to see you while we are in Washington to confirm the value of our transaction. And you are to be available to me should the need arise at any time. My other two assistants, Jorge and Felix, are already engaged on another project in the U.S., so you are the chosen ones for this mission."

Vasquez and Davila nodded, hoping to disguise the fact that they were already aware of their mission and that Philip Cox, their DEA contact, had presented it quite differently than Belsasso. Quite differently. Sweat popped out on the upper lip of Vasquez. Things were moving along at a faster pace than he had bargained for. He wondered if his partner had the same misgivings.

* * * *

Pat Beason hung up the phone from her conversation with Belsasso and stretched, then shook her arms to relieve the tension. A lot of irons in the fire this Saturday morning, and tired from the last-minute scurry to Crossville the day before. Thoughts of Jenny were crowded out by the morning *Tennessean* which was resting untouched on her desk. A quick scan of the front page left her cold, so on to the next. There was a short follow-up article on the priest's death in Alabama:

CLUES SOUGHT IN PRIEST'S DEATH
Huntsville, AL

Huntsville police and FBI officials are saying little about their findings so far in Monday's unexplained death of Father Grant Stone, Episcopal priest who was to be a star witness for Senator Jonas Crockett at the Senate Armed Services Committee hearings on the closing of Ft. Campbell, Kentucky. A coroner's report is pending and foul play is suspected.

Informed sources within the Police Department have indicated, however, that the identities of two Mexican military men allegedly attached to Redstone Arsenal's Army Missile Command in Huntsville are being sought. According to these sources who asked for anonymity, two such persons were seen leaving church services with the priest on Sunday. He was not seen alive after that and was discovered dead by his maid on Tuesday morning. The maid has refused to talk to reporters.

Beason blanched at the word "Mexican," her heart picking up the pace.

She leaned forward in her chair with elbows on the desk and head in hands. *My God, what if...what if Belsasso's behind this? Why wasn't I more curious about the way information was being used? I thought I was helping a business partner with strategic moves…not with murder, for God's sake!*

She stood up and paced the room, pushing all the mental buttons she could find.

Her mother's words of yesterday flashed boldly: *He won't let you do anything to hurt that precious Jenny. She'll be proud of her mother.*

She stopped pacing while those words repeated. Then she went to her desk again to open the top drawer.

She shuffled through miscellaneous papers and finally came up with the item she was looking for: the calling card left at her office just a few days ago by "Phillip A. Cox, Special Agent, United States Drug Enforcement Agency." The man she had been too busy to see. She noted the telephone number, paused just a moment, then picked up the phone on the chance he would be working on a Saturday.

Chapter 18

▼

It was women's week at the monastery. That meant Rachel got to stay in the main guesthouse while Scott was put up in the south wing of the cloister. They were informed that, for the last two years, women had been accorded equal status with men, alternating weeks at the guesthouse with them.

To compensate and allow for more male visitors, the abbot had decided to expand guest capacity. Declining numbers of resident brothers had freed up several rooms in the monks' quarters, so eight rooms in the south wing had been designated as auxiliary overflow space. That wing was adjacent to the church and nearest the guesthouse, so it was naturally suited to the purpose. Intrusion into the monks' routine was minimal and any inconvenience seemed to be offset by the enhanced spirit of hospitality.

What was not publicized was the corollary: revenues were enhanced also. Though guests—"retreatants," they were called—were not charged room-rates, freewill offerings were encouraged. To those in the know, it was no secret that the retreat business was more and more providing needed revenue to balance the monastery's budget. The farm and bakery operations with cheese, fudge, and fruitcake sales were the chief income-producers, along with Merton royalties, but hostelry was growing rapidly. Guests were generally generous.

On this Saturday afternoon there was a full house. So said Brother Brendan when Rachel and Scott checked in.

"Looks like you two were late additions," the receptionist-monk said, perusing the list before him on the desk. "Jacob was asking about you just a while ago."

"Yes, sir," Rachel answered, "I got lucky. I think we got a couple of late cancellations."

"This your first time here?" Brendan asked gently.

"Yes, it is." Scott was letting his sister do all the talking so far. "But our father's been here lots. Do you know him? Trey Crockett? Doctor Crockett from Nashville?"

"Oh yes, of course I know Doctor Crockett. Our psychiatrist friend." Brendan nodded and smiled.

A voice came from behind the two guests. "You must be Rachel and Scott."

They turned to see another monk standing there. He had arrived so quietly they hadn't heard. Scott knew immediately who he was.

"And you must be Brother Jacob," Scott said. They shook hands, as did Rachel and Jacob. "Dad showed me pictures of you, so I cheated."

"Good. Maybe I haven't aged so much after all. I think I'd have recognized you, too, Scott. You favor your father. Rachel's a different story. She has her own particular beauty."

Rachel blushed but managed words finally. "Thank you. People say I look more like my mother."

"Here. Let me help you with your bags and show you to your rooms. I'll orient you to the place. You'll get the hang of it quickly. We try to keep it simple here. Quiet and simple. Just like God's truth." He raised his eyebrows and his eyes gleamed.

They followed the lithe, gently animated guestmaster to the elevator.

"I know you're here for a special purpose, Rachel. I'll do what I can to help with the abbot and the papers, but no promises. He's the boss, you know, and he knows that for sure. You do have one thing going for you, it seems. Dom Philippe has agreed to talk with you."

"That's great! What convinced him?"

"Well, after hearing about the priest being murdered in Alabama and the possible connections with the Delores Project, he became quite disturbed. Then when I told him Doctor Crockett's son and daughter were coming for a visit, he offered to talk with you, said he was pleased the doctor's children were going to bat for him. Well, that's a paraphrase. He was especially interested when he heard about your family's researches into Merton."

Just as the elevator door opened, they were startled by Brother Brendan's voice. He was almost shouting, a rare phenomenon in these surroundings.

"Jacob! Jacob! Get to the infirmary! There's a code on Dom Philippe!"

"Sorry, folks, I'm being paged," he said, breaking into a trot.

Scott and Rachel looked at each other in a moment of silent but instant agreement. They ran after Jacob.

Approximately forty-five seconds later they were at the door of Dom Philippe Flaget's room. There were four other monks already there, two of them kneeling at the foot of the bed in prayer and one of them, Brother Thaddeus, the infirmarian, was administering CPR.

Jacob was surprised at what he was witnessing. The fourth monk, Brother Matthew, met them as they approached the bedside and pulled Jacob aside. Jacob whispered, "What's going on here? I thought we weren't going to do this. Did I miss something?"

"I guess we all missed it except for Brother Thaddeus. Apparently a couple of hours ago Dom Philippe told Thaddeus he wanted to make it through this weekend; he wanted to be kept alive; he felt himself slipping, but there was something he needed to do before he died, and this was the time to do it. Said you'd know about it, Jacob."

"Me? That I'd know about what he needed to do?"

"That's what Thaddeus said. Maybe he can illuminate the matter when he has time." He nodded at the monk's figure hunched over Dom Philippe's body, hands pressing rhythmically on the sternum.

Thaddeus spoke up at that moment. "Hey, Jacob, give a hand. Want to alternate on mouth-to-mouth and compressions?"

"Sure. Hold up a second, and let's see if he's doing anything on his own."

Thaddeus ceased pressing while Jacob checked the carotid pulse and reached for the stethoscope. He listened a moment, shook his head, and said, "Let's get back to it." The pair worked in tandem for another three minutes. Rachel's bold voice interrupted the tension with an offer. "If you need to rest a minute, I can spell you. I know CPR."

Scott looked at her with eyebrows raised.

Thaddeus paused and stepped aside, motioning for Rachel to take his place. "Thank you, dear child. I'll take you up on that for a few minutes. These old arms aren't used to this."

After another several intervals, Jacob suggested that they check the patient's responses once more. The assemblage held their collective breath as they watched Dom Philippe's chest. And then it happened. He was breathing by himself! He made a groaning sound and moved his arm.

Jacob listened to his chest and smiled at Rachel. "Regular rhythm, about sixty or so," he announced. "Good work, young lady Crockett. You have the beauty of your mother and the healing gifts of your father."

Rachel, embarrassed, backed her way to her prior position next to Scott on the outside of the group. She took her brother's hand and he promptly gave her a squeeze.

Brother Thaddeus asserted his role as monk-in-charge and suggested that all except Jacob and he retire from the room. Scott said they would wait in the infirmary sitting room just down the hall, to which Jacob nodded accord.

Dom Philippe's vital signs were good. He opened his eyes once and mumbled the words, "*la societe de Bossuet,*" then closed them again.

Jacob and Thaddeus talked in whispers.

"What'd he say?" Thaddeus asked.

"It sounded like '*la societe de Bossuet*'—the Bossuet Society. You know what that is, don't you?"

"Not off-hand, no. Should I?"

"Not necessarily," Jacob said. "But never mind. Probably just some mindless recollection coming out of the coma. Tell me about Dom Philippe's request. Matthew said you knew about it."

"It's about that young couple. He said he wanted to see them, they wanted to talk to him. He wanted to be kept alive. I was shocked. When I looked up and saw all of you, I guessed who they were." He paused and crossed himself. "Then, when the girl offered to help, Mother of God, I got chill bumps. It was like the Blessed Virgin herself had come among us. What's going on, Jacob?"

"Clearly more than meets the eye. My eye, anyway. I'm as shocked as you are. Tell you what, I'll go tend my little flock out there and check back with you in half an hour. Let me have your beeper, just in case."

Jacob collected Scott and Rachel and the three retraced their steps to the elevator in the guesthouse. The bags were on the floor just as they had left them.

They were alone in the elevator. Jacob took the opportunity to set the stage. "I'd opine you weren't expecting this sort of welcome, were you?"

Both shook their heads.

"Let me assure you it wasn't planned that way, at least not by any of us mortals. But it could be the beginning of a memorable weekend for us here at the farm. For some reason Dom Philippe takes quite seriously his intention to meet with you. Enough so, it seems, that he came back to this life from another, which by all accounts is much to be preferred, just for that purpose."

Rachel interrupted. "I don't understand. What are you saying?"

Jacob explained what Thaddeus had confided to him about Dom Philippe's determination to meet with them.

"Wow!" Scott sighed and looked admiringly at Rachel. "I guess you knew what you were doing when you decided to come here. And you were sensational in the resuscitation."

"Just lucky. We had another class in CPR last week, so it was fresh on my mind."

"Luck by any other name," Jacob injected, "is God's grace, Rachel. If you stick around here long enough, you'll begin to understand." He led Rachel to her room. "For now let's plan to talk with Dom Philippe tomorrow morning before Mass. Give him time to recuperate from the near miss. About 9 o'clock, if that's okay. We'll meet in the lobby. Then I'll see about an audience with the abbot."

Before taking her leave, Rachel inquired of Jacob, "Did anything else happen with Dom Philippe after we left his room? Did he say anything else?"

"Nope. He was resting quietly, recruiting strength I reckon for whatever he needs to accomplish on this side. Yup, he's a masterful specimen of God's persistence. He's been a beautiful addition to our community since he arrived. A treasure-trove of historical data. That's his hobby, church history. Must be the reason he made that reference to Bossuet after you left the room. Yeah! That's right! He did say that. Curious."

"What's that? Bossuet? What is it?" Rachel asked.

"The Bossuet Society. A renegade gang outside the mainstream of the church. I'd tell you what I know about it, but I'm running close on the clock. Look it up in the guest library if you like. *Roman Catholic Encyclopedia.* Top shelf on the right as you get off the elevator. B-o-s-s-u-e-t."

"I'll do that," she said and entered her room.

After leaving Scott at his room in the south wing, Jacob retired to his own quarters to collect himself. He wasn't exactly sure where this was leading. He wondered how the Bossuet Society had surfaced from Dom Philippe's unconscious. The abbot was returning this very evening from a convocation somewhere in California. Jacob would be glad to see him back at his post. Dom Philippe had told Jacob yesterday that he needed to see the abbot as soon as he returned, something to do with the visit of Scott and Rachel.

Jacob decided to leave a note taped to the abbot's door, which read:

> Saturday 3 p.m.
>
> Dear Father Abbot,
>
> I was asked by Dom Philippe to let you know as soon as you returned that he wishes to speak with you. It seemed very important to him. I believe he wants your consent to talk to two of our guests about some rather sensitive matters.
>
> You probably are not aware of his near-death this afternoon. He was brought back by CPR at his prior request. Hence his time with us is tenuous at best. You might want to see him tonight, considering all.
>
> Grateful for your safe return to us.
>
> Your humble servant,
>
> (Bro. Jacob)

Arriving back at his office on the second floor of the guesthouse, Jacob checked the messages on his machine. One was from Brendan indicating that there were going to be two late-late weekend arrivals, two Trappist brothers who were traveling the USA and visiting abbeys. They had called from Louisville and would be arriving via rental car soon. Brendan assured them of a place to stay. Jacob didn't recall any advance notice, but St. Benedict's Rule required hospitality to all, most especially to sojourning brothers. They were Mexican, said Brother

Brendan, and expressed a particular interest in seeing how the infirmary was set up at Gethsemani.

Jacob reckoned that he really didn't need that. He had his hands full already. He sighed and looked out his window over the cemetery and up the hill to St. Joseph's statue. He had a good view of the patron saint of the abbey standing proudly with the infant Jesus in his arms, overlooking the monastery from his vantagepoint on the rise just south of the buildings.

He pulled a portable radio from behind a stack of books and clicked on 90.3 FM, public radio out of Louisville. The small but powerful radio was Jacob's last vestige of rebellion. He kept the volume low enough so only he could hear. It was Garrison Keillor. He thought he could catch a few minutes of the Lake Wobegon monologue before he had to check with Brother Thaddeus on Dom Philippe's condition.

* * * *

The south wing wasn't as comfy-looking as the guesthouse. Smaller room, community bath and toilet down the hall, more like the college dorm Scott stayed in his first two years at Davidson. More like the monastic cell that it was. He deposited his bag and looked around the room. There was a Bible on the small reading table and a sheet of orientation instructions for guests.

Scott scanned the sheet, noting the times for meals and daily offices as well as mass. Supper at 6:15. He looked at his watch. He had a couple of hours to look around the place before feeding time.

He needed to hook up with Rachel so he went first to the guesthouse lobby. He found her inspecting the painting on the far wall, a three-part mural that depicted the progression of Christian monasticism through the Benedictine line. Trappists were third-generation Benedictines, having branched from the Cistercians who in turn had left the mainstream order sometime in the 12th century. The colorful mural told of that evolution all the way to the modern era and the American foundations of which Gethsemani was the first.

Scott joined his sister in this graphic bit of monastic education before they walked outside to survey the grounds.

"Now that the excitement is over we can act like normal tourists," Scott said.

"Maybe you can, but I don't think I feel very normal after that. Look." Rachel held out her trembling hands.

"You were plenty cool under pressure, sis. I was proud of you. Dad would have been too."

Rachel shrugged her shoulders and said, "Think so? I still can't get used to talking about him without getting all tight."

"Yeah, it still shows on you," Scott observed.

"You know why."

"Yes, I know why. But not three years' worth of why, I don't. A year or two maybe, but are you going for a record? An unforgiveness record? I'll call up the Guinness guys right now and get them over here."

"So give me a break, okay? I'm trying. I'm here, aren't I? I saw him last week, didn't I? I don't need you on me. My dreams and Mom and now you! Huh!!" Rachel folded her arms and scowled.

"Look. I don't mean to be on your case. But I guess I am. Dad's messed up bad in his time. I've been furious with him before. Sometimes still am. But I love him. Love him better without his alcohol and his women, sure. I wish we could all be back together. That none of that had ever happened. I remember that session at the hospital, too."

"You do? I thought you'd probably just blanked all that out." Rachel's tone softened.

"Hardly. I can still see Mom's tears." Scott looked away and squinted.

"Me, too."

They both sighed.

Scott cleared his throat. "Let's find Merton's grave. They brought the body here for burial."

"There's the cemetery," Rachel said.

The pair looked through the uniform, small, metallic grave markers, finding eventually the one with "Fr. Louis Merton" on it.

"It's just a plain one like the others," Rachel said.

"The Trappists don't believe in glorification of this life. They'd say it's a life of simplicity, and all are of equal importance, at least in God's eyes."

After a brief walk through the gardens, Rachel announced she was going to find the library. Scott elected to sit on the patio and soak up some rays. They agreed to meet again at supper.

* * * *

"Brothers" Jorge and Felix had paused on the shoulder at the off-ramp of I-65, studying again the map provided by the National Car Rental agency. The Buick Cutlass didn't seem to want to turn off at this intersection, so Felix the driver asked to check directions one more time.

The nice lady at the desk at the Louisville airport had highlighted in yellow their route to Bardstown. She didn't know about the monastery though.

"Yes, this is the correct exit, number 245, Clermont, *tonto*." Jorge said in perturbed Spanish. "See, it goes to Bardstown, and then we have the instructions from the monk from there. I told you I've studied this map carefully." The smaller Jorge flipped his hand in the air in disgust.

"Okay, okay. I just don't want to get lost in Kentucky. These people may not like strangers. I still think we should be wearing those robes we brought," Felix answered while maneuvering through the exit and on to the two-lane state road.

"I will tell you once more, Brother Felix. Monks do not wear their frocks while traveling. We will put them on when we get there. And don't worry. These are civilized people." Jorge always walked a fine line between pacifying and castigating his partner. Felix's bulk was extremely useful for this type of assignment but he was dumb as a post. He definitely needed to be led.

* * * *

Trey returned to his original AA home group for the five o'clock meeting. He was on the schedule to chair this one, so he was there a half-hour early to open up and start the coffee. Chairing meetings looked good on his record.

This particular office building at Blakemore and 21st Avenue was closed on Saturday afternoon, and the only people around were there for the meeting. As usual, there were the early birds arriving for the "meeting before the meeting." Trey recognized most of them.

Bob R. was there. After greetings and housekeeping, Trey approached him. Bob was Group Chairman this month and kept the schedule of assignments.

"I'll have to beg off chairing the other meetings this week until Tuesday or Wednesday. Got to go out of town tomorrow. Sorry, it was unplanned," Trey said.

"Sure, Trey, no problem. We've got some one-year-chippers who've volunteered to start chairing. We'll just put 'em to work. Where you going?"

"Oh, just business. Nothing special," Trey hedged. So far his predicament had escaped public scrutiny. The climax was fast approaching, and visions of sensational headlines plagued his thoughts.

"You just don't look yourself tonight. Got that hangdog face. Am I right?"

Bob was distracted by another member, leaving Trey alone to fix the coffee and to correct his face. His thoughts were elsewhere, wondering where Scott was this weekend, whether he had told Rachel yet. He was worried about how she took it.

He also wondered where Pat Beason was and how she was calculating to make political hay out this mess.

He wondered if life was worth it.

*   *   *   *

"Volume 2, BAA-CAM." Rachel fingered the binding of the volume of the encyclopedia on the top shelf just where Jacob had said it would be.

She found an unoccupied corner and flicked the pages until she came upon "Bossuet, Jacques Benigne, 1627–1704." There was a one-paragraph capsule of his career to begin the biographical piece that in toto covered a full page and a half of the volume. The sketch read:

> Bishop Jacques Benigne Bossuet, Jesuit priest, graduated from the College of Navarre in 1652. He became Cathedral Canon at Metz and then Preacher of the *Chapel Royale* under Louis XIV. Later Bishop of Condom and Meaux, he was inducted into the *Academie Francaise* in 1671, honoring his literary career. He was a champion of orthodoxy and purity in doctrine and a leading proponent of the Divine Right principle, thus placing him in opposition to a strong papacy.

Rachel went on to the body of the article, scanning parts of it until she came to the last section with the subtitle, "*La Societe de Bossuet.*" The French title gave way mercifully to standard English:

> Bishop Bossuet left a legacy of orthodox conservatism and a body of writings to undergird it. He also left another legacy of which he was never aware and which he likely never would have endorsed. This movement sprang up after his death and has come to be known as the Bossuet Society with roots in French priestly and monastic communities. It is a secret, unsanctioned, apostate fellowship of ordained priests and monks whose alleged purposes are to undermine what they perceive as excessive papal authority and to stem the tide of liberalism wherever it appears in Church circles.

Its membership is unknown but inferred by reactionary attitudes particularly among the French clergy. Most Church authorities have denied the very existence of this society, but others see it as a real and vicious threat to Church unity. Rumors were widespread during the First Vatican Council of 1865 that this Society's members might defeat the doctrine of papal infallibility. These fears were never realized as the Declaration passed the voting body by a 533 to 2 margin. Such a resounding victory might have been forced, in part, by an anonymous tract that was circulated the day prior to the vote which exposed the names of suspected members of the Bossuet Society.

After Vatican I, little was heard about this group until the Second Council, which convened in 1961. Vocal opposition arose in response to the pope's *Declaration on the Church's Relations with Non-Christian Religions*, and the Bossuet group once again was blamed by the media covering the Council. When the proposal passed the Council, storms of protest and rumors of threats of retaliation reverberated around the halls of the Vatican, all of which were attributed to the Bossuet Society.

The hierarchy of the Church traditionally has avoided official statements regarding the Society, preferring instead to relegate its existence to the realm of rumor.

Hmmm, Rachel thought, if it was just a rumor why would Dom Philippe mutter that name at a time like this? Could Dom Philippe possibly be a member of this maverick gang? After all, he is French.

She couldn't wait to see Brother Jacob to quiz him about it.

* * * *

"Brother" Jorge was saying something about "Brother" Felix's mother. Judging from Felix's expression, it was not complimentary.

They were parked on the dirt shoulder of a small county road somewhere in Nelson County, Kentucky, and, to top it off, the Cutlass' air conditioner had chosen that moment to die. Jorge opened the door, sweating and swearing and waving his arms. He stood beside the car with the much-maligned map spread on the hood, pointing at marks and swearing again.

"I knew we shouldn't have turned right back there, *cabron. Chinga tu madre.*"

"I did just as you said. First you said right, then left, then right again. What was I supposed to do? There was a line of cars behind me." Felix also was standing beside the car now. "So where are we…BOSS?" He smiled broadly and stood with arms akimbo.

"Arrrgh!" was Jorge's response. He spat and looked around. Not a hundred feet away were two girls playing in the front yard of a house, one of them swinging on a tractor tire suspended from a large tree while the other watched. "I'll find out." He walked toward the girls.

The swinging one's bare feet caught the ground to halt the homemade swing as Jorge approached her. She looked at him with squinted eyes while the second girl edged closer to her companion.

"Excuse me, please. May I ask you for directions, young ladies?" Jorge asked with his most engaging voice, coarse as it was by nature.

They didn't answer but stood together, wary of this strange-sounding person approaching.

Jorge sensed their caution so halted his approach.

"My friend and I are lost it seems. We are looking for the monastery that is near here. Do you know the directions? Do you know the place I'm talking about?"

They looked at each other, then one of them spoke. "Ya mean the monkeytory? That's what my ma calls it."

Jorge was confused. "Excuse me, I'm not sure what you said. It's called a monastery, I believe. You know, where the monks, the brothers, stay."

"Yessir, the monkeytory. I know whatcha mean."

"Good, very good," Jorge beamed.

"Where ya from, anyways? Ya talk funny."

"We're from Mexico. Do you know where that is?"

"I reckon." She giggled at the other girl. "We studied that in school this year. Miz Johnson taught us all about it, the Spaniards an' Aztecs an' ever'thin'. Do you speak Spanish, seenyor?" She giggled again and was joined this time by her friend.

"Yes, I do." He was trying to be patient. "Could you tell me how to get to the...the mon-key-to-ry?"

"Yessir. Ya must've took a wrong turn back on the highway. Ya go back to it, turn left and go to the store, then take a right. It's down that road a spell."

"Thank you, *gracias*, young ladies, *Señoritas*," he said, backing and then turning to trot to the car and the waiting Felix.

"*Vaminos, tonto!* I'm driving this time."

*   *   *   *

There was only a handful of men at dinner in the guest dining room. Tables full of women, but not many men. Scott looked around in the silence, spotting Rachel at the window table and wondering about these assorted people who were choosing to spend their weekend in such a manner.

They finished a meager meal of tomato soup and grilled cheese sandwiches. After returning trays to the clean-up table, they exited to the lobby where they could talk.

"I wonder how Dom Philippe's doing," Rachel said.

"Me too. Let's see if we can meet up with Jacob after Compline. That's the last service. If we sit downstairs we can probably catch his eye leaving the church."

They did catch his eye and met Jacob just outside the church, but he didn't have much time. He had to play host to the two surprise guests who were supposed to be waiting for him in the south wing. But he was able to give Scott and Rachel an encouraging report on Dom Philippe. He had eaten a decent supper meal and was conversing rationally.

"See you two pups in the lobby at nine in the morning. Sleep well, my friends," Jacob added and turned away.

"Can't I see your monk's quarters?" Rachel asked.

Jacob stopped and answered thoughtfully. "That's usually not done. We try to keep the genders separate. Not exactly '90's PC, I know, but the abbot has quaint ideas."

"I'll do exactly what you say, I promise."

Jacob looked around. "Okay. Come on." Scott excused himself.

Entering quietly through the main door of the cloister, Jacob and Rachel approached the passageway that led past the abbot's office. Jacob was surprised to see two strangers at the abbot's door. They were turned the other way so did not see the two approaching. Jacob held out his hand to stop Rachel. The men were reading the note he had left on the door.

Jacob approached them and they turned abruptly, leaving the note taped to the door and looking embarrassed. They were dark-skinned. One was small and wiry, the other tall and bulky.

Jacob broke the uncomfortable silence. "You must be Brothers Jorge and Felix."

"Yes," the smaller one with a coarse heavily accented voice replied, "and are you Brother Jacob?" He held out his hand in greeting.

"I am. Welcome to our abbey."

Jacob introduced them to Rachel, who remained in the background. He was cordial and showed them to their rooms. They apologized that their visit was unexpected, explaining that their abbot in Guadalajara had assured them it had been cleared a month ago. Perhaps, they conjectured, the correspondence had been lost or never arrived.

"Never mind," Jacob consoled them, "I'm sure we have adequate accommodations for you. No problem."

They expressed their desire to inspect the infirmary, explaining that they were planning to build one soon at their abbey, Our Lady of Fatima, and would like to learn from the experience of Gethsemani which had a reputation for being state-of-the-art in that department.

"Of course, I will arrange a tour for you tomorrow."

"If I may beg you," Brother Jorge said, "would it be too much trouble for us to see it tonight? Our schedule is very tight tomorrow, and we will need to leave soon after mass to catch our plane in Louisville."

Jacob hesitated, uncomfortable with the whole deal for some reason.

"Why, yes. Yes, we can do that right now if you wish."

The two guests bowed graciously, Felix taking the lead from Jorge. "Bless you, my brother," Jorge added as an afterthought and nudged Felix.

"Uh...bless you, my brother," Felix parroted.

"If it's okay, I'll just head on back to the guesthouse," Rachel said. "Nice to meet you. Uh, Jacob, could I speak to you a minute?"

She pulled him out of hearing range.

"Jacob," she whispered, "I've seen those Mexicans before. I can't place it, but I know I've seen them. That's weird."

"Maybe it will come to you. I need to attend to them."

Jacob took them on a brief tour through the infirmary and then escorted them back to their rooms. They took notes all the while and thanked him for his trouble.

Just as he was about to take his leave, Jacob turned to Felix and asked, "Tell me, is Dom Miguel still the abbot at Our Lady of Fatima?"

Felix looked at Jorge, who appeared to be busy with the door to his room. "Uh...yes, yes, he is," Felix stammered. "Still abbot. Do you know him?"

"No, not personally. Just by reputation. Good night."

Chapter 19

Jacob had a difficult time getting to sleep. Not only the stress of Dom Philippe's close call, but a gnawing unease about the Mexican brothers kept him tossing and turning in his narrow bed that didn't accommodate very well to that sort of thing. Finally he drifted off.

He awoke at 1:15 a.m. with a fright and pulled himself up squarely thinking that something was wrong. He had to get to Dom Philippe.

The halls were quiet as tombs. He passed the abbot's office and saw that the note had been removed. When he turned the corner of the hallway to reach the outside door, he was startled by a figure approaching him rapidly from the other side. In the dark he couldn't make out the face.

"Jacob," the figure said.

"Rachel!" Jacob said. "What are you doing up this hour?"

She was now directly beside him. "I was coming to get you. I couldn't sleep. It's those Mexicans."

"You, too? Come on. Follow me."

Swiftly they walked to the infirmary, which was unlocked. Brother Matthew was asleep in his bed with the door open. Jacob and Rachel burst into Dom Philippe's room.

What they saw and heard was a blur of shadow and muffled sounds. The room was faintly lit by a candle burning on a corner table. They saw two figures at Dom Philippe's bedside, and there were grunts coming from the bed where the monk was struggling. The door opening allowed only a smattering of additional illumination upon the scene.

The two onlookers froze. The men at the bedside turned and walked toward them slowly in silence. Jacob wanted to speak, but his throat closed. Only a few feet away their features were distinct. Their fears about the Mexican brothers were confirmed.

Without having a chance or the wits to invoke his martial arts training, Jacob felt the cold steel of a pistol handle sharply against his skull and he collapsed in a heap with his lights out. Rachel was mugged by the larger of the pair, one large hand over her mouth and the other arm lifting her off the floor.

The other man left Jacob where he fell then turned around to finish the task. Dom Philippe was awake and praying aloud but was too weak to resist. A pillow was pushed onto his face while Jorge used his body as a restraint, draping himself across the arms and torso of the helpless victim.

Just then a flashlight beam caught the back of Jorge's head, and a stern voice barked out: "Get your hands up and get away from that man or I'll shoot." He indicated to Felix to do the same.

The imposters could see the barrel of a pistol gleaming toward them in the aurora of the flashlight, so they complied. Rachel backed against the door, gasping.

"Move over to that wall and face it, and put your hands behind your head." They did that.

"Now lean against the wall and spread your legs."

He frisked them, removing revolvers from each frock pocket, then backed away toward the bed.

"Down on the floor face down and stay there."

The rescuer then moved to the side of the bed to check on the condition of Dom Philippe. The pillow was off his face and he was breathing. Pulse was weak but steady.

Just then Brother Matthew appeared in the doorway, stunned and still half-asleep.

"Brother, could you turn on a light in here and see to Jacob. He's been hurt."

The room light played upon the bizarre scene. The interlopers were lying face down as directed. Dom Philippe opened and blinked disbelieving eyes and surveyed the surroundings that used to be his peaceful dying space. The man with the gun knelt beside the would-be assassins and methodically cuffed their hands behind their backs while reciting Miranda. Rachel stayed put.

Jacob in the meantime had raised himself up on one elbow and gingerly felt the side of his head which was oozing blood. Matthew assisted him to a chair.

"I bet your head feels like the inside of the church bell," he said.

"More like the Liberty Bell with this crack in my temple. I haven't hurt this bad since a kidney stone."

Jacob rose to attend Dom Philippe but quickly fell back into the chair. "Guess I'm not quite ready for the upright position."

Matthew went to the monk with nine lives and raised his head to offer some water from a glass. Dom Philippe gratefully sipped, crossing himself and murmuring a prayer in Latin.

"Wh...what happened?" Jacob finally asked.

"You'll have to ask this gentleman," said Matthew, nodding at the one who was obviously some sort of officer of the law. "I was asleep until I heard a thud. That must have been you hitting the floor."

Rachel walked to Jacob's side.

"Who are you, sir?" Jacob ventured through the haze of blood and pain. "Didn't I register you today as a guest? Is it...Bishop...Mr. Bishop?"

"That's right, brother," the man replied, not taking his eyes or his gun off the Mexicans. "Your memory hasn't suffered any from the blow you took. My name is Claude Bishop. I'm an agent of the Tennessee Bureau of Investigation here on special assignment with the

Federal DEA." He pulled a badge from his pocket. "They called me Saturday, emergency-like. Said they'd been tipped off about a possible incident here. Looks like the tip was a hot one. Sorry I was a little late arriving at the scene. Picked the wrong time to go for a cup of coffee."

Then he cast a half-smile at Jacob and Matthew. "I want to thank you, brothers, for your hospitality. I'd say you've gone above and beyond tonight. You, too, young lady."

Jacob looked up at Rachel. "You okay?"

"Yeah, I'm okay." She hid her trembling hands.

* * * *

Trey Crockett arose Sunday morning surprisingly refreshed. No bad dreams to disturb him. Not even the last-minute harassment call he had received from Big Al Horton the previous night had perturbed him. Curious, he thought, that he felt so good.

After loading the coffeepot, he fetched the *Tennessean* off the driveway. Beautiful clear September day. Just a hint of fall in the air. A good day to be alive. Amazing what a good night's sleep can do.

The newspaper managed to take the sheen off the morning. He read the headlines about NAFTA, then scanned to the bottom of the front page where the expected article on Ft. Campbell was located.

"Campbell vote too close to call" read the headline with the subheading: "Panel expected to vote Monday." Trey read on.

Washington, D.C.

Senator Jonas Crockett's Armed Services Committee is expected to wind up hearings Monday on the resolution to block President Clinton's proposed closing of Ft. Campbell, Kentucky.

The month-long collision between the senior senator from Tennessee and the president will come to an end, according to reliable sources on Capitol Hill. Polling of Committee members indicates a very close vote with two members switching sides only Saturday. These same sources say that Senators Wilford (D-WA) and Jansen

(R-AK) are now voting against the resolution, which could be enough to defeat it.

Asked for comment, Senator Crockett said, "I haven't heard anybody banging a final gavel yet, and until that happens it's still open to question. But, yes, I do think we can get a decision Monday. I hope to God we can. And God will rap the gavel that really counts, you know."

Good old Uncle Jonas, Trey thought. Give 'em that ol'-time religion. He could have been one helluva preacher.

Trey's mood dampened as his thoughts continued apace. *So the old political warrior is going to be defeated and Billy Boy will gloat. My skin will be saved through none of my own doing. The resolution will be defeated, Fort Campbell will be closed, the Screaming Eagles of the 101st will have their wings clipped forever, Delores will buy Middle America, and U.S. citizens will be blessed with yet another entertainment venue with which to amuse themselves to death.*

Jonas will be defeated...and I will be off the hook...an Episcopal priest war hero is dead...Pat Beason will be elected governor keeping her hands clean...Manuel Matsaku becomes richer than Croesus...and Hopkinsville and Clarksville, two all-American, apple-pie towns, become satellites of Tokyo and Mexico City.

Trey's thoughts ran on and on. Images of Uncle Jonas and Aunt Jeanne at their farm came to him. Thoughts of his father, of Scott, of Rachel. Particularly of Rachel. He couldn't shake the memory of the Mexicans' parting comment about Rachel that night at his house. Could his children be in danger?

For a moment he could feel Rachel's weight in his arms and remember when she was "Puddin'" and he was "Pie." A great pain pierced his heart thinking of the hurt that he had caused her. Caused by his recklessness. He wondered if he could ever win her back, if he would ever measure up with her again.

And can I measure up to whatever is the best in me?
What is the best in me, anyway?

He recalled Brother Jacob's recent admonishments to him in the cloister's garden. "At some point you must experience amendment of heart. I don't see that happening."

He was pouring coffee on automatic pilot, still in a reverie, the newspaper with its story lying on the kitchen counter. He recalled his unusually good mood just a few minutes ago. A burden had been lifted from him in a way he couldn't explain. And now his shoulders were feeling the weight again.

His hand rested next to a book. It was Merton's autobiography.

Then it suddenly came to him. He knew what he had to do. Putting down his cup, he flipped the cardex and dialed Georgetown.

His uncle answered.

"Uncle Jonas, this is Trey. How are you and Aunt Jeanne?"

"Fine as frog hair, son, fine as frog hair. How about you?"

"I don't know. I really don't. There's a lot at stake these next two days. A lot, for a lot of people."

"I know, son, I know." The senator's voice dropped noticeably. "And I'm not fine as frog hair either. The truth is I've been worried sick about you and the outcome of all this. Whenever I think we have the votes we need, I can't help but feel the pinch of where that puts you. Right now it looks like somebody has gotten to Wilford and Jansen. Probably that Mat-see-oo-koo feller. So you might be saved right here at the bell. It makes me sick, though, to think that the 101st will be lost forever. Who knows what that might spell for our country's security."

"That's what I'm calling about, Uncle Jonas. We can't let that happen. I don't want the resolution to fail. I'm flying to D.C. today to help the DEA nail Belsasso, but I want to do more. I want to help you, to testify for you tomorrow at the hearings. To tell everything I know about 'Delores'." The weight was gone once again from his shoulders.

The senator was at a rare loss for words and the conversation ended, the phones in their cradles.

Trey stood motionless, staring at the checkered pattern on the wallpaper.

It will be the end of my career. What will mother think? Can she be shielded from it? What would my father be saying? Scott and Rachel? My colleagues?

I do have other options. For one, I could drink. Or...

He pondered the other, Option Two.

*   *   *   *

Sunlight broke over the Kentucky knobs and the abbey's steeple, penetrating the light blue fog that lay in the low places. Dew sparkled on bluegrass. The monastery came to life as usual on Sunday morning, quietly and prayerfully, notwithstanding the unsettling commotion of the previous night.

Dom Philippe was sitting propped up in bed eating his breakfast with Brother Matthew assisting. One could not have guessed from the serenity of the room that this was the scene of an attempted murder just hours previously.

A light sedative had eased the ailing monk's anxieties so that he had slept until around 8 a.m. under the watchful eye of Matthew, who chose to spend the remainder of the night at the bedside.

"Tell me," Dom Philippe asked hoarsely, "Is Brother Jacob all right?"

"I believe so. He went into Bardstown to the emergency room for attention to the laceration. Came back here with a bandage on. It was sutured. You were asleep."

Dom Philippe was only picking at his food, and he indicated to Matthew to take the tray away.

A knock at the door startled Matthew. The door opened and the head of Dom Raphael Keating appeared.

The abbot had returned from his trip to California the previous night to find Jacob's note on his door, but the hour was so late that he had not tried to talk to Dom Philippe. Then, of course, all hell had broken loose, and he was up the rest of the night coping with the sheriff's deputies and Special Agent Bishop who arranged for safekeeping of the Mexicans in the county jail.

Dom Raphael entered the room and knelt beside Dom Philippe's bed, crossing himself and kissing his hand.

"My beloved Dom Philippe, I'm so happy to see you looking well this morning. There's no way for me to express my regret that you had to endure such trauma and anguish and especially at such a time when you are so weak. Angels are watching over you, and who am I to question the path set out for each of us by the Almighty?"

"I agree, dear Dom Raphael. I am puzzled by the power of life in me. By all rights I should be the angel now looking down over you. Clearly, though, that is not the case. I still lie here in this bed with my brothers attending, awaiting, I suppose, the final test."

"Test?" Dom Raphael asked.

Dom Philippe was taken with a fit of coughing, requiring a pause for a sip of water.

Then he was able to reply hoarsely: "Dom Raphael. A weighty matter is upon me this hour. I need your counsel. I have come to rely on you for such these last years. Not only that but I need you to hear my confession."

The abbot looked around at Matthew who silently bowed and removed himself from the room, closing the door behind him. Dom Raphael then pulled a chair closer, crossed himself, and nodded to his colleague.

"I am at your disposal, Dom Philippe, as always."

"First, let me ask you: Have you never entered the locked file of Merton papers in your safe since I entrusted them to you? I know that you made the pledge to me, but I must now hear from your own lips that you have honored that charge."

"You may be assured. You have my word on it. It is my understanding that only you and Mme. Matsaku and Cardinal Swenens have seen the papers. Further, that only one of those three could ever order their unsealing. Since the other two are deceased, that leaves only you. Is that not correct?"

"Yes, yes. You remember well. And now, Dom Raphael, I amend that charge. I hereby grant to you the privilege of reading them. Further, the responsibility of the decision as to their disposal upon my death rests with you alone.

"I believe, Dom Raphael, it is now the time for you to open that file and use it to prevent the perpetuation of evil deeds. I have been led to that conclusion after much prayer these last days." His voice grew hoarser, requiring another sip of water before continuing. "I will explain that to you after I make confession. Which I am now ready to do."

They both crossed themselves.

"In the name of the Father, the Son, and the Holy Spirit, come now my brother and humbly make your confession to Almighty God, seeking His forgiveness and absolution."

"Father," Dom Philippe proceeded carefully, "I have sinned against God and my neighbor. I have committed the most grievous of sins even against my saintly friend and God's humble servant." His voice broke and he had to collect himself before continuing.

He then pulled himself up, took as deep a breath as he could, and said, "I...I conspired in the death of Father Louis Merton. I betrayed his trust and friendship."

He mumbled on with the details for some minutes.

Tears streamed down the faces of the two men who held hands in silence.

After an appropriate interval, Dom Raphael broke the silence with the ritual question, "My brother, are there other sins you wish to confess?"

"No, Father."

"Your penance has been extracted a thousand times over through these years of anguish, so I prescribe no more." And then he concluded, "Now rest in peace in the full knowledge that your sins are forgiven. And pray for me, a sinner. In the name of the Father and the Son and the Holy Ghost. Amen."

After another respectful silence, the abbot said with great difficulty, "Now, Dom Philippe, let me hear of your plan and how I may help you."

"It has to do with Doctor Crockett, one of your frequent guests here. I first turned aside his plea for help only to realize later how much it is needed." Dom Philippe looked at the desk clock on his bedside table. "But perhaps now," he said, "you could see if my guests have arrived. It's after 9, and that was the appointed time for the audience."

"Who is it you are expecting?" Dom Raphael asked.

"Brother Jacob and the two children of Doctor Crockett. They are here to pry from this wretched old dying man his heinous secrets in order to save their father's medical license and to put a stop to the murderous binge that appears to attach itself to the ventures of Delores Matsaku's son. And also, with God's grace, to bring a redemptive ending to this man's life."

Dom Philippe waved permission for Dom Raphael to attend to that task which he did. He found the expected delegation in the sitting room: the bandaged Jacob with his two guests, Scott and Rachel.

"Father Abbot, I'd like you to meet Scott and Rachel Crockett from Nashville, Tennessee. They're here to visit with Dom Philippe."

The three exchanged greetings.

"So pleased to have you here as our guests. I'm sorry that there's been so much distressing activity to greet you. I assure you it's not the routine here."

"Yes, sir...uh..." Scott stumbled, "I'm sure that's true. My father speaks very highly of your abbey."

"I believe it's your father who is the stimulus for your visit here. I've heard just enough of the matter from Jacob and Dom Philippe that I'm sure it's a most worthwhile mission. I will assist in any way I can."

"Thank you, sir," Rachel said.

"It's time for us to proceed." He turned and led them to Dom Philippe's room once again.

Brother Jacob handled the introductions.

"Dom Philippe, I don't think you recall these two. They were here yesterday when you went into cardiac arrest. This is Scott and this Rachel Crockett, the son and daughter of Doctor Trey Crockett whom you have met."

Dom Philippe held out his hand and greeted them. "Yes, Brother Jacob. I was not conscious of their presence, but I believe I owe a debt of gratitude to this young lady. I am told you assisted in the resuscitation." He held on to Rachel's hand.

"Yes, sir," she replied and blushed. "I helped just a little."

"Just enough, it seems." The gentle man smiled and she also. Dom Philippe shifted in his bed and gestured for them to sit.

"Let me begin by saying that your mission is providential. You are not aware at this moment of my reasons for saying that, but it will become clear as we engage in more dialogue. God has sent you here that I might die with a great burden lifted from my soul. I am as sure of that as I am that I have seen my last escape from the arms of death."

The room was still and expectant.

Dom Philippe continued. "After I have told you the story of my association with Delores Matsaku you will doubtless be shocked and disturbed. I have just a few minutes ago made confession to Dom Raphael about the matter. You will be the only living people to know the entire story. My sole request of you is that you use this information with the greatest discretion possible. You must at all costs keep it from the media, and," his voice broke at this point, "I beg you to do so. It would shake the foundations of the Church."

Rachel spoke up. "Sir, you have our word that we will treat your confidence with the greatest care." Scott added in a whisper, "Yes."

"Very well. Now, where should I begin? I am weak and need to conserve my strength. I can't rattle on forever as is my pedagogical custom, but it is important that you hear the historical relevance…"

Jacob interrupted. "Would you like a break first, Dom Philippe?"

"No, no, I haven't many breaks left. Let's go ahead. Yes, where shall I begin?"

He began in the seventeenth century.

He told them of Jacques Benigne Bossuet, the eminent French priest about whom Rachel had read the previous evening in the library.

"His stance upholding the divine right of kings was openly nationalistic and contrary to the pope's position, and that set the stage for the formation of *La Societe de Bossuet*."

He described the inner workings of this underground group as being consistently reactionary to papal authority and as having evolved over the past three hundred years into a mysteriously foreboding presence. Much of the mischief in the politics of the Church was likely to be laid at the door of this organization.

"The Vatican Council of 1869 provided the first major threat to the Society. It had to do with the doctrine of papal infallibility."

Dom Philippe explained that this issue quickly had become the most hotly debated one of that First Vatican Council. Initially it was not even scheduled to be introduced, but everyone knew that such was only a ploy by the pope to attempt to play down the matter. Once it was on the table the battle lines were drawn. The chief opponents of the doctrine were Ignace von Dollinger of Germany and Bishop Dupanloup of France. Everyone suspected the latter of being a member of the Bossuet Society along with many of the other "anti-infalliblists," as they were called.

As the time for a vote drew near, the numbers were in favor of the doctrine, but there were at least 150 nay-votes. However, on the day of the vote, July 19, 1870, there were only registered two dissenters.

"What happened," Dom Philippe explained, "was that most of the nays left town the day before the vote. On July 18, an anonymous pamphlet was distributed naming fifty or more members of the Bossuet Society who were voting delegates. Though this could never have been proved, the tactic worked. Dollinger later was excommunicated."

Nothing was solved for long, however, as the angered Bossuets were driven further underground.

"You will see the point in this palaver soon." Dom Philippe paused to shift and also to wet his mouth.

The narrative continued. He explained that the next obvious and open reappearance of the Society came almost a hundred years later at the time of Vatican II in 1965. This time the issue was concerning the *Declaration on Relations with Non-Christian Religions*, titled *Nostra aetate* in the official document designations. John XXIII, who called the Council, was determined to accomplish two things by this edict. He wanted to appease the Jews who had been so damaged by the Nazis. Many of them blamed the Church, in part, for sitting on its hands. But more importantly in the long run, he also had in mind a major rapprochement with the Eastern Orthodox Church, the first such reconciliation since the Great Schism.

These intentions were considered anathema by the ultra-conservatives in the Church who had already suffered defeats on other reforms passed during the two years the Council had been in session. The name Bossuet came to be prominently whispered about once again.

The untimely and unfortunate death of John XXIII in 1963 prior to the completion of the work of the Council did not dim papal enthusiasm. Paul VI, his successor, was bold in pursuing to the last detail the ambitions of his predecessor. Not only that, but Paul had the political instincts to match his ideals. He immediately created a new body, the College of Moderators which was chaired by Cardinal Swenens and whose task it was to set the agenda for Council sessions. These were four handpicked Cardinals who bypassed the delays and contrivances of John's committee structures. This maneuver allowed Paul to ramrod the documents to completion.

"It was at this time that I first met Madame Delores Matsaku. I was a delegate from my Order. She attended the sessions of the Council having to do with the ecumenical document, not as a delegate, but lobbying for its passage. She was a most persuasive advocate, and I was immediately taken with her devotion to the Church and its larger mission in the world."

"I was also taken with her political abilities," Dom Philippe continued. "She somehow managed to be invited to meetings of the College of Moderators during this time. It became clear that she was very close to the new pope, a datum that will have more importance as this story comes to its completion. Which it will do soon." He coughed and asked for his pillows to be rearranged, hoping those present were ready for what was to come.

The story continued into the post-Vatican II era. Dom Philippe explained that Pope Paul VI wasted no time in capitalizing on the momentum offered him by the overwhelming passage of the *Nostra aetate*. He visited Istanbul, the first pope to do so since the Great Schism five hundred years previously. He officially lifted the excommunication of all Orthodox communicants that had been invoked by prior administrations and that had been a source of great division between East and West.

"Many were happy to see these developments. Many were not. Thomas Merton and I were in the former category. He and I had become friends during this time, enjoying a...shall we say spirited...correspondence. I was witnessing the evolution of his thinking into a mature personal spiritual theology that embraced all mankind in the family of God, no matter the outward trappings of institutional religion. He was becoming a Universalist in his theological outlook. A Universalist with a Christian foundation within a Christian monastic community which he found increasingly oppressive to his growth. He was far ahead of me in this regard as well as in his social activist views which had gained him such renown—and scorn from the conservatives.

"More and more he looked to the East and particularly Buddhism for inspiration, just as Paul VI was looking in that same direction for his own purposes.

"Merton had in mind becoming a hermit monk, an ambition which was no secret to anyone. For the last three years of his life at Gethsemani he lived in a hermitage away from the cloister. His burning passion was to find a truly isolated spot to which he could retreat, and he had his sights set on Asia.

"That is why, my friends, he was intrigued with the idea of attending the International Monastic Convocation in Thailand when Madame Matsaku invited him. She enlisted my aid in persuading him to deliver the opening address, but that was an easy task. He wanted to use the meeting as an excuse to explore the East for a personal hermitage site."

"What he didn't know," and Dom Philippe paused at this point to look individually at each person beside his bed, "was that he was walking into a conspiracy. A conspiracy contrived by members of the Bossuet Society in collaboration with others. A conspiracy to silence him because he was a...I think you say a 'loose cannon'...outside the constraints of his Order."

Dom Philippe reached for a tissue to wipe away tears before he was ready to conclude his narrative.

With anticipation his audience waited, Rachel included. She awaited the revelations that had brought her here. Less than twenty-four hours ago. It seemed like days had passed since she and Scott first drove up to the parking lot of this strange yet curiously compelling place. This Trappist monastery. This Abbey of Gethsemani which was providing the healing link between her and her father.

* * * *

After four rings the tape clicked in.

"I'm not here right now, so please leave your message." Trey Crockett's voice was as clear as it was predictable on his answering machine. The equally predictable beep sounded on cue.

"This is Scott, Dad, about…uh…one o'clock here…that's twelve noon your time on Sunday afternoon. I need to talk to you real bad. I'm in Kentucky at Gethsemani, and some pretty heavy stuff is coming down. Call me here. It's, uh, it's 502-549-4133. I'm staying here 'til I hear from you."

"Where do you think he is?" asked Rachel, perched on the arm of an easy chair usually reserved for more formal use by visitors to the abbot's office. Scott had received Dom Raphael's permission to use the phone in his office after the intense morning's work dealing with Dom Philippe's confessions and the contents of the safe.

"Beats me. Could be anywhere. At a meeting, at lunch, the lake. Dammit! We've got to reach him." Scott slammed his fist against his thigh, then reddened, realizing swear words were decidedly out of place here. "Why'd you have to be so cute and keep our trip a secret from him anyway? He wouldn't have stopped us."

"Cute, huh?" Rachel shouted. "You don't like how this is going, you can always bug out. Just leave now. I can handle it myself."

"Calm down, calm down," Scott said quietly. "I'm sorry. I didn't mean that. He probably would have stopped us."

He rose abruptly. "What the hel…heck. That's all history now. What to do?" He looked helplessly at Rachel.

Rachel crossed past a wall covered with photographs of important persons. John and Ted Kennedy were probably the only ones she would have recognized had she been paying attention. She got to the window thinking out loud. "We've heard the whole story now, I mean the whole story! This is something, Scott! Wonder what Dad'll say about it."

"We're staying here 'til he calls. There's got to be a way he could use this information to his advantage. We have Dom Philippe's permission to use it with discretion. Keep it out of the media, that's all."

"Does that mean we're spending another night here? I'll have to call Mother and get permission to miss school tomorrow."

"Yeah, yeah, you better do that, just in case." He raised both fists and face toward the ceiling and yelled, "Where are you, Dad?"

Claude Bishop's face appeared in the open doorway with the announcement, "I can answer that question. He's in Washington, D.C., or at least on his way there."

Scott and Rachel wheeled in the direction of the voice, surprised and unaware that the door was ajar.

Bishop interrupted the stunned silence by stepping into the room and introducing himself. He had met Rachel but not Scott.

"It's okay. I'm a friend. Rachel will vouch for me"

"Yeah. Sure. I told Scott about you. With the Tennessee Division of Drug Investigation, right?"

"Correct. The FBI and DEA put me here. I may be making history. Those two agencies aren't famous for cooperation, you know. But here I am, folks, living proof of bureaucratic harmony.

"Looks like my friends in D.C. had a good tip. It all fits when you consider the connections with Matsaku's project. The FBI traced those two imposters from Mexico City to Dallas to Louisville. Had me waitin' on 'em at the airport, and I followed 'em here to the abbey. Even had to get lost once with 'em." Bishop chuckled at the recollection. "For a while I thought we'd end up in Saint Louis." He slipped both hands in his pants pockets and rocked on his heels, enjoying the mental image of the two Mexicans lost on the county road.

"I took up vigil outside the infirmary last night." He shook his head. "Picked the wrong time to go for a cup of coffee. You and poor ol' Jacob took the brunt of it. Brave fellow. Sort of fellow I'd like to've had with me in the Mekong Delta.

"But," he pulled himself up taller and hitched his suspenders, "you'd like to know about your father, wouldn't you?"

"Yes, sir," they answered in unison.

"I just got off the phone with Phil Cox in D.C., and your father's name was in the thick of our conversation. Seems Doctor Crockett is assisting the DEA with a sting operation. At least he might be. He's sort of playing back up, you know, Plan B? Did he tell you anything about it?"

"No, no, sir, he didn't. I'm lost. What's going on?" Scott queried.

"Not sure how much I should tell you. I can tell you where to call him, though, and let him make that decision. He's at the Capitol Holiday Inn, or will be, this afternoon. What you kids have in mind?"

"We...uh..." Rachel looked at Scott for a signal to proceed with this stranger. He nodded. "We think Dad should know what's happened here with the attempted murder, and we have some other information he might be able to use. You see, he's...well, he's sort of in a fix."

"You don't have to be coy with me, miss. I'm fully aware of the blackmail in process against your father, the Delores Project, his Uncle Jonas' dilemma, all of that. And if you've uncovered something else that could help him, you might want to tell me about it. Seems to me we should all be on the same team here, huh?"

Rachel asked, "Doesn't that work both ways, sir? I mean shouldn't you tell us what you know too?"

Bishop smiled broadly. "Nothin' slow about you, is there? Yeah, you're right."

Bishop proceeded to explain the plan to apprehend Fernando Belsasso with the aid of defected members of the Mexican Mafia, Vasquez and Davila. He included the backup plan to use Dr. Crockett for identification of Belsasso's suspected henchmen in blackmail and murder, the two "monks" now in the county jail just up the road in Bardstown, Kentucky. He told them Cox had learned that Matsaku was in D.C. for the hearings to lend weight to his interests and that the Delores Project team was being summoned to Washington for an impromptu meeting.

In return for these disclosures, Scott and Rachel took turns divulging the alarming discoveries made that morning from Dom Philippe and the surprising involvement of Delores Matsaku.

"I can see," mused Bishop after listening to the narrative, "why you want to talk to your father. This could save his ass—uh, hide—excuse me, miss."

"In fact," the agent continued, thinking intensely and pacing in front of his two newly recruited confederates, "this leads me to believe that all of us should be in D.C. tomorrow. I'm including the Mexicans. Now that we've got 'em red-handed, they could be real useful to us with *Dineros*."

"Who?" Rachel asked.

"*Dineros*. That's the code name for Belsasso."

Rachel's voice brimmed with excitement. "Say, while we're at it, why not take along the letters? You said Matsaku was in D.C. They could be real important, couldn't they? If he could see them, see his mother's own handwriting, I mean. Wouldn't that make him think twice about this deal?"

"Whaddaya mean?" Bishop asked.

"Well," Rachel haltingly explained, "He got into this Delores thing mainly to honor his heritage, his mother, her Catholic Church, didn't he?" She looked at Scott for consent.

"Yeah, supposedly he made a promise to her on her deathbed." Scott nodded.

"So, if that's his reason, these letters could turn it around. See what I mean?"

"I don't think the abbot will let you use them. Remember his pledge to Dom Philippe," Scott cautioned.

"Yeah, I know, but we'll see about that. Don't forget what Jacob said about the way things happen around this place. You never know." Rachel beamed a smile like Scott hadn't seen from her in a long time.

CHAPTER 20

▼

*The New York Times
December 13, 1968*

MERTON DEATH RULED NATURAL OR ACCIDENTAL, BODY TO RETURN HOME

Associated Press

BANGKOK—The death of Thomas Merton, noted Trappist monk, social activist, and literary giant from the Abbey of Gethsemani in Kentucky, has been ruled natural by police investigators and other authorities here. An autopsy was judged to be unnecessary in spite of rumors that foul play might have been involved.

Two Frenchmen who were seen near the building at the time of Merton's death were cleared of any wrongdoing when it was learned they were maintenance employees.

Speaking for the Roman Catholic Church, Dom Philippe Flaget, a fellow Trappist and friend who was accompanying Merton on his trip to Bangkok, issued the following statement: "All the evidence points to either natural death by heart attack or accidental electrocution from an electrical fan in his room which had faulty wiring. The Church does not wish to pursue any other rumors with a prolonged investigation that would do nothing but hamper plans to return his body for burial. We need to celebrate his life, not tarnish his death."

Merton was in Thailand speaking at an international convocation of eastern monastic leaders when he died suddenly three days ago. One of the promoters of the meeting, Mme. Delores Matsaku of Tokyo, also issued a statement on behalf of the sponsoring organization: "I join with the officials of this convocation and admirers from around the world in a deep sense of loss at the passing of a good friend and inspirational leader. We are satisfied with the investigative report of the authorities and are ready to see the matter put to rest."

Tentative plans call for a private funeral on December 17 at the Abbey of Gethsemani in Bardstown, Kentucky.

Chapter 21

▼

Trey left early for the airport Sunday afternoon giving himself enough time to visit his mother whom he had neglected of late. A few years back when it became clear that arthritis was soon to demand she have full-time assistance, the decision was made for her to move to Nashville.

His younger sister, Abby, had made the obligatory attempt to have her close to her home in Virginia, but it was evident to everyone that she had her hands full with five children. Not to mention that she struggled with chronic fatigue syndrome. Trey and Evelyn had agreed the seventy-five-year-old Ruby was better off in their keep in the St. Cecelia Episcopal Residence.

Now eighty-five, she was managing to hold on to her faculties but not her walker. She had graduated to a wheelchair.

Evelyn continued to be attentive, even after the divorce, sharing duties with Trey. Lately she was doing more than her share. Trey needed to see his mother. For many reasons.

"There you are," he said, approaching her in the day room. She turned and smiled.

"I've been wondering where you were," she said in her barely audible, hoarse voice. Her vocal cords were withering, too, according to her doctors.

"Sorry I haven't been around lately. There's been a lot of things happening all of a sudden. How you been?" He kissed her on the forehead.

"Pretty good." Her usual response.

With her permission he rolled her to apartment 303, the small efficiency type common to assisted living facilities. Everything was in its place—the family pictures, console television, motorized lifting chair that she had fussed about initially but was now her favorite piece of furniture.

After more pleasantries about her friends and favorite staff members Ruby asked, "What's kept you so busy?"

"Well," Trey hesitated, "it's a long story and probably not very interesting to you."

"Let me decide that," she said. She could still muster a twinkle.

Trey sat down on a stool beside her. It was time for him to pull out the explanation he had rehearsed on the way to see her.

He cleared his throat. "Okay. Actually, I'm on my way to the airport. I'm going to Washington, D.C., to help Uncle Jonas. You've probably been reading about him in the papers, the Fort Campbell thing."

Ruby nodded and frowned.

"You see, I have some information that could help him with the resolution to save the army base. So I'm probably going to testify for him, if he needs me, that is. He might not."

"Oh, my, Trey, I hope not. You don't need to go through that now, do you?"

"Honestly I'd rather not because it could, well, it could get nasty and turn out badly for me. I debated whether to tell you about it today, but you might see it in the papers so I thought you ought to hear it from me first."

Her head fell making it even harder to hear her. "After what you went through I'd hate to see you get hurt again."

Yes, her memory was still good. She knew about his problems with the bottle. She wasn't asking for more details of his new problem, wasn't eager to store up more bad memories.

"Me, too, Mother. And I know how it hurt you. I...I don't want to disappoint you again."

She glanced at him long enough to see his eyes moisten, and then her head fell again.

He reached in his jacket pocket and pulled out an envelope. "Mother, there is a note in here for you. I don't want you to open it, though, unless something happens to me. You just never know these days, flying in airplanes and all. I'll pick it up from you when I get back. Unopened, okay?"

She nodded and took the envelope. His rehearsal had paid off.

Trey straightened himself up and looked at his watch. "Well, I've got to scoot on out of here. Can't miss my plane." He kissed her and said, "I love you."

"I love you, too. Please be careful."

They parted.

* * * *

Within two hours' time on Sunday afternoon Washington National was host to the arrival of thousands of passengers on dozens of flights from dozens of places. Among the throng with its sundry lives unfolding were a number of persons who were converging upon each other for the particular purposes of either doing or undoing NAFTA or Ft. Campbell, Kentucky, of either shoring up or killing the Delores Project, of either enabling or disabling the drug traffic from Mexico.

Not a bad afternoon's work for the busy metropolitan airport.

Two of those passengers came from Nashville, Tennessee. One—the man, the psychiatrist—flew American Airlines and immediately found a pay phone to announce his arrival to Phil Cox.

The other—the woman, the politician—arrived a little later by private charter jet paid for by the individual she was now calling from the plane just before touchdown.

"Mr. Matsaku, this is Pat Beason. I'm arriving at Washington National. Very nice flight, thank you."

"Ah, Honorable Madame Beason, so glad you arrived safely. I am pleased you could arrange to come for this hasty bit of business away from your office. It seemed such an opportune time for us to meet. I hope it hasn't inconvenienced you too much."

"Not at all. Glad to be here. You said you'd have instructions for me now."

"Indeed. I have arranged for adjoining suites at the Hyatt Regency for all of our out-of-town partners. There is a limousine awaiting you at the private hangar where you will land. Just ask for the Matsaku Enterprises limo at the charter desk. Then if you will ring my room, number 2430, when you arrive at the hotel, we can detail further plans."

"This is all quite convenient. Oh, could you tell me, are you expecting Señor Belsasso to be here?"

"Yes, our friend from Mexico is scheduled to join us. He should be arriving any time."

"That's good. Very good. I'll see you in a little while." The Tennessee lawyer-politician hung the phone up and inhaled deeply, savoring the exhilaration of the scent of power that filled her nostrils. She liked being catered to by one of the ten wealthiest men in the world. She liked it as much or more than sex. Though she couldn't help but wonder what the trilogy of sex-power-money would feel like next to her in bed.

The sting of anxiety disallowed any extended ruminations such as that, however. Her mission, after her call to Phil Cox the previous day, was now tainted with mixed motives. She was no longer feathering her political nest but attempting to salvage her name and career from the mire of Belsasso's murderous tactics. She and Cox agreed to keep her new alliance with him to themselves so that no suspicions could leak to Belsasso. Not even Trey Crockett was to know that she was now a mole, aligned with the same team he was on.

She barely missed running into Belsasso whose private jet pulled up to the same hangar. It was after he had already made plans to honor President Clinton's invitation that he had been called by Manuel Matsaku, asking him to join the Delores group for the hastily called meeting in Washington. Belsasso's boss, President Salinas, was quick to grant permission for both activities, implicitly trusting his *Ministro de Comercio*, trusting him much more than he should have.

Certainly Salinas had not the foggiest notion as to the events awaiting his high-profile cabinet member on Monday. For all he knew, Belsasso would simply show up with Clinton and other key personages in the pro-NAFTA contingent to enhance the feeling of solidarity between the two nations.

And he couldn't possibly know that Belsasso was expecting two members of *Ojos Negros* to meet him in D.C. for nefarious purposes. No, for all the taints on the high offices of Mexican government officials in recent decades, none had yet reached the depths of overt drug trafficking. And while political payoffs and kickbacks south of the border were as common as adultery charges were becoming in the American presidency, the murder of aging Episcopal and Catholic priests definitely was frowned upon.

Nevertheless, such were the circumstances of Fernando Belsasso that Sunday afternoon. His *Ojos* contacts, Vasquez and Davila, arrived commercial carrier as planned, filled with apprehension about their dangerous mission. They were about to betray their boss, their compatriots, their country.

These two operatives had been "turned" by the DEA's secret agent in Mexico City, allowing themselves to be targeted because of their growing discontent with *Ojos* security and distrust of their superiors. Then there were promises of substantial monetary reward by the U.S. government, one-half million dollars apiece to be specific. The clincher for their decision to defect from the Mexican Mafia was the guarantee of personal security from the President of the United States—a new identity, U.S. citizenship, and the Witness Protection Program.

Their contact person was none other than Phil Cox who awaited their call at 3:15 p.m. in his office. He also awaited Trey Crockett who would arrive soon via taxi from the airport. Cox had left word with security to personally escort the doctor from Tennessee up to his office.

Spike Field leaned back in his chair and asked his partner, "You got any doubts they'll show?" He didn't have to wait for a reply.

"Any doubts? Any doubts?? Are you fuckin' crazy? On drugs? Of course I have doubts. Any man in his right mind would have doubts. These are Mexican scumbags we're dealing with here, Agent Field, not the Boy Scouts. Their pledge probably goes something like, 'On my honor I will do my best to do my duty to the Devil and my own black soul.' No offense about the 'black' part, but you get my point."

Field poked a potato chip in his mouth and smiled his impish Cosby smile. The phone rang and Cox pounced on it. It was the Mexicans, Vasquez the spokesman.

"You made it in okay, huh? Very good. My partner and I would like to meet with you right away to detail the plan. We have in mind a quiet little park, the Basin, on the river. There's a statue there of a horse and rider. Can't miss it. Any taxi driver will know it."

"Just a moment, Seññor Cox, if you don't mind." Vasquez sounded nervous.

"What is it?"

"My partner and I, we want to inquire again of the payoff arrangements before we are seen with you. Just when will we receive the cash? I think you said it would be ready immediately at the time of the contact with Señor Belsasso tomorrow."

Cox cleared his throat and frowned. "Uh...well, can't we discuss that when we meet in a few minutes?"

The door opened and a uniformed security officer appeared with Trey Crockett in tow. Field motioned him to come in and shook hands, putting his finger to his lips and motioning toward Cox. Cox nodded at the familiar, newly arrived guest but was clearly preoccupied.

"No, Señor Cox, we want to be very clear about this before proceeding."

"Well, there has..." Cox shrugged his shoulders at Field. "There has been a slight change in our plan on that. What we want to do is to pay you one-half tomorrow...and then the other half after your testimony at the trial which should be no longer than six to nine months." Cox delivered the last statement with pseudo-confident rapidity, hoping it would just sail through without comment.

His hopes were dashed.

"What? What testimony? What do you mean? No one has mentioned testimony. It is our understanding we will be paid and then immediately go into the protection program, and that's it. What testimony, Señor Cox?" Vasquez was clearly shaken.

"It's just procedure, Señor Vasquez. Nothing to get upset about."

"It's not as we agreed. We cannot take such a risk being seen at a trial. Our lives would be finished. No. We will not agree to this. No."

The phone clicked on Cox's end and went dead while he was saying, "But...but..."

He held the phone in his hand and stared at Field who was on the edge of his chair. "What happened? What'd he say? Did he hang up?"

Cox's head was hanging now. "Yeah, yeah," he whispered, "He hung up. We've lost 'em. We screwed up. I told you we should've given the whole layout before now." The phone dropped into its cradle.

"Don't panic," Field soothed. "Let's just sit tight right here. Let 'em think about it. They'll call back, I bet."

"You're on." Cox pulled a quarter from his pocket and slammed it on the desk. Then he greeted the psychiatrist from Tennessee with the most somber of demeanors. "Looks like Plan B arrived just in the nick of time. Welcome to the world of international intrigue. Intriguing, isn't it, Doctor Crockett?"

"What was that? What do you mean?"

"What I mean, dear doctor, is that Plan A just went down the tubes. Unless that phone rings in the next minute with a contrite and conciliatory Mexican on the other end, which I would bet my pension plan in addition to the quarter that it doesn't happen, then you're the man of the hour. So glad you're here. Sit down. Let's talk." Cox was now the practical man. He wasn't dwelling on misfortune.

The phone rang and locked the three into a moment of catatonia. The bet was on. Cox recovered after the second ring and answered.

There was an accent of the Southern variety but not quite far enough south for Field to win the bet. Cox picked up his quarter, brandishing it at his partner. "It's Bishop," he whispered, covering the mouthpiece while he listened.

He listened for at least two minutes without speaking, taking notes on a pad, nodding, and grunting the occasional, "Yeah, yeah."

Then it was his turn. "Sure. I like the plan." He was smiling for the first time. "I'm sure Smithers will approve. We'll get the necessary clearance from this end from him and the Fibbies. Then we'll fax the paperwork to the sheriff in...is it Bardstown? The prisoners will be released to your custody. Why don't you go ahead and charter a flight from there for tonight. Surely there's a charter service nearby. How many of you will there be?"

"Six? It's you, the two kids, and the two Mexican prisoners, and who else?"

"Brother who? a monk? Brother Jacob? Why a monk?"

"Oh...okay, if you say so...yeah, as a matter of fact, Doctor Crockett is sitting right here with us. Do his kids want to speak with him?"

Cox handed the phone to Trey. At the other end, Scott held the phone out to Rachel who took it momentarily only to shake her head and return it to him without a word.

There was much explaining to do on both sides for the two parties who had been on their own missions and trying to make contact with each other. They talked for ten minutes, covering all the latest developments including Rachel's part in the action.

Scott explained that the abbot had given permission, with Rachel being the most effective in persuading him, for the previously-secret letters to be removed from the abbey only in the personal custody of Brother Jacob. They would be bringing these documents, along with Jacob, to Washington to use with Manuel Matsaku. They hoped their impact would sway the industrialist to abandon his obsessive passion for the Delores Project, a passion that was evolving into a murderous nightmare, outside of his awareness, one assumed.

"Well, Scott, I'd like to see those papers myself. But I wouldn't count on them deterring Matsaku. He is a businessman first and foremost."

"I know, Dad, but I just can't explain it on the phone. The abbot was real clear that the letters be handled with strict stipulations. They can't be discussed on the telephone, can't be copied or faxed, can't be released to the press. And only Brother Jacob can decide if anyone is allowed to see them. So maybe you'll have a chance to read them. I hope so. You wouldn't believe it unless you did. Hey, I've got to get off the phone. Mr. Bishop has some arranging to do."

Cox and Bishop finished up their plans while Spike Field offered chips and cookies to Trey.

"Tell me," Trey asked aside, "why has this gotten to be such a have-to situation with Belsasso tomorrow? I mean, if the case is that shaky, isn't it risky to move in so fast?"

Field cleared the cookie crumbs from his mouth. "It's the *Post*. Jack Bergman, ace investigator, has been like a dog on a bone the last few days confirming a leak about our case on the guy. He's that close to having it nailed down. You can expect to see it on at least page two tomorrow or Tuesday. Maybe page one. Clinton's decided he'll look better if we nail Belsasso before the press does. It's chancy though.

Hard to figure the reaction among Congress as to the NAFTA vote. It's due the next day."

Cox was finished with Bishop.

"Okay you guys. Here's the plan for tomorrow morning." He wrote the essentials on a note pad as he talked, handing sheets to the other two for them to do the same. "There's still all the fine details to work out with the Fibbies tonight. We should have him in handcuffs by 1100 hours. That'll be just enough time for the President to call a press conference at noon to announce the arrest."

"And," Trey interrupted, "in time for me to get to the Senate hearing. I'm testifying at two o'clock for the resolution, you know."

He was answered with quizzical looks.

"Oh. Guess I hadn't told you that. I, uh, volunteered to help Uncle Jonas by telling all I know about the Delores Project." He nodded weakly and sighed.

Cox said the obvious. "I don't get it, Crockett. I thought that would be just what you wouldn't want to do, to expose yourself, to make public your relationship to Pat Beason. Not to mention exposing Eisenberg which will tie straight into the president. Talk about risky!"

"Yeah, and now," Field broke in, "after the arrest, assuming it comes off, the Delores thing will be in the open anyway. That could just take care of your problem, couldn't it?"

"Yeah, been thinking about that. I'm not so sure. The vote on the resolution will come tomorrow. The time limit written into the law is running out. Uncle Jonas has assured me of that. So the arrest will be fresh news with a lot of questions around it. It'll take someone like me to supply those answers quickly and directly to the Armed Services Committee. I doubt Belsasso would agree to do that in handcuffs four hours after he's arrested. Somehow I believe he'll have counsel by then."

"Hmmm." Cox shook his head. "It's your medical license, so we'll just have to let you spin your own web. I've got a busy afternoon and night ahead of me, so please excuse while I call the boss." Dialing, he continued, "I'm not asking for much. Just an order from the FBI releasing two attempted murderers from a Kentucky jail to the custody of Claude Bishop plus permission to charter a plane for six from Bardstown to D.C. tonight..." Someone picked up the phone on the other end, so he covered the mouthpiece to finish. "...and a Justice Department promise of no death penalty for the Mexicans if they help us nab *Dineros*.

"Hello, Mr. Smithers. This is Phil Cox calling from headquarters, sir. Agent Field is here, too. Sorry to bother you at home, sir, but we need your help with our project tomorrow..."

* * * *

The Nelson County, Kentucky, sheriff seemed skeptical. Even after speaking personally to the state Attorney General, the county's Presiding Circuit Judge, and the Director of the FBI, he was still skeptical. When the fax machine finally chattered its confirmatory message, the beer-bellied, shirt-sleeved, cigar-smoking officer of the law breathed a long, stale sigh and shoved the piece of paper at Claude Bishop.

"Waal, sir, I guess that's what I need. Let's go ahead in there and tell them two what you're a-plannin'. And you better make it quick. I dunno how much longer I kin keep the reporter from the paper from findin' out about this arrest. Freedom of information and all that stuff."

He waved Bishop to follow him to the cellblock, clattering keys and gesturing his deputy away from the door. Bishop in turn motioned for Scott and Rachel to come along. It was a dank place with concrete floors and an odor admixed of cigarette smoke and disinfectant. Most of the cells housed at least two inhabitants who glanced with less than enthusiastic interest at the party passing before them.

The sheriff stopped at the last cell on the right. "Hey, you two banditos. This here agent wants to talk to you." Jorge and Felix looked up from their pallets then arose slowly to a standing position, arms akimbo, squinting.

Bishop addressed them. "I have here an order signed by the chief law enforcement officer in the United States, the Director of the FBI, James Stennis, releasing you from this jail into my custody. You're bein' asked to help us with an important matter in Washington, D.C. tomorrow, something that involves your boss, Señor Belsasso."

The two disheveled prisoners looked questioningly at each other as if to ask the other if he had squealed.

"Don't try to figure out how we know about him. We just do. And we're goin' to arrest him with your help. In exchange you get some special considerations in your case."

"Special considerations?" Jorge growled. "We haven't had much of that yet with your American justice system. We haven't even been able to call anyone." The words came spitting out.

"I know. I think you'll be interested in what we have in mind for you. I'll explain it all on the flight to D.C. We have a plane waitin' for us in…" He looked at his watch. "…in just 45 minutes at 6:30. So we'll be movin' right along now."

There was an airfield just east of town where Brother Jacob would join the entourage, and an eight-seater was supposedly on the way from Louisville to pick all of them up.

Bishop backed away from the bars to allow the sheriff and his deputy to do their handiwork which in this case involved not only handcuffs behind their backs but leg chains as well. Rachel and Scott, excited but fearful, looked on silently. Rachel was beginning to think about a career in law enforcement.

With those thoughts pulsing through her reverie, and with the two subjects visible in the rear view mirror of the van, a sudden flash hit her. She was outside Holy Spirit Catholic Church in Nashville with her friend Phyllis, and two Latino men were leaning against the wrought iron fence. Those were the same men in cuffs in the back seat. She finally recognized them. What did this mean?

At Rachel's suggestion they stopped at Hardee's on the way to the airport. It had occurred to no one to eat since breakfast, and there was a three-hour flight ahead of them. She and Scott fed the prisoners their burgers and fries in the car, and she couldn't help but wonder what would happen when they had to answer nature's call. Law enforcement as a career suddenly had less appeal to her.

Jacob was waiting for them at the hangar, locked briefcase cradled close to his bosom. Rachel told him and Scott of her recollection regarding the Mexicans, that she had seen them lurking outside the church in Nashville that September evening.

Scott was first to put two and two together. "That places them in Nashville the night Dad was accosted in his driveway. Those are the messengers. And they were tailing you, too."

"You're right," Rachel answered. "Maybe I can help with their identification."

Boarding the twin-engine Beech Kingair, Rachel was curious about something else. "Jacob, how'd you happen to be up at 1:30 this morning?"

"Good question, my good friend. I think it was because the two Mexican monks flunked the test."

"Huh?"

"I was a little suspicious of them at first sight. So I simply asked them a simple question to see if they were simpletons. I asked them if Dom Miguel was still the abbot at their monastery. They told me he was."

"So?"

"Dom Miguel died two years ago." Jacob shrugged his shoulders.

CHAPTER 22

▼

Monday morning broke on the nation's capital without a sign of any kind to indicate the day would be different from the last one. Early morning fog was confined to the low grassy areas and bodies of water. A pale blue-white cloudless sky welcomed the sun. The Potomac basin sent an ever-so-light breeze with its scent abroad for those with specially attuned nostrils.

The night had been equally quiet to all outward appearances.

Trey Crockett had taken a stroll outside his hotel at eight o'clock Sunday evening, relieved he didn't have to be putting up appearances at an AA meeting. He did spend a few minutes, though, inside St. Peter's Cathedral. It seemed to him quaintly appropriate to be in that environment, the Roman Catholic Church, the church of Delores and Manuel Matsaku, the church of Thomas Merton, of Dom Philippe Flaget and Brother Jacob.

He came upon the sexton in the center aisle. He must have been the sexton. Who else with jeans and khaki shirt and a tool kit swinging from his left hand?

Just as the two strangers exchanged greetings the mellow harmonics of the organ swept over the nave. A Bach fugue transfixed the space. Trey's pace slowed to a crawl. He worked his way to the altar and knelt, now alone except for the unseen organist who played the accompaniment to Trey's prayer.

He found himself softly chanting *Praise to the Father, the Son, and Holy Spirit*...and gathering in the presence of the choir monks of Gethsemani. Brothers Matthias, James, Brendan, Jacob, and all the rest in their white and black were at his side at that altar....*the God who is, who was, and is to come, at the end of the ages.*

Merton must have come to a reckoning with himself in those last days. His journals spoke of his raptured interest in eastern sirituality. How was he to reconcile the unstructured, apersonal paradoxes of Buddhist truths with the dogma of his own faith? If he confessed his true leanings, his new yearnings, all of his followers would know the truth about him: that he wasn't what he had appeared to be.

Could Merton have taken his own life? There wasn't an autopsy. Or could he have made himself so vulnerable that he was murdered. On purpose? Is suicide all that bad when your time has come?

An hour was consumed before he realized that the organ was silent and that his knees hurt.

Once outside again he passed a couple of bars. Even paused in front of one of them long enough to test his salivary glands. They passed the test.

Cross off Option Number One.

He returned to his room at ten to decide about Option Number Two.

*   *   *   *

As for Manuel Matsaku, he had gathered remnants of the Delores confederation in his suite for a light buffet dinner, which was more than satisfying to Pat Beason, Fernando Belsasso, and Leon Eisenberg. General Perkins and Governor Turnbow could not be there. Matsaku had asked each of the assembled to be on hand at the Senate committee hearing the following afternoon. He had explained that he planned to watch on C-Span from his hotel suite, that his actual presence would be too obvious. Unless, of course, last-minute exigencies demanded he be there. His aide had given each of them cellular phones with which to communicate along with a list of their names and numbers. Nice attention to detail.

Secretary Eisenberg made very clear President Clinton's uneasiness about the Delores Project and any negative effect it might have on the NAFTA proceedings.

* * * *

Phil Cox and Spike Field had spent most of the night nailing down final details of the next day's operation with the FBI agents assigned to work with them. They had grabbed a few winks after 2 a.m.

The charter flight from Bardstown had arrived at Andrews on schedule at 10:30 p.m. with its unlikely cargo of the Tennessee Drug Enforcement agent, two Mexican goons, a couple of starry-eyed youngsters, and a briefcase affixed to the hand of a monk in blue jeans wearing a Phillies baseball cap. This group spent the night in a suite of rooms located in the DEA office building and designed for special security occasions such as this. It came close to being a jail, but no one complained.

Rachel didn't ask, didn't want to know, about procedures for attending to the prisoners' nature calls. She was grateful to sleep on the sofa in Phil Cox's office, comfortably separated from the others and thinking her own thoughts. She had plumped a makeshift pillow and wondered what the morning would bring to her father's plight. How she could figure into the plans. Whether she would actually see him. How she would act if she did. Still confused, she was.

* * * *

"This has got to come off just right," President Clinton explained. "As you all know, the House votes on NAFTA tomorrow morning. Belsasso is meeting with the Vice President and tiebreakers for breakfast as we speak. We don't really think his presence will add that much, but it keeps him from being suspicious of our real purpose in having him here. We're just lucky as hell the *Post* hasn't printed it yet. Has anyone seen the morning paper? Hell, it's supposed to be here on the table. Why can't anything be done right around here?"

There were three shaking heads around the table belonging to White House Chief of Staff Marshall Counts, DEA Chief Harvey Smithers, and FBI Chief Jim Stennis. These were the invited guests of Bill Clinton in the White House breakfast room at 8 a.m.

"I heard this yesterday: Where do you take a leak at the White House? Just like any cur dog—to the *Post*." Clinton broke through his irritation and smiled. The others snickered politely at his poor joke, Counts while muttering an order on the intercom to the receptionist on duty to fetch a newspaper.

The Chief of Staff commented: "Mr. President, it seems like a gamble, going ahead with this the day before the House vote. There's still time to rethink the thing and postpone it to later this week if we can get Dineros to hang around on some pretext."

"Marshall, I don't think so. If we do it right, it will work in our favor. Principles above politics, and all that sort of stuff."

"Jimmy Carter sort of stuff, it sounds to me like, and you know what he's doing now, building houses." Counts could get away with jibes like that, largely because no one expected anything better of him. Certainly not those around the table.

The server passed among them with fresh coffee. Continental was the order of the day with fresh fruit, Danish, and bagels being the highlights. Clinton looked famished nursing a bowl of oatmeal, his penance for sporting an ever-swelling waistline that television-viewing audiences all over the world were privileged to witness whenever his jogging was on exhibition.

The receptionist entered bearing the morning edition of the newspaper. Counts motioned for her to deliver it to him. While the others ate he quickly scanned the front, then the second page.

"Ho-ly crap!" Counts exploded. "Excuse me, gentlemen, but," he handed the twice-folded paper to the main man on his left, "I'm afraid the cat's out of the bag. One paw, anyway."

Clinton frowned and read aloud:

DEA MAKES MEXICAN CONNECTION

> According to reliable sources within the administration, illegal drug traffic into the United States has been traced to one or more high-ranking officials in the Mexican government. The sources, who requested anonymity, confirmed that the *Ojos Negros*, an organization often referred to as the "Mexican Mafia," has been responsible for a major influx of cocaine and marijuana into this country in the last few years. This underworld syndicate has been directly under the protection of one of the cabinet members in President Salinas' administration, according to these same sources who declined to name the cabinet member.
>
> Attempts to reach President Salinas for comment have been unsuccessful. Chief of Staff Marshall Counts, when contacted late Sunday afternoon, said he had "no knowledge" of such accusations, and he refused to speculate on the impact of such a development on the imminent NAFTA vote.
>
> Drug smuggling from south of the border has often originated from Mexico as well as South and Central America...

Clinton's voice trailed off and he scanned the last two paragraphs silently.

He handed the paper back to Counts who was already planning strategy. "What do you think about me getting Al Gore on the line, like right now, to see if Belsasso has seen this? Maybe, just maybe, we'll get lucky."

"Good idea. Go ahead. We'll be finalizing our plans here anyway," indicating with a nod to the others around the table. He shook the paper at them. "You see, we've just got to plow ahead with this thing. There's no time." He asked Jim Stennis to outline the plan.

"We're going to get him on tape, audio and video, acknowledging his association with the known criminals. You are aware, I think, Mr. President, that the original plan has been modified because of the...well, the disappearance of the two operatives from *Ojos Negros*." Smithers studied his napkin.

"But fortunately, another possibility fell into our laps at the same time." Now he smiled at Smithers. "Harvey's men have nabbed two other operatives with direct connections to Belsasso. Not for drug smuggling but for murder. This may be plowing old ground for all of you, but we now have in custody two Mexicans who are being held for a) attempted murder, a monk in Kentucky, and very likely for b) murder, the priest in Alabama. We're still working on that charge. If we can get a positive ID from someone at that church in Alabama who saw Father Stone leaving with them, along with Doctor Crockett's identifying them as his blackmailers, we should have enough to pin that one on them too."

"Yes, Jim, I've heard all that." Clinton shifted again in his chair. "Has to do with the Delores Project, doesn't it?"

"Yes, sir. Definitely. Both victims could have been—could be, I should say, since the vote isn't in yet—helpful to your opponents in the Senate."

"Now tell me," Clinton asked, "when and how does this come off? So I can be ready for a press conference at noon to declare victory over the forces of evil and lead the media to extol the virtues of an administration which is willing to risk a political setback in order to drive out the hideous specters of drug smuggling and murder from across our border?"

"In..." Stennis glanced at his watch. "...in just over two hours we've arranged for a meeting between Belsasso and his accomplices. With a guarantee of our help in arranging a reduced sentence on the murder charges, these two have agreed to wear body mikes and meet Belsasso at a designated place at 1030 hours. Videocameras will be in place. They've told him this is a rendezvous to show him some important materials they claim to have lifted from the monk at the monastery. I won't go into detail about the significance of these materials, but they supposedly had something to do with the reason they wanted to wipe out the old monk, important enough that Belsasso will want to see them."

"And Belsasso agreed to meet them? That's all set?"

"Yes, sir. That is, unless he's seen the morning paper."

On cue, Counts reentered the room and all eyes followed him to Clinton's side. He smiled. "Al says the breakfast is going famously, that there's not a newspaper in sight, and that Belsasso is conducting himself like a diplomat, not a suspect. Even says the vote on NAFTA is looking good at this point."

Clinton visibly relaxed. "Good. That's real good, Marshall. We'll just have to pray he doesn't see the paper. Maybe they sold out of copies early. Be ready to announce the press conference about 10:45 or 11 then, and you and Jobe get to work finishing my text."

Clinton stood and walked around the table. "You know, men, I've been thinking a lot about this thing with the 101st. I believe, if that resolution passes, we'll call off the dogs. I don't want to see it fought out on the Hill."

All arose to allow him to shake hands with each in turn. He took his leave inviting them to stay and finish eating.

* * * *

Phil Cox pulled up to the Capitol Holiday Inn entrance at 8:45 a.m. on the nose. Trey Crockett was pacing the concrete. "Hey, Trey, get in, it's time to scram. We're on a tight schedule. It's okay to call you Trey, isn't it?"

Trey knew about the schedule which required him to be escorted by Cox and Field to DEA headquarters where he expected to meet Raspy and Large Hands face-to-face for the first time since that August night in his driveway in Brentwood, Tennessee. That night when he was at the mercy of the unknown, when fear had burst upon his life once again.

Within fifteen minutes, 9 a.m., they had met Spike Field and were in the elevator punching the button for the fourth floor.

"You think Scott and Jacob and Rachel will be here?" Trey asked.

"Don't know for sure. Kinda doubt it, though." Cox checked his watch while Field flipped through his notebook.

"Yeah," Field added, "according to my notes, we wanted everyone cleared out of here and scattered by now, everyone except the two goons. We suggested those three get down to the House chambers to watch the NAFTA debate. They were sort of getting in our hair; Rachel kept begging to let them help us in the operation today. Had to keep telling her we can't let untrained civilians get in harm's way. She finally accepted it, grudgingly. Yeah, they should've left here by now."

"I'm sorry Rachel gave you a hard time. That surprises me."

The elevator stopped and the door opened. "Yeah," Field continued, "both your kids are real winners. Scott wanted to help with the cameras at the site of the operation, the coffee shop. We're planning to have two angles recording Belsasso going in and coming out. Then we'll have the audio for the actual meeting with the two guys, and the whole thing will be on synchronous electronic clock timing. Scott got real fired up hearing about it. We had to wave him off, too."

"Man!" Trey was impressed. "You got all this arranged since last night?"

"Let's just say we didn't get much shuteye, pal." Cox led the way to the office they were seeking.

Field opened the door and Trey entered the room where the two Mexicans were waiting, still shackled and under armed escort by Federal marshals. He recognized them at once and vice-versa.

Cox and the marshals escorted the prisoners out of the room and on to their assigned mission. They would be coached further in the dos and don'ts of the upcoming rendezvous with Belsasso.

Spike Field and Trey Crockett were left with their task: composing and completing a formal statement from the good doctor which detailed his encounter with Mendez and Gonzalez, the blackmail plot against him, and his communications with Pat Beason, all of which could be used circumstantially in the charges against Belsasso as well as in the case against these two murderers.

"How long will this take?" Trey looked at his watch.

"Oh, I'd say about forty-five minutes if we do it right and don't have to rewrite too much. Why?" Field flipped the switch on the computer. He would type as Trey wrote so there would be a backup copy.

"I have a lunch date with Uncle Jonas at noon at his office."

"You'll make it. I can run you over there. We should have some exciting news by then." The IBM was booted up and ready to roll.

* * * *

The sun streamed in from the east windows of the executive suite on the twenty-fourth floor of the Hyatt Regency. The occupant had requested the morning sun in his accommodations; rather, his staff had requested such knowing of the ritual habits of their employer when away from home.

Manual Matsaku carefully arranged the silk tablecloth on the small lamp table provided in the suite. The lamp had been removed making way for the framed picture of his mother with Cardinal Swenens and Pope Paul VI and the crucifix. Adjusting the picture so that it caught the sun's rays, he knelt and crossed himself, rosary in hand.

It created an intriguing tableau, this scene with the powerful industrialist, the Japanese/Mexican Roman Catholic, the man possessed of a passion to perpetuate his mother's life work through the medium of his father's, kneeling in prayer in the light of a window which looked out eastward over Washington, D.C.. His mumbled words of devotion reverberated against the glass of that window, competing on the other side with the hum and horns and hosts of humans that typified a Monday morning in the nation's capital.

He arose slowly, draped the rosary beads over the picture, stepped back and bowed, then went to the window to survey the scene. His peaceful frame of mind was disrupted with thoughts of the day's project. He had been disappointed with the gathering of his team last evening. Eisenberg had been noticeably silent during most of the discussions except for his warnings about the president's unease. Even when the two were alone, the Secretary of Defense had nothing further to report to Matsaku about Belsasso and the murder of the priest.

And as for the Mexican team member, Matsaku had watched him closely for any signs of deceit. He saw none. Fernando Belsasso comported himself coolly throughout the evening.

Too coolly, Matsaku thought. The man's too smooth. But could he be capable of ordering the murder of the priest in order to promote this deal? Would President Salinas have offered for me to coordinate the Delores Project with his Secretary of Commerce if he were a murderer?

Of course not! Impossible!

But then not necessarily. Salinas might not know everything about his cabinet members. Stranger things have happened in the world of politics and international business.

Matsaku sighed and determined to himself, gazing out the window at the street scene below, that he would not condemn the man based on rumor alone. He would not interrupt the course of events that day which were moving toward the defeat of Senator Crockett's resolution. The votes of Senators Jansen and Wilford would assure that defeat, and he would not call in their votes based on what he knew.

With renewed resolve, he stepped away from the window, picked up the picture, and kissed his mother's image as well as that of her beloved Pope Paul. He felt in his heart they both would approve his decision.

He would now bathe and prepare to await developments of the day.

CHAPTER 23

▼

Belsasso was tagged by the FBI tail as he left the breakfast scene hosted by Vice President Gore. A taxi was waiting to return him to the Hyatt Regency some ten blocks away. Using a two-way radio from his unmarked car, the tail notified the observer on duty at the hotel, ready to pass the baton to him as soon as their subject disappeared into the revolving front doors.

"He's yours and without a newspaper in sight." The voice came through distinctly to Claude Bishop from the tiny speaker that masqueraded as a hearing aid. He was seated nonchalantly in the hotel lobby, looking bored. Not a difficult assignment for this man who had survived the horrors of V.C. massacres. Most of life could be classified as boring to him after those years.

Unseen by Bishop were three other persons at the other end of the hotel lobby trying to look equally nonchalant. One was a pony-tailed redheaded teenager in skirt and Reeboks holding a cup of diet cola, another a clean-cut collegiate-looking young man, and the third a lean, bluejeaned man with salt-and-pepper short-cropped hair covered mostly by a Phillies baseball cap which also partially covered a gauze bandage on his scalp. This third one was clutching a briefcase.

"You know we've got no business being here. Whose idea was this, anyway? Bishop told us to keep our noses out of it," Jacob whispered to the other two.

"It's no harm," Rachel argued. "We're just hanging out and watching."

"Just stay put and don't let him know we're here and it's cool," Scott added.

"Cool, yeah," Jacob said, "like I don't think Dom Raphael would say it's cool."

"He's not here," Rachel countered. "He's there. You're on your own."

Then she added, "Say, how'd you get to be a monk anyway?"

"You want the short version? It happened in college when I had a summer job with my brother at a publishing house in New York City. I was assigned to work on a collection of Merton's unpublished writings, and I caught the bug. My early Catholic upbringing primed me for the call."

"What was your real name?"

"Nick. Nick Sudack. Polish. Lots of Poles in Allentown."

"Oops," he said, interrupting himself, "I think I see him."

Belsasso walked straight to the elevator with the casual Bishop following. Rachel, Scott, and Jacob watched the procession, standing and idly chatting at their safe distance.

"So that's what he looks like," Scott murmured. "Maybe we'll see Matsaku too. They said this hotel was Delores headquarters."

Scott had to excuse himself to go to the men's room. "I'll be right back. Don't move."

There were two other people already in the elevator. Belsasso pushed button 24; Bishop followed with 23. Just as the automatic doors began to close, Belsasso suddenly snapped his fingers, excused himself to the others, and exited back into the lobby. Bishop decided not to follow. Too obvious. The door closed and he left the quarry temporarily unwatched, planning to stop at the next floor and return immediately to the lobby.

Rachel punched Jacob when she saw what had transpired at the elevator door. They followed Belsasso down one corridor of the lobby and stopped when he entered the notions shop. He bent down to the *Washington Post* pile and lifted the one off the top, walking then to the cashier where there was one person ahead of him.

Rachel turned her back to the shop and whispered to Jacob, "We've got to stop him from getting a paper. You heard what they said." Her voice now was nearly a squeal.

Jacob saw Belsasso reach into his pocket to remove some bills while he casually perused the front page. "How?"

"I don't know." She nervously turned her head to see the first person complete his exchange and Belsasso move up to the counter. "Yes, I do. Move toward him with me and argue with me."

"Argue? About what?"

"Anything. Raise your voice." She pulled him by the front of his shirt and moved toward the cashier, cola in hand. He followed.

"I can't let you do that to me again, Lisa. I won't let you!" Jacob complained, raising his voice on the second statement and flailing his briefcase in the air.

"Who says you won't, you jerk! You don't own me, you know!" Rachel turned to Jacob as she delivered these lines, then jerked herself around leading with the cola hand just as she reached the gentleman trying to pay for his paper. Belsasso had turned to look at the commotion along with all others in the shop, only to meet a half-full cup of soda pop and ice emptying unceremoniously on his shirtfront and tie.

Next came a scene of profuse apologizing and blaming, with some swearing thrown in, including the man in the Phillies cap who didn't stop to think what the abbot would say about that.

"Lisa" insisted that her boyfriend, who by then was tabbed "Greg," take the victim to the men's room to help him clean up, manhandling Jacob and Belsasso in the process away from the cashier and out into the hall. Belsasso protested the entire way, finally wresting himself from the grasp of his assailants.

"Please, please, just let me go to my room upstairs and clean up. I assure you I can manage that myself. I'm sure you meant no harm. Please. Thank you. Thank you." He backed away from them, brushing at his tie, then almost sprinted to the elevator.

The recently-quarreling couple watched him disappear, then turned to see the newspaper still resting on the counter, the cashier shaking her head in disapproval.

"Sorry," Rachel shrugged.

Bishop had arrived to catch the last few seconds of the encounter, surprised to see his Kentucky team members at the hotel but feigning non-recognition. Rachel and Jacob walked by him without comment. Scott appeared at that moment.

"What was that all about? Did Bishop see you?" Scott asked, catching up with their pace.

"We'll talk later about it," Jacob whispered. "Rachel just earned an Oscar. For both acting and directing."

The threesome walked silently the rest of the way out the revolving doors to the street.

"Whew!" Jacob exclaimed. "I'm not sure my heart can take much more of this. I'm older than you, remember."

"Not buying that line, Jacob," Rachel answered, chuckling. "Anybody who can pick up dialogue and improvise like you just did including the profanity is ready for action. PG, I know, but mild profanity, anyway. What do we do next?" She rubbed her hands together in delight.

Scott intervened. "Hey, wait a minute. What happened with you guys while I was in the men's room?"

Jacob and Rachel high-fived it and then proceeded to describe the events while removing themselves from the immediate area of the hotel entrance.

Claude Bishop stationed himself in the lobby again. His task was to follow the subject to the rendezvous coffee shop and then assist FBI officers with the arrest when Belsasso emerged. He saw the large clock over the registration desk. It said 10:10. Probably another ten minutes or so in which to ponder the meaning of the episode with Rachel and Jacob, only the tail end of which he had caught.

And to wonder about the outcome of this morning's operation. Would Jorge Mendez and Felix Gonzalez—if those were their real names—perform as specified? Would Belsasso smell a rat before the cameras and tapes could spring the trap?

And if all that went well, how about Fort Campbell, the Delores Project, Doctor Crockett, and…

Pat Beason. Just as Bishop was thinking the name, he saw the woman herself walk by from the elevator across the open space toward the door. He recognized her but doubted she would him. He'd had very little personal contact in Nashville with the lady legislator. Not to worry; she didn't see him huddled on the easy chair behind the overgrown fern.

She carried herself with the same assurance that had been her trademark. Stylish hairdo, smart tailored business suit, tasteful makeup. She also carried herself right out the door and down the street. About fifty feet away she was distracted by the contents of a shop window, a chic ladies-wear shop. She didn't recognize any of the three persons standing only a few feet from her, but Scott and Rachel knew her instantly.

Scott had memorized her features ever since his father had confessed the liaison. He had cut her picture from the newspaper and pinned it to the bulletin board at his apartment at school. He even threw darts at it occasionally.

When she had walked on by several paces, Scott ventured to identify her to Jacob and Rachel.

"I recognized her," Rachel said.

"Oh, Pat Beason, yes, I've heard of her," Jacob volunteered, not knowing exactly how much more to say about how he had heard of her. He opted to say no more.

Rachel was curious, though. "What's she doing here, I wonder."

"You know about her, don't you, Jacob?" Scott asked opaquely. He knew his father had confessed these things to Jacob.

"Uh, I think so, Scott." Jacob frowned at Scott, shuffled his feet, and hugged his briefcase tighter.

"Look, sis, there's one thing about Dad's dilemma I haven't told you. I've been chicken." He sighed and looked away, gathering courage. "But it's time I should. It's got to do with Pat Beason and Dad."

"I'm not sure I want to hear it," Rachel interrupted.

Scott's attention was caught just then by the figure of Fernando Belsasso exiting the hotel wearing sunglasses as well as fresh shirt and tie. Time had flown; it was 10:25 already. Bishop was not far behind, following his subject in the opposite direction from where the three were standing.

Rachel and Jacob turned to see what had transfixed Scott in mid-thought.

Rachel grabbed Scott's arm. "Later about Pat. Let's tail 'em."

Jacob tugged at Scott's shirt. "Maybe we shouldn't." His fearless companions weren't listening.

Around the corner and midway down the block on E Street, Belsasso paused short of the entrance to the Midtown Coffee Shop and examined the neighborhood. Bishop suddenly became interested in the poster display in a travel agency. Two video camera operators, unseen in second-floor windows across the street and spaced to record different angles, became interested in the scene below. A radio receiver, equipped to record the anticipated conversation, was wired to a synchronous timing device with the cameras. The electronics specialist sat with headphones and monitored the process while the hum of coffee shop activity came through on the speaker for the camera operators to hear also.

Mendez and Gonzalez were inside and behaving so far.

Belsasso, satisfied with the environs, opened the coffee shop door and entered. Bishop leaned his back against the brick siding of the travel agency and swept the scene, at the same time receiving a message from across the street that he was to sit tight and to work with the agents standing just on the other side of the coffee shop entrance. Yes, he knew that, thank you.

He did a double take on the three people who were slowly approaching him from a short distance to his left.

"Just what the hell do you bozos think you're doin'? You're s'posed to be acting like tourists and attending the House debate," he muttered when they were close enough to hear.

"We're just law-abiding citizens here to give a hand if we can," Rachel answered. "We already saved the operation once."

"I don't know what you're referring to, and I probably don't wanna know either. So just keep your traps shut and stay outta the way." Bishop turned back to his surveillance.

Belsasso seated himself with Mendez and Gonzalez at the table they had picked in the rear of the shop. A waitress took his order for espresso and refilled the cups of the other two.

"So you have successfully completed your mission in Kentucky?" Belsasso noted beads of sweat on the upper lip of Jorge Mendez.

"Yes, you will be happy with the outcome, I believe," Mendez replied. Belsasso didn't recall ever seeing him perspiring from nerves. The temperature of the shop was comfortable.

"Which was...?"

"The subject was eliminated, and we have these papers which were the object of interest at the monastery." Mendez pulled from the empty chair a large manila envelope, handing it to Belsasso. Gonzalez was quiet, as usual, except for a nervous frog in his throat.

Belsasso reached for the envelope, noticing at the same time an opened newspaper that had been left on the chair, apparently by the previous occupant.

A minor headline caught his eye: "**DEA makes Mexican connection.**"

The conversation went dead at the receivers on the second floor across the street, leaving only the background clatter of the shop. The electronics specialist adjusted his earphones and frowned.

Belsasso read the article without comment, leaving his companions wondering why he had lost interest suddenly in the contents of the envelope.

He coolly folded the paper so that page two didn't show and tucked it under his arm, noted again the signs of nerves in his underlings, started to speak once, thought better of it, then looked around the shop for a few moments.

"Just hold this and wait. I'll be back in a minute." He returned the envelope to Mendez and walked slowly to the door at the very rear of the shop with the sign, "MEN."

Nerves were beginning to show on the agents stationed across the street too. They wondered what was going on.

Soon their puzzlement ended. Mendez' subdued voice came through to them, "If you're wondering what's happening, he picked up a newspaper that was lying here, read it for a minute, then excused himself to the restroom. He left the envelope."

By the time the agent was able to spread the alarm, Belsasso was already perched sitting backwards halfway out the small window he had found in the men's room, getting ready to jump to the alleyway as soon as he could maneuver his legs around.

Bishop received the message the same as the other agents on the ground.

"They think he's escaping out the back through an alleyway," he shouted at his uninvited accomplices. "I've been told to secure the prisoners. Stay where you are!" He rushed to the coffee shop door.

"Alleyway?" Scott began sprinting, retracing their path on the sidewalk until he came to an alley he had noticed when they were trailing Bishop. "Come on, it probably connects," he shouted, waving to

Rachel and Jacob who obeyed. They were all sprinting now to the intersection ahead that they figured connected with an alley behind the shop.

They were met abruptly with Belsasso's frame falling toward them from atop a tall wire gate that had slowed his exodus and separated him from a piece of his jacket. Two FBI agents could be heard and seen running toward them from the other end of the alley.

Scott lunged at the fleeing man, knocking him to his knees and halting his progress momentarily but also disabling himself when he stepped in a pothole and felt a lightning pain and crunch in his ankle. Scott fell to the side, groaning with the familiar sensations he had first known on the basketball court in high school.

Belsasso's faltering recovery was stopped next by a running sidekick to his midsection delivered by the lean and agile Jacob. The well-placed karate blow succeeded in knocking the wind out of its target, sending Belsasso to the asphalt and stunning him further when his head struck the brick wall of the building behind him.

Gasping for air and doubled over in pain, he looked up through glazed eyes at the man and young girl standing over him, vaguely recognizing them. "You…(gasp)…you two…(gasp)…at the hotel."

"Yes, sir, sorry about your shirt and tie." Rachel went to her injured brother, seeing that the FBI agents had scaled the gate and were ready to take over.

Jacob in turn retrieved his briefcase and Phillies hat that had been abandoned in the fray. It was the first time he had been physically parted from the documents, the security of which he has vouchsafed to Dom Raphael. He had even slept with them the last night.

The agents handcuffed their subject and repeated Miranda after assuring themselves that he could understand English. Belsasso simply nodded and said nothing.

Standing him up, the agents then turned to the others in the alleyway. "Thanks. Good show. Who are you, and how bad is he hurt?" one of them asked.

"I'm Jacob, Brother Jacob, a Trappist monk, and I'm here, you might say, on special assignment. And this is Rachel Crockett and her brother Scott, from Tennessee. We're all here together, as you see." Jacob was stumbling over the words. "How bad is he hurt? Let's see." He bent down and looked at the ankle Scott was holding, gently removing the shoe and sock. It wasn't pretty. The already-developed swelling and blue coloration indicated trouble.

"It's probably a sprain. I've had them on that ankle before. It feels like a bad one." Scott grimaced.

One of the agents spoke into his radio. "Harry, this is Ike. We're back in the alleyway with the subject apprehended. There's a civilian who assisted us in the capture who's injured an ankle. How about calling an ambulance to get him and getting our car to the alley entrance on E Street? Someone'll need to accompany him and the other two civilians to the hospital to get statements.

"Hey, Brother Jacob? Is that your name? You did a number on the man here. I saw that karate move. Do they teach monks that sort of stuff?"

"No, not really, I mean, not all of us."

Jacob and Rachel each shouldered one of Scott's arms so that he could hop with them toward the street while the two agents maintained flanking positions walking on each side of the still-stunned Belsasso. An ambulance could be heard in the distance, and the Channel 12 Live-Eye van pulled by the alley entrance just as they reached E Street.

Chapter 24

Mondays were usually among the slower days at Capitol Hill Hospital, the calm after the weekend storm.

The police officer who had accompanied them to the hospital had collected written statements from Rachel and Jacob, had taken names and addresses, and was now waiting in the hall for Scott to be available for a statement.

Jacob fetched sandwiches from the vending area and brought them to the treatment room where the orthopedic assistant was gathering materials for the doctor to apply a cast. It was more than a sprain. X-rays showed a hairline fracture. Such required a cast, not a splint as Scott had been used to seeing on that ankle in times past.

"How's it feeling now?" the castman inquired.

"Not so good. Of course, the dope helps. Don't know what I'll say when it wears off."

"I'm sure Doctor Horn will give you a prescription for something to take with you. You'll be on crutches for a while too. Just wait here 'til he comes back to put the cast on and check everything out."

"Crutches. Wonderful." Scott thanked the aide as he exited.

"It's not so bad," Rachel consoled. "I had crutches last year after knee surgery."

"Yeah, but you're no judge, sis. You're the 'crutches queen'." Scott grinned. "Jacob, you'd never believe what this girl asked Santa for when she was eight years old."

"Not what I think you're going to say."

He nodded. "Yep. Crutches. One of her classmates in school was using them that year, and Rachel thought they were so cute that she wanted some for Christmas. Got 'em, too. Dad borrowed a pair from the hospital, and she used those things for a few days until the new wore off."

"You didn't have to tell that. That's embarrassing. If you weren't hurt, I'd get you good."

"Here you go, children. Eat your sandwiches. The doctor might be a while, and methinks we're not done with this day yet." Jacob passed out the food and drink. "Or it's not done with us."

"What time is it?" Rachel looked for a clock on a wall, finding none.

"Twelve-fifteen," Scott reported. "Not very long before the hearings start up. Mr. Cox said they typically resume a little after 2 p.m., so Dad will be testifying soon. Doesn't give us much time to get to Matsaku. Damn this ankle!"

A pensive moment, then Scott continued. "Look, no telling how long before I get released, so you guys get on with it. Get back to the hotel and find Matsaku. I'll follow as soon as I can. Time's a-wasting."

Jacob and Rachel exchanged looks. "Golly, Scott, I don't feel right leaving you in the lurch here on crutches and everything. What do you think, Rachel?"

She gave her brother a hard stare. "I think Scott's right. We've got to find out if he has moved any from his position as a result of Belsasso's arrest. If not, then...well that's what you're here for, Jacob. You and that briefcase. You wouldn't want to come all this way for nothing, would you?"

"Rachel, before you go, I never got to finish telling you about Dad and Pat Beason."

Rachel held up her hand and interrupted her brother. "No time for that. I think I know anyway."

Scott hugged Rachel a big one and bade goodbye to his two comrades.

* * * *

"So your kids are here, too," Jonas observed, standing over the table where his aide had deposited lunch for Trey and him. "I hope you don't mind eatin' in my office. It just seems to me this is shaping up as one of those gulp-it-and wash-it-down-with-buttermilk sort of days. Except you can't find real buttermilk 'round here. Leastways not the kind your grandmother used to churn."

"I'm sure this is fine. Looks like a good sandwich, and I never acquired a taste for buttermilk."

"Don't know what you're missin', son." Jonas turned to his desk. "Hey, better turn up the volume on that TV. Looks like a news bulletin on Channel Twelve." He picked up the remote.

The newscaster announced, "Downtown Washington was the scene this morning of a most unusual arrest by FBI agents. At approximately ten forty-five, Fernando Belsasso, Secretary of Commerce of Mexico, was arrested on two charges of conspiracy to murder."

Film footage of the scene on E St. was being shown as the report continued. It showed Belsasso being escorted into an automobile by two men and next to them could be seen a man and a girl assisting another young man in walking toward an ambulance.

"Look!" Trey pointed out. "That's Scott and Rachel and Jacob!"

"Really? Aw, surely not! Let's listen."

"According to Tennessee Drug Investigation agent Claude Bishop who was here on special assignment, the arrest was a planned operation of the FBI in cooperation with the Federal DEA, based on confirmed evidence of the Mexican official's direct involvement with the murder of an Episcopal priest in Alabama and the attempted murder of a monk in Kentucky."

There was then some footage of Bishop and his two prisoners.

"We've learned that three bystanders were instrumental in the capture of Belsasso who was fleeing the scene by way of an alley. One of these persons was injured, but the extent is unknown. More details on Channel Twelve's Prime News at six."

The newscaster continued. "And now stay tuned for a Special White House news conference called by President Clinton, which is now in progress."

Trey and Uncle Jonas settled into their chairs, having lost interest in the sandwiches.

"I have a statement to make, and then we will have time for a few questions." Clinton's hoarse voice continued. "In a carefully planned operation this morning, the FBI in collaboration with the Drug Enforcement Agency has arrested Mexico's Secretary of Commerce, Fernando Belsasso. He has been charged with conspiracy to commit murder on two counts: one having to do with the murder just a week ago of a priest in Alabama and the other the attempted murder two days ago of a monk in a monastery in Kentucky.

"At the same time that I am proud of our agencies and their brave and competent agents, I am saddened by the circumstances and the persons involved. At this moment in time when most of us are concentrating on the important passage of the North American Free Trade Agreement bill in the House tomorrow, we are pained that one of the high-ranking officials in our NAFTA partnership must be arrested on such heinous charges. I have already been in touch with President Salinas to inform him of the events and to express my regrets.

"I have been working closely with Jim Stennis and Harvey Smithers the past week in order to bring this matter to a conclusion. Nothing would have pleased me better than for the entire matter to have simply disappeared into limbo until the NAFTA agreement was assured. But politics cannot take precedence over justice. Human lives are more precious than legislative victories. How hollow all the trade agreements in the world would be if the world, and especially priests and monks, were not safe from cold-blooded murderers.

"Mr. Belsasso is now in custody. The criminal justice process will move forward, and he will be allowed the full protection of our laws. Likewise, the legislative process will move forward. The House and Senate must approve the NAFTA agreement. I place my trust in the good judgment of your elected representatives. I know you do too.

"I'll take questions now."

The usual ritual of raised arms followed. There was a question about the drug-smuggling suspicions and whether Belsasso was involved in that, to which Clinton had no comment.

Jonas turned the volume down so they could talk.

"Not a bad country speech. Made himself out to be plum pristine, didn't he?"

"Right. Not a mention of the pressure put on him by the press. But then you really wouldn't expect that, would you?"

"Depends. On whether he wants to leave an out for himself in the event his case against Belstosso doesn't hold up. Then he could say the case was about to be lost with publicity and that with a foreign suspect you can't let that happen."

"So," Trey speculated, "he must be pretty confident of the government's case."

"That's one conclusion." Jonas returned to lunch and Trey followed. They were silent for a minute. Jonas looked tired.

"That doesn't help you any with the vote this afternoon, though, does it?" Trey asked.

"What? What doesn't help? Oh, you mean the arrest."

"Yeah. The arrest. Doesn't change things for your cause. For Fort Campbell and the 101st."

Jonas stopped in mid-mouthful, pensive. Then, softly, "No, son, no, it doesn't, not that I know of."

"So when should I be there to be sworn in?"

The senator wiped his mouth with his napkin and leaned back in his chair. "Trey, son, I don't want you to do this. I've been anguishing over it since Saturday. It's just too much to ask of you, to ruin your career. Oh I'd love to see Billy Boy squirm when you tell about Eisenberg and Perkins, his boys involved in this mess, but it's not worth it to do that to yourself. All that about the Delores Project will come out anyway in Belstosso's trial, assuming there is one.

"You haven't been subpoenaed. You're a voluntary witness, so you can just say you changed your mind. We need to leave things in the hands of the Good Lord now. If He wants Fort Campbell to be closed and the Screamin' Eagles decommissioned, so be it. If He doesn't, then so be it the better. But whichever the way He chooses, let's let it be His show now, okay?"

Trey got up and faced his uncle, bending to a crouch to lock into his eyes. "Uncle Jonas, I'm following what I think is God's will. I felt it so strongly when I decided to do this before I called you. It's a personal decision for me. In keeping with honesty and integrity and all those things you and Dad always stood for. Just...just believe in me."

Jonas reached out and grasped his nephew's hands, eyes glistening.

"Two o'clock. Be there about thirty minutes ahead of time. Lou Lazar is our committee's counsel and he wants to brief you on procedures before you testify."

"I will be. Now," Trey concluded, standing erect again, "let's see if those three bystanders who helped capture Belsasso are who I think they are. Who can we call?"

*   *   *   *

The policeman deposited Jacob and Rachel at the entrance of the Hyatt Regency, promising to return with Scott as soon as he was released and had signed his statement for the police records.

The clock in the lobby said 12:35.

Rachel spied the house phone near the registration desk. She lifted the receiver and dialed operator.

"Please ring the room of Mr. Matsaku." She spelled it.

"I'm sorry, but that number has a 'No operator ring-through' specification."

"What does that mean?"

"It means the caller must know the room number already. It's a privacy protection option we offer for VIP's in the suites. I'm sorry."

"What?" Jacob asked the crestfallen Rachel.

"They won't ring through. How will we find his room number?" Rachel's hopes of coming to the aid of her father were fading. She recalled the horror of her nightmare of last Thursday night and recaptured the resolve that had mounted within her mind over the last two days. A resolve energized by the events at the monastery, the shocking discoveries in the Merton papers, and then the excitement of the morning's arrest. She didn't want to give up yet. She could picture herself again on the tennis court with her father, could even taste the chocolate milkshake afterward.

They walked toward the registration desk to ask for suggestions. Jacob stopped and grabbed Rachel's arm, halting her forward progress.

"Whoopsie. Look who's here. That's Pat Beason isn't it?"

"Yeah. It is."

"I betcha she's here for the hearing. Maybe she knows what we need to know."

They reached her just before the elevator. "Excuse me, Ms. Beason. You are Pat Beason aren't you, from Tennessee?"

"Why, yes, I am." Her patented smile flashed automatically.

"We're…uh…I'm Rachel Crockett, Ms. Beason. You know, Doctor Trey Crockett's daughter. And this is Brother Jacob from Kentucky. Gosh, Jacob, I forgot your last name." she said, suddenly embarrassed and awkward-feeling.

He held out his hand and smiled. "I'm Jacob Sudack, Ms. Beason. Pleased to meet you."

Beason was a little flustered. "Well now, what a nice surprise. Nice to meet you both. I think I've met you before, Rachel, last week. Right?"

"Yes, ma'am. I hope I behaved myself."

"Of course you did. Your question was very appropriate."

There was an awkward silence, broken finally by Beason. "And what are you doing in D.C.?"

"We're here to help my Dad. You do know him, don't you?"

Beason could contain a blush no longer. "Yes, of course." Then she looked around nervously and suggested, "Tell you what. This is a little noisy. Would you like to come up to my suite and we can talk easier."

They agreed, relieved.

Safely behind the closed doors of her suite on the 24th floor, Beason asked her guests to have a seat and offered liquid refreshments from the well-stocked bar, which they politely declined.

"Now, that's better. So tell me again what Doctor Crockett's daughter and friend are doing here." She had regained her composure.

"I'll get straight to the point, Ms. Beason. Jacob and I and Scott, my brother, when he gets here from the hospital—but that's another story—we need to see Manuel Matsaku like right now! It's crucial that we talk to him about the Delores Project which I know you're familiar with. Right?"

A sigh, then: "Yes, I am." The sincerity of the young lady captured Pat Beason's best instincts, and she decided to be open with them.

"We have some papers, letters, from the monastery that could mean a great deal to Mr. Matsaku. Jacob has them in his briefcase. I really shouldn't tell you any more about the papers because we're sworn to secrecy. We know he's staying in this hotel but we can't get through to him. Have you seen him? Do you know his room number?"

"Yes. Yes, I know where he is. As a matter of fact, he's just next to this one, number 2430. I think I know a little about those papers from the monastery. From Dom Philippe, I think? Trey told me about them." A nod from Jacob confirmed her conclusion. "Shall we see if Mr. Matsaku is there?" She stood and extended her arm in invitation.

The door was answered by Matsaku's aide. "Just a moment. I will see if he is available." They waited impatiently for his return. "Yes, Mr. Matsaku will see you. Please come this way."

The stately gentleman with the bold, mixed facial features greeted them. Beason handled the introductions.

"What a pleasant surprise. I hope you come with good news. So far the day is not going well for me. As you might suspect, I am not a fan of the NAFTA accord which by latest count might pass the House by a narrow margin. And then I was greeted with news of the arrest of a business associate, Señor Belsasso. I am sure Madame Beason is aware of these developments." He looked inquiringly at his junior partner.

"Yes, I saw the TV coverage and Clinton's news conference. I'm as shocked as you are."

"I must say it leaves me stunned. But tell me, who are your friends here?"

"Rachel is the daughter of Doctor Trey Crockett, the nephew of Senator Jonas Crockett with whom I believe you are familiar. Jacob is a Trappist monk from a monastery in Kentucky."

"Oh, from the Abbey of Gethsemani?" Matsaku broke into a smile.

"That's correct. All of the brothers there are very much aware of your family's connections with our abbey, and we are most grateful for the support."

Matsaku bowed ever so slightly. "My beloved mother's memory is forever linked with your monastery and with the legacy of her dear friend Thomas Merton. Did you know him?"

"No, he died a few years before my entry into the order. But in truth I do know him. His presence is with us still."

"Of course. But tell me, just what is a monk from Gethsemani doing here in Washington, D.C.? Surely not to merely reminisce with me about my mother's affections."

Rachel spoke up. "No, sir, if I may explain. My father, Trey Crockett, is in Washington today too. He's planning to testify before the Senate Armed Services Committee about the Delores Project and the way he was blackmailed by the Mexicans to help defeat the resolution to keep Fort Campbell open. I think I said that right. Anyway, they were the same Mexicans that murdered a priest and were caught trying to murder another one this weekend. The same Mexicans who were working for Mr. Belsasso. Don't you see?"

Matsaku looked at Pat Beason. She nodded affirmation. "And...?"

"And we know that you control votes that can defeat the resolution. At least that's what we've been told."

"And...?"

"And we—Jacob and I and Scott, my brother—he's coming later." Rachel was rattled momentarily, suddenly remembering that Scott wouldn't know how to get to this room. "We were just wondering—hoping, really—that your mind would be changed by what's happened this morning and you would...well, would arrange for those votes to be changed." She blew a big sigh.

"And why is this so important to you? Because your father is testifying?"

Rachel, choking up, found it hard to continue.

"What she's trying to say, Mr. Matsaku," Beason injected, "is that Doctor Crockett's testimony will ruin him professionally, not to mention what it could do to President Clinton when the committee hears about Eisenberg and Perkins. And to me, for that matter. I stand to get a black eye out of this thing too. But that's not the point. Doctor Crockett will have to divulge the reason he's being blackmailed, and it will probably cost him his medical license. If you plan to use your influence on the committee and, well, abandon the plans for the Delores Project, this very moment is the time it would be most advantageous to do so from everyone's perspective." She looked at her watch. "Doctor Crockett is scheduled to testify in approximately one hour."

Matsaku paced stiffly to the window and the altar with its picture and rosary beads.

"All right. That explains the presence of the young lady. But still our Trappist friend's presence is a puzzle."

"Well, sir, my presence is necessary here only if you remain persistent and unchanged in your plans."

Matsaku's voice was raised this time. "You leave me with such a conundrum. No, a demand? You three people, two of you strangers, walk into my suite and ask me to reverse my plans on a project of which I have been dreaming for years? A project which will reconnect me to my heritage and complete a destiny to which I have been driven?" He was almost shouting at this point and pacing before them. His aide appeared at the door.

"No, Ikama, it's all right." And then, suddenly quiet, to his guests: "Please forgive me. I know I become too outspoken at times. I do not mean to be offensive to you."

"Of course, Mr. Matsaku, no offense taken." Beason tried to smooth things over. Rachel had retreated further into her upholstered easy chair. Jacob clutched his briefcase.

"It would be very difficult, as you can see, for me to give up this project. Even the events of this day do not compel me in that direction. At least not to this point. Of course I do not condone murder, but these are charges which as yet are unproven. It is just too great a decision for me to make so quickly. I hope you understand."

There was a lengthy silence. Rachel could hear her pulse in her ear. Pat clenched her fists. Jacob chewed his lip. The tension was broken when he reached into his pocket and retrieved a key. He used it to open the lock on the briefcase he had held so faithfully for his abbot. He removed an accordion-type folder and began unwinding the string that held it closed. All watched intently.

"These, sir, are papers removed yesterday from the abbot's safe at Gethsemani. I was given custody of them with instructions to use them only if absolutely necessary to convince you to give up this project.

They are not to be copied, discussed over the telephone, or shown to the press. They are now for your eyes only. Rachel and Scott and I have seen them. My abbot, Dom Raphael, and Dom Philippe Flaget, if he is still alive, are the only other living persons who know what they say. Cardinal Swenens, author of two of the letters, and your mother, author of the other, are deceased." Jacob had removed and was holding the several pages that filled the folder.

"You will find here three primary documents which are letters in their original handwriting and language which was French. Two are from Cardinal Swenens, an official on the Vatican College of Moderators, to your mother, Delores Matsaku. The other is from Madame Matsaku to Cardinal Swenens. The rest of documents that you'll find here are typed English translations of these same letters that were rendered some time ago by Dom Philippe Flaget in anticipation of a need such as ours. And in addition there's a cover sheet by Dom Philippe that explains why the documents were kept.

"Sir, these are now yours to read." Jacob handed the papers in the direction of Matsaku who had been listening, dumfounded, to the speech by this stranger. It all seemed surreal to him except for the presence of Pat Beason who lent a foundation in reality for him to find anchor.

Hesitantly he walked to Jacob and took the papers in hand then sat in a chair next to a table with a lamp on it. He took eyeglasses out of his shirt pocket, put them on, and leafed through the pages. Next he studied the first page carefully after which he looked around the room to find the others studying him just as carefully.

He read silently the cover page:

> I, Dom Philippe Flaget, on this date September 12, 1991, submit the following statement:
>
> I have translated into English the three letters enclosed herewith to the best of my ability. These letters will now be in the safekeeping of the

abbot of Our Lady of Gethsemani, as my failing health demands that I place them in responsible hands. I was asked to preserve them by Cardinal Swenens and Delores Matsaku, both now deceased. It was their wish that such a record of the events leading to the death of Thomas Merton be maintained in case the occasion ever arose when they should be used for the good of the Church.

(signed)
Philippe Flaget

Chapter 25

▼

Bangkok, Thailand
December 10, 1968

The two men quietly and methodically surveyed the bedroom. They opened drawers, the suitcase, the briefcase, careful to leave everything as they found it. The floor fan offered background noise as well as relief from the tropical heat.

"This is his room," one of them whispered, pointing to the stationery with Thomas Merton's letterhead. The other nodded, then checked out the bathroom. It was as he expected: very small with a shower stall separated from the rest of the cubicle only by a curtain and a slight rise in the concrete basin that served as the bottom of the stall.

"Look...Pierre...here," the second beckoned the first. He pointed to the water spillage that represented vestiges of Merton's bath that morning. "If he takes a shower this afternoon, all we have to do is rig the electric fan, wait outside for him, then come back with the water when he is in the shower."

Pierre nodded and motioned for Gerard to follow him back to the bedroom. "Here, you take care of the wiring while I stand guard at the window." He handed Gerard a pocketknife.

* * * *

Only a few hundred yards away, Merton was being introduced to the assembled group of Eastern and Western monastics. His was the opening presentation at this gathering of leaders of the Benedictine and Cistercian orders, a conference sponsored by the international Benedictine group, *Aide a l' implantation Monastique.*

His introduction by the moderator was low-key as was the entire affair. Merton sensed a sort of stillness, an air of tension surrounding the proceedings, born perhaps of the political overtones arising from the topics to be addressed. Merton's speech was to be on the relationship between Marxism and monasticism. Many of the other participants were from Communist countries and all these words were being reported to the authorities back home. The war in Southeast Asia was at its peak. The Roman Catholic Church, much to the dismay of Merton and others, did not want to appear to be taking sides.

* * * *

Pierre stood lookout, clutching in his sweating palm the crucifix that hung around his neck while his partner went to work setting the stage. Gerard unplugged the floor fan, turned it on its side, found a part of the wire that lay just along the metal edge of the fan's base, and used the knife to fray the insulation exposing the bare copper. He stood the fan upright, plugged it in, and turned it on. He lightly touched the metal and jumped at the harmless but definite test jolt he received.

Pierre watched and nodded approval. "Now the fuse box."

Gerard walked outside to the electric utility box located on the back wall of the building. One by one he unscrewed and then replaced the fuses that broke the circuits, waiting for a sign from his partner that the fan was off. Finally it came. He pocketed the fuse then pulled the main switch, which cut all juice to the fuse box and the building. Quickly he took a short piece of copper wire from his pocket and jammed it into the empty fuse space. He then threw the main switch back to the "ON" position and closed the box, knowing that he would return the fuse to its place after the deed was done. He walked back to the room where Pierre was waiting, relieved to get that part finished without alerting anyone in the vicinity.

They left as quietly as they had come after opening the blinds of the window on the back wall of the room just enough for them to be able to see from outside. They also left the door bolt locked in the open position on the back door to allow quick entry later. Then they took their observation positions in the woods just behind the cottage. The bucket of water which would be used to leave a deadly trail of 220-volt electricity from the fan to the bathroom door was at hand.

Pierre crossed himself and glanced anxiously at Gerard. "Mother of God, forgive us."

"And *la Societe de Bossuet.*"

* * * *

Merton was well into his speech by this time. He spoke in English, and there were interpreters translating into French and Japanese for the headsets that were provided the participants. He addressed issues head-on, including in his remarks his views of the positive as well as negative aspects of Marxist doctrine. He spoke of the similarities between a monastic community and a communist society.

No applause interrupted the speech. Muted applause accompanied the ending. Nervous shuffling seemed to be the body language of the day. Tension filled the room, reflected also in the strained look of Mme. Delores Matsaku, his benefactor and friend, who sat in the audience. Merton's attempts at light-heartedness, as few as there were, fell on unresponsive ears. Maybe they lost something in the translation, or maybe they lost everything in the pool of political uncertainty that permeated the atmosphere.

Merton welcomed the 11:30 lunch break inasmuch as he had made plans to spend it with Dom Philippe Flaget. It would be a respite from the unexpectedly tense morning.

On the way to lunch the two traded observations about the morning's session, Flaget comforting his friend with encouragements. They took in the countryside and the neatly arranged homes and shops on the twenty-mile drive from the village of Samut Prahan, the site of the conference, to downtown Bangkok.

The taxi driver deposited them at their chosen destination. They were seated at their table among an assortment of patrons, gathered, it seemed, from all over the world. Merton savored the occasion. It wasn't often he had the opportunity to converse in French over an *aperitif* much less in a setting such as Nick's Hungarian Diner in downtown Bangkok. The controversial Trappist monk, the nemesis of the Roman Catholic hierarchy, was now in his element.

"Thomas," Dom Philippe was saying in his native tongue which seemed well suited to his physical features, the classic angular jaw and Roman nose, "I must admit I thought this time would never arrive. It seems we've been corresponding and planning this trip forever, doesn't it?"

"The truth is I think I've been planning this all my life. Or that is to say, rather, that God's been planning it for me." Merton hesitated a moment, choosing his words carefully. "It's safe to say that this trip has been the culmination of my life as a religious. I could die this moment and know that there was nothing more needed. There is something about my being so close to the ground of the Hindu and Buddhist spirit..." His voice trailed off and he sighed, shaking his head.

"If I should never have the privilege of treading the ground of my Kentucky knobs at Gethsemani, if I should never read another word of Holy Scripture, if I should never write again of the contemplative life, I should die a happy man, my dear brother Philippe."

"It is touching to find you so satisfied but disturbing to hear the finality of your tone," Flaget said uneasily. "I hope you do not feel that the rigors of your journey have brought you to the brink of your mortality."

Flaget was referring to the non-stop pace of Merton's trip since he left the Abbey of Gethsemani in Kentucky more than two months previously. His travels had taken him from Gethsemani to California to Bangkok to India where he had an audience with the Dalai Lama and then back to Thailand. The primary objective of the trip had now arrived: this international convocation of monastic leaders.

"No, no, I didn't intend to sound morbid, only profound." He laughed. Merton loved to laugh. The fifty-three year old balding monk who thrived on wearing blue jeans and listening to jazz and who looked more like a short-order cook than a Trappist delighted in humorous repartee. "Now don't be so serious, Philippe.

"In fact," Merton continued, "if anything were to have done me in, I think it would have been the preamble to the journey: the incessant wrangling with my bosses which you tire of hearing about, I'm sure."

"I know, I know," Flaget sighed. "Of course, you'd never be here at all if Dom James were still abbot. I sometimes wonder if he retired from his position in order to relieve himself of his self-imposed one-man mission in life to keep a harness on you and your unorthodox ideas."

Merton and Flaget had visited this theme before. The monk from Kentucky was probably the most controversial figure in the Roman Catholic Church. His liberal and activist positions and writings having to do with the Vietnam War and nuclear weapons had brought down the wrath of censorship from the church, and in particular the Trappist, hierarchy. Lately, his personal interest in eastern religious practices and philosophy was also suspect. Dom James, his recently retired superior at the abbey, had used all the energies and prerogatives of the abbotship at his disposal to clutch this tiger's tail. This included intercepting and reading every piece of mail to and from Merton.

Merton shook his head. "Poor Dom James. His obsession with what he called my 'willfulness' just about consumed him. I'll never forget the letter he wrote you expressing concern about how I was placing my will before God's. I've committed one passage to memory. You'll probably recall it: 'But the final solution is for good Father Merton to try more and more to conform his will to God's will than to try to make God conform His will to that of Father Merton.'"

"Yes, yes, I remember it well!" Flaget sipped the pungent liquid in his glass. "But now is another time. Dom Flavian appears to be more lenient with you and your marginal ways."

"I owe a great deal to his courage in allowing me to come. He took a lot of heat from the right. I heard it went all the way to the Vatican, that the Holy Father had to break up the opposition personally."

"I heard those same rumors," Flaget agreed. "I also heard," and he lowered his voice, "that without the intercession of Madame Delores Matsaku the Holy Father might have blocked your approval. Did you hear anything of that?"

"No, no, I didn't. But it doesn't surprise me. Without her influence and financial backing none of us would be here doing this!" Merton sipped and savored the flavor of the golden liquid, a rare treat and welcome change from the bourbon of his adopted home. "*Touché!*" He clinked glasses with Dom Philippe.

"She met me at the convocation center last night. Seemed tense and tentative from the set of her jaw. Probably just the strain of all this. Sort of like you seem, Philippe. Are you okay?"

Dom Philippe waved off that remark with his hand. "Must be the morning's session."

Their conversation went on like this, sometimes serious, sometimes lighthearted, always entertaining to the gregarious Merton.

After lunch he retired to his cottage before the afternoon session. The rooms were only slightly larger than those of a monastery, but he had his own bathroom at least and the beds were comfortable.

He went to his knees on the floor beside the bed, the breeze from the fan flowing over him. His head ached. Sinuses. A glance at his watch told him it was 1:15. The afternoon session began at two.

His eyes focused on the unadorned wall of the cottage room; he closed them and breathed deeply and rhythmically.

"Most Gracious Father," he began, whispering, "grant me peace and understanding and wisdom to speak Your truth, and to hear Your truth, and above all to live Your truth here in this holy gathering. May the trust of the Holy Father and Mme. Matsaku be not misplaced. In the name of the Father, Son, and Holy Spirit. Amen."

He knelt silently for a few minutes then debated with himself as to whether he should nap or shower. His love of midday showers was well known to his friends.

* * * *

At 1:55 p.m. Philippe Flaget knocked on the door of his friend's cottage. There was no answer. He waited a few seconds and knocked again. Still nothing. There was a window beside the door, and he shaded his eyes to look. A crack in the blinds allowed him to see only a portion of the room, but he could see enough.

He could make out the lower half of Merton's body lying on the floor with an electric fan across him. He wasn't moving. Dom Philippe could see water on the floor also.

He yelled for assistance from others nearby and the front door was forced open. Merton was lying there motionless with only a towel wrapped around his waist, the electric fan still going, the motor casing resting where it had fallen on his bare chest.

Flaget rushed to remove the fan, receiving an electric shock as he did so. He jumped away from the water, unplugged the fan, removed it from Merton's body, and felt for a pulse.

Thomas Merton was dead.

Holding his friend in his arms as others crowded into the room in disbelief, Philippe Flaget wept openly.

Chapter 26

Trey walked slowly along Constitution Avenue, soaking in the midday Washington sun. It was a beautiful fall day, eighty degrees, ten-mph breeze from the southeast, billowing clouds.

He had been able to confirm that yes, indeed, those were his son and daughter and friend on the television news clip and that Scott had injured his ankle. Uncle Jonas had used his well-honed connections to ferret out these facts. Trey had even spoken to Scott via telephone in the emergency room of the hospital, enough to satisfy himself that his son would be okay.

It wasn't far from Uncle Jonas' office to the committee hearing rooms, and he could have taken the tunnel train with his uncle, but he elected to get some fresh air. He inhaled it like precious perfume refreshing his spirits. Spirits that were alternately in a state of agitation and resignation.

Last night he had been at his hotel desk for some time composing the note he would carry on his person to the hearing. He wanted it to be with him in case he carried out Option Two, the one he had decided upon, the option that involved a small bottle containing 100 tablets of the antidepressant amitriptyline that he would also carry in his jacket pocket.

He fingered that bottle while he walked, recalling several times the emergency room had notified him of cardiac arrest from this drug. He had always considered it ironic that the medication used to relieve depression was also one of the most fatal.

There were crowds of demonstrators on the capitol steps with placards that mostly reflected anti-NAFTA sentiments, from the trade unions, one supposed, such as "AFTA NAFTA, NO JOBS". He turned up to the steps of his destination building and looked at his watch. 1:20. He was early for the briefing before the hearing.

* * * *

Matsaku read on:

> By courier to Mme. Delores Matsaku
> from Cardinal Swenens
> Vatican City
> 12 November 1968
>
> Dear Mme. Matsaku,
>
> This letter is being delivered to you via courier to assure that no eyes but yours will see it. The same courier will return your reply to me under lock and key in his valise. You will keep the key he brings; the only other copy is in my possession.
>
> What I will say to you will be most alarming. It will not surprise me, nor would I blame you, if you roundly reject what I ask. Nevertheless I ask your indulgence.
>
> In my position with the College of Moderators I recently have been approached secretly by certain members of the Bossuet Society. Let me acknowledge that you, Madame Matsaku, might be one of those who disbelieve in the very existence of that organization. To that assertion I can only say that I too have had my doubts, that is, until recently. My doubts are now erased. There is a Bossuet Society and it is very strong. Strong and determined.

Their communication with me has produced the following astonishing data:

1) Their purpose is to undermine any efforts toward liberalization of the Church, and this often requires drastic measures.

2) One such measure was the murder—yes, murder—of our beloved Pope John XXIII in the midst of the Second Vatican Council. Already stricken with cancer, he was poisoned in such a way as to hasten his death, and there were co-conspirators in the Vatican to squelch any thorough investigation. (The hasty embalming was always a puzzle to me.)

3) The Society is determined to impede the current liberalization trends as exemplified by the conciliatory actions of Pope Paul with the Eastern Church. They fear that the Mother Church eventually will be diluted and blended into a nebulous, universalist position, accepting of all religions as equally valid.

4) The Society has targeted another exemplar of their fears, your beloved Thomas Merton. His writings are becoming ever more popular with clergy and laity, and his recent leanings toward embracing the religions of the East are anathema to the Society's members.

5) I have been told that our beloved Pope Paul VI is now the object of an assassination plan. It is scheduled to take place before the end of this year. I have been told further that the only deterrence to the plan would be the sacrifice of Merton's life, an eventuality that the Society is prepared to assure while he is engaged on his current Eastern journey.

This, Madame Matsaku, brings me to you. I know that you have been instrumental in arranging the conference in Bangkok next month and particularly in arranging Merton's participation. The Society has made preparations for his death while at that conference. They expressly state their insistence that there is to be no extensive investigation into his death. They require that, in fact, as a guarantee.

I see what I am writing, and I can't believe it. Yet on I go.

Your position as organizer of the conference would allow you certain influence in determining the course of events after such an occurrence. The Society suggested I enlist your aid.

My conscience is heavy with this matter. I pray unceasingly for guidance. If I attempt to expose the Society, it is my word against theirs. And I am already branded a near lunatic among my colleagues because of my oft-heard predictions of doom.

If the pope is assassinated, I will feel like an accomplice. In order to prevent such, I must be an accomplice to yet another atrocity. I beg your forgiveness for involving you, and at the same time I anxiously await your reply.

Your servant,

(Cardinal Swenens)

Manuel Matsaku, blanching, placed the typed and handwritten pages of that letter aside on the tabletop. He then picked up the pages with his mother's handwriting; the script and stationary he recognized right away. He leafed through the three pages and glared at the signature, clearly hers also. He then picked up the English translation.

The other three persons in the room watched silently, noting the faintly trembling pages in his hands.

* * * *

Trey Crockett walked to the end of the hall where a crowd was gathering for the afternoon session. He saw the placard on the tripod stand that announced, "Senate Armed Services Committee Hearing."

Press badges were flashing as well as special passes such as the one given him by his uncle. He showed his to the security guard outside the chamber doors, explaining that he was to meet with Counsel Lou Lazar. He was told to wait while the guard checked inside.

Trey recognized a couple of the men as senators. He couldn't exactly place them, but a senator without a name is still impressive, he thought. They were talking to one another and other waiting participants. Trey overheard one of them relating that Clinton's office was now tallying up the House NAFTA vote in his favor, that the arrest of Belsasso that morning had resulted in two reversals nay and four yea. Just enough to tip the balance in favor of the treaty.

It was 1:32 when the guard reappeared and motioned Trey in for his briefing with Committee Counsel Lazar.

* * * *

14 November 1968
Cardinal Swenens
Vatican City

My dear Cardinal Swenens,

My reply to your letter will be, I trust, shorter than was yours. I asked the courier to stay over a day so that I, too, could "pray unceasingly," as you say.

As I read your letter, I found myself wanting to pinch myself or expecting you to suddenly interrupt the text with a giant confession that it was all a bad joke. Then I had to come to terms with the fact that you were in dead earnest.

Came flashing back to me then all the recollections of the Second Vatican Council, of the supposed natural death of our Pope John, of the rumored threats of the Bossuet Society. I recalled my efforts on behalf of the Nostra aetate, the collaborations with supporters and opponents, the suggestions that the Society was instrumental in opposition to the document which eventually passed.

I am ashamed of myself now for taking so lightly the rumors. I am crushed that such monstrous happenings were, and are, occurring under our very noses. I am fearful for the future of our Church if deeds like these are perpetrated by supposed holy men of God, by believers who daily kneel at the altar of our Blessed Virgin Mary and recite the liturgy and consume the host.

In short, your news is indeed appalling to me. Every fiber of my being shrinks from involvement. The thought of betraying my friend Thomas Merton chills my marrow. And yet, my dear Cardinal Swenens, I cannot bear to face the death of another of our Holy Fathers knowing that it could have been prevented.

With a grieving heart I agree to do as you ask. I await further instructions.

Your servant,

(Delores Matsaku)

Matsaku's hands were quivering in sympathy with the words he was reading. He held both copies of the letter, the original and the typed translation, side by side. Though his French was meager, he could compare a few of the words just enough to satisfy himself that the translation was correct.

He was ready for the final document.

* * * *

The security guard announced that persons with passes would be admitted into the hearing chambers. Perhaps fifty persons crowded toward the door. Those without passes were asked to wait until all the others were seated and were told they would be admitted first-come, first-served.

Inside the chamber, Trey had already emerged from the side office where he had been given a short course in the committee's procedures, the swearing-in, the fifth amendment which didn't really apply in Trey's case since his testimony was voluntary anyway, and assorted tips as to testimonial etiquette. Such as: don't swear or pick your nose since you're on C-Span and CNN; don't take offense at the committee's questions since they're just doing the job they're paid to do. Namely, to humiliate ordinary citizens. Lazar had a sense of humor.

Trey took a seat just as the crowd began to surge through the door. He spotted Uncle Jonas at the table up front with the nameplates and microphones. He was one of five committee members already present. The chairman was too preoccupied with his aide Robert Hughes to notice his nephew in the back of the room.

Trey tried to settle down and look calm. His heart rate was about 90. He could feel it in his throat and time it by the sweep of the second hand of the clock on the wall that now registered 1:45. Jonas looked up, saw him, and smiled.

Trey managed a smile back at him. He was relieved that he still had the small bottle in his jacket pocket along with the note addressed to Rachel and Scott. No one had searched him before being admitted.

C-Span and CNN were warming up their equipment.

*   *   *   *

Via courier to Mme. Delores Matsaku
From Cardinal Swenens
Vatican City
20 November 1968

Dear Mme. Matsaku,

I wept as I read your letter, knowing the pain you are feeling.

I have informed my contact person with the Bossuet Society that you have agreed to assist in the matter. With this assurance they have now vowed to me that the plan regarding the Holy Father has been canceled. If, then, the word of these people means anything, we have successfully stanched the threat upon Pope Paul.

You and I will not be privy to any further details of their plan. Perhaps it is better that way. I am told, however, that there will be another confederate in Bangkok with whom you will participate in the matter. It seems that Dom Philippe Flaget, Merton's good friend and fellow Trappist, has been enlisted also by the Society. Their powers appear to be limitless. Between the two of you, there should be little difficulty convincing Bangkok's law enforcement officials to eschew any formal investigation of the death.

I am returning your letter with this one with the request that they be saved. Who knows when they might be needed to document what has happened. I suggest you hide all of them well and arrange for their safekeeping if the time should come that you were no longer able to safeguard them. Perhaps Dom Philippe would agree to serve in that capacity.

Pray for me, as I do for you.

Your devoted servant,

(Cardinal Swenens)

Manuel Matsaku sat for a moment staring at the still-surreal words on the paper. He turned to his guests and spoke in a monotone. "How long is it before your father testifies?"

"Just fifteen minutes," Rachel answered.

He nodded and paused pensively before speaking.

"It...it is a great deal for me to digest." He spoke as much to the air in the room as to his guests. "My mother...my Church." The words faded so that the others could not hear them.

Then he gathered himself and stood up.

"May I ask you all to leave me alone for a short while? No, may I ask you simply to leave, to go on to the hearing. Your father, your friend, needs you there." He handed the papers to Jacob who returned them to their folder and briefcase.

He spoke to Jacob: "My mother...Delores...you never knew her."

Jacob shook his head.

Matsaku then turned from him. "Madame Beason, you should accompany them. They need your support it seems." He attempted a smile. "Thank you. Thank you for your devotion to your father, your friend, your Church, your God. I know this has not been easy for any of you. I am sorry, so very sorry."

His voice fading again, he escorted them to the door and asked his aide to see them out. The door closed. The Japanese industrialist multimillionaire walked slowly toward the window of the room that faced the east. His jacket brushed against the altar, almost knocking over the picture and beads. The closed window insulated him from the world. Tears were streaming down his face.

For the first time since his mother died, he wept. He walked slowly to the door of the sitting room, which separated him from his aide. Pausing a moment, he reached to the lock and turned it.

Just as deliberately, he walked back toward the window. His mother's deathbed words flooded his memory. "My son, our wills may be firm, our intentions lofty, but God's plan is mysterious and humbling." Words with new meaning.

Chapter 27

▼

"I'm Pat Beason, room 2420. Was there a young man on crutches here just now trying to find Mr. Matsaku? Or me?" She was at the front desk of the hotel.

"Just a moment, please. I believe I saw the other clerk handling that. A brown-headed, nice-looking fellow, about six feet, leg in a cast?"

"Yeah, that's him," Rachel answered.

The other clerk finished his business with a patron and then attended to his co-worker's request. "Yes, oh, yes. He left a note." He reached under the counter and pulled out a folded note with "Rachel Crockett or Brother Jacob" written on the outside. "Is one of you either Rachel or Jacob?"

"Yes/Yep," came the simul-answer.

Rachel opened it and all read:

> It's 1:30 and I can't find you. I'm headed for the hearings, and maybe you're there already. If so, disregard the note. If not, regard the note and get your butts there.
>
> (signed) Scott

"Maybe I should stay with Mr. Matsaku," Brother Jacob said. "Maybe I can influence him in the right direction. And...he looked rather despondent. Who knows? The oriental mind. It wouldn't hurt for him to have company. What do you think?"

Rachel looked at Pat, who took it as an invitation to speak. "Well, if you want my opinion, I'd say Mr. Matsaku isn't the type who can be influenced any further. And he does have his aide with him for comfort and safety, if that's what you're worried about." Pat shrugged her shoulders and returned the look to Rachel with raised eyebrows.

"Okay, let's go." Jacob put his arm around Rachel's shoulder and they all went to hail a taxi.

The cabby started the meter at 1:55.

*　　*　　*　　*

All twenty members of the Armed Services Committee were present at the head tables and in varying states of readiness for the final session on this matter. Most recent polls had the resolution failing by a vote of ten to nine with the chair's vote in abeyance according to rules. The swing votes of the senators from Alaska and Washington remained confirmed. They—Wilford and Jansen—were seated and ready.

Senator Crockett received a final word of clarification from Counsel Lazar and then gaveled the meeting to order. The murmuring died to a trickle.

"Ladies and gentlemen, let this hearin' come to order." He gaveled again and repeated, "Ladies and gentlemen, please, let this meetin' come to order. Before callin' the final witness in this matter, I have an announcement to make. The committee has agreed that it's time to vote on the question. The statute under which these hearings are proceeding specifies time limits, thank God Almighty, under which we are to operate. That limit has been reached; at least it will be two days hence. We've agreed that to prolong the matter would not add any more to our deliberations, and instead would just make testy varmints out of us, which most of us are already, of course, speakin' for all but myself."

A ripple of laughs filled the room. Jonas smiled and a few of his colleagues joined him. The others had heard his homespun humor a few too many times.

"I have another announcement too. It has to do with today's witness. He's a relative of mine, a very close relative, my nephew in fact, and more like a son to me. So I'll relinquish the chair to the chairman-pro-tem, Senator Nunn of Georgia. And you'll also be surprised to learn that I'll excuse myself from questioning the witness at all. No applause, please."

There was scattered applause and laughter accompanied by some noise at the door to the chamber. The guard was opening it to allow entry of more spectators, one of whom was on crutches and causing the bulk of the noise. Rachel, Jacob, and Pat had caught up with Scott outside and they now entered and were allowed to stand at the rear, all seats being taken. They stood only a few feet from where Trey was seated.

The gavel was taken by Senator Nunn. "Is the next witness, Doctor Crockett, in the chamber?"

Trey stood and moved forward through the rows of seated spectators. "Yes, sir, I'm here."

"Please be seated at that table there in front of the microphone. Thank you."

Trey sat in the appointed seat, spotting the TV cameras and crews trained on him. His heart rate was probably about 100, he thought. He could feel the looks of his children and friends on his neck. Friends? How about friend, singular. Brother Jacob. Pat didn't quite fit that description according to his latest calculation.

"Would you raise your right hand and be sworn in?"

Trey lifted his right hand.

"Do you solemnly swear that the testimony you are about to give is the truth, the whole truth, and nothing but the truth?"

"I do."

Senator Nunn continued. "Please state your name."

"Winton Sevier Crockett the Third. I'm most often called Trey."

"We'll just stick with Doctor Crockett, I believe. Tell us about yourself. Where you are from, your age, profession, etc."

Trey launched into a mini-bio. A muted phone-ring could be heard in the room. It came from the rear where the SRO's were located. Pat Beason opened her purse and removed the small cellular phone that had been given her by Matsaku. It was ringing. She pushed the "Talk" button and turned toward the wall to speak in a whisper. This created a minor disturbance but not enough to interfere with the proceedings.

After listening a half-minute, she held her hand over the speaker and whispered to Scott, "It's Matsaku. He wants to speak to either Senator Jansen or Wilford. How can we do that?"

Scott called upon his summer's experience with Jonas. "You get a guard to take the phone to one of them."

"I'm in the private practice of psychiatry in Nashville. I also hold appointment at Vanderbilt University as a Clinical Professor in the Department of Psychiatry where I teach residents. My office is near the University."

Trey was moving ahead with his introduction without interruption so far.

The guard took the phone and walked to the end of the table where Counsel Lazar was seated. He spoke to him, motioned toward Pat Beason in the rear of the room, and waited for a response. Lazar nodded and shrugged his shoulders. This was a bit irregular, but he walked down the back of the chairs until he came to Senator Wilford. He whispered a message to him and handed him the phone.

"…am divorced with two children, who happen to be here with me today. I am a recovering alcoholic, having…"

Senator Nunn was irritated at the commotion. "Would you…Doctor Crockett," he interrupted, "would you excuse us a moment, please. We'll let you continue shortly." He covered his mike and turned to address Senator Wilford, who was whispering into the cellular telephone. "Mike, if you don't mind, that's not the way to treat our witness. What's going on?"

Senator Mike Wilford covered his mike too. "Sam, could we have a short recess? It's real important to what we're doing here."

Senator Nunn snorted into his mike and gaveled a recess. He invited Senators Crockett and Wilford and also Lazar to join him in the adjoining chairman's office. Wilford asked Jansen to come along, too.

Trey sat back and looked to the rear of the room. It was his first opportunity to catch the eyes of his people. Rachel was watching him, and he thought he saw the hint of a smile. He got a catch in his throat. He wondered about the association of Pat Beason with the others.

The murmur picked up again and followed the four senators and their counsel through the crowd to the office. Once inside, relative quiet greeted them. "What's up?" Jonas asked.

Wilford held up one hand. "Wait a minute. Let Bob have the phone first." He handed it to Senator Jansen and explained while the latter talked to Manuel Matsaku.

"We're speaking with Manuel Matsaku, the Japanese industrialist. I believe you know who I'm talking about." Crockett and Nunn nodded. "He's been...let's say instrumental in Bob's and my vote on the resolution. He's asking us now to reverse our position and vote in favor. Something important has changed his mind on the matter. He wouldn't say what it was."

"Yes, sir. I understand perfectly. I believe I can do that. Thank you for your concern, and I hope to see you soon," Jansen said, finishing the conversation. He collapsed the antenna and pushed the "Power" button.

"Did you tell them what it was about?"

"Yes. I'm voting 'yea'. What about you?"

"Same here."

"Well, gentlemen," Jonas chimed in, "accordin' to my calculations that clinches the resolution. Would somebody go and fetch my nephew off the witness stand? And get those kids of his and their friends in here too."

Jonas shook hands with the three senators and they left the room while Lazar fetched for the chairman.

Soon the entourage was assembled. Jonas covered Trey with a bear hug to beat all bear hugs while the others looked on. "You don't have to testify now, son. It's all over. We won. Matsaku called and got the two votes to swing our way. That's what all the commotion was about."

A scream from Rachel—"Yessss!!"—pierced the air and caused Trey to turn to her. He saw her laughing and crying at the same time, and he held out his arms to her. Without a moment's hesitation she threw herself into her daddy's arms with a vigor that bespoke years of pent-up emotions. He mingled his tears with hers, holding her tightly and repeating softly, "My puddin', my puddin', how I've missed you."

After a few moments the father-daughter embrace broke up to let Trey celebrate with the others. Scott hobbled over with his crutches and received his well-deserved and warm hug. "I want to hear all about your war wound, young man. Do you get a commendation?"

"I'm not sure. Bishop might put me in jail for meddling in police affairs."

"And you, Jacob, what in the world? You get a black eye using karate?"

"Nope. Guess again. Just the opposite. Should have used it when I didn't. But I wish you'd seen me disable the crook this morning. You'd have been proud of this middle-aged monk, yessirree."

"You should be proud of all of them, Trey," Pat said. "Even me. I'll tell you all about it later. We have a lot to talk about." She winked at him and they hugged too.

"Okay," Trey replied, "I'll take you up on that, governor."

"I've gotta get back in there for the vote. Wouldn't want to miss that." Jonas left them.

"Tell you what," Trey said, moving them all to the door that led to the hall that led to the elevator that would take them outside, "let's all go have a good stiff milkshake. I want to hear about...let's see...the black eye, the sprained ankle...just for starters."

"And you'll want to know how I got mixed up with these guys." Pat was holding tight to Rachel's hand while addressing Trey.

Trey was holding his daughter's other hand, but she broke away in front of them and turned facing them all walking backward. "I've got the best story of all. Somebody owes me a diet cola. I had to use mine as a prop. It was awesome!"

Jacob piped in. "Yep, that was a corker, but the most awesome of all was Dom Philippe. I wonder if he's still kickin'. He'd enjoy hearing this tale."

"Uh, Trey," Pat said, stopping and motioning for him to speak to her aside. She pulled him a few steps to the wall of the corridor.

"What is it?"

"I'm going to split. You guys need to be to yourselves, you know?" Her eyebrows went up.

"No, it's okay. Stay with us," Trey said.

"It's not just that. I've got to catch a plane out of here this afternoon, so time's a factor. Need to turn in this phone, too. It's served its purpose."

"What's your hurry to get home?" Trey quizzed.

"Oh, just something..." She turned her head away then looked at her feet.

"What?" Trey put his hand on her shoulder.

"I've got a family meeting of sorts in the morning. With my sister and niece. You know, Jenny? You saw her picture the other day."

"Yeah, yeah. What's going on?"

She pulled his arm away. "No time to go into that right now." She looked over to the others who were waiting impatiently. "I'll tell you all about it later," she sighed.

Trey looked at her, puzzled, but rejoined the others.

"Pat's got to scram," Trey announced.

She said her good-byes and walked briskly away.

Passing a trash can in the hallway, Trey unobtrusively emptied his jacket pocket of a small bottle and envelope.

Soon the group was on the street. Trey stopped a policeman and asked, "Would you happen to know the closest place we could get a milkshake?"

* * * *

The breeze from the east moved softly through the curtains on the window located on the 24th floor of the Hyatt. That same breeze brought street noises from an excited crowd below that was gathering around a man's body on the sidewalk. The quiet of the suite was broken by the insistent calling for his master and knocking on the door by Ikama. All was in order in the vacated room except for the broken picture lying on the floor, leaving fragments of glass in the vicinity of the altar.

And the rosary beads were missing.

THE END

About the Author

Bill Goodson is a psychiatrist living and practicing in his native Alabama. He finds time for family, church, the homeless, bicycling, and retreats at the Abbey of Gethsemani in Kentucky.

0-595-27971-6